Praise for the novels of Jill Shalvis

"Clever, steamy, and fun. Jill Shalvis will make you laugh and fall in love."
—Rachel Gibson, *New York Times* bestselling author

"Shalvis writes with humor, heart, and sizzling heat!"
—Carly Phillips, *New York Times* bestselling author

"Animals and hot heroes. How could you not love a romance like that?"
—Jaci Burton, *New York Times* bestselling author

"Fall in love with Jill Shalvis! She's my go-to read for humor and heart."
—Susan Mallery, *New York Times* bestselling author

"A fun, sexy story of the redemptive powers of love. Jill Shalvis sizzles!"
—JoAnn Ross, *New York Times* bestselling author

"Witty, fun, and sexy—the perfect romance!"
—Lori Foster, *New York Times* and *USA Today* bestselling author

"Fast-paced and deliciously fun . . . Jill Shalvis sweeps you away."
—Cherry Adair, *USA Today* bestselling author

"A Jill Shalvis hero is the stuff naughty dreams are made of."
—Vicki Lewis Thompson, *New York Times* bestselling author

"Shalvis makes me laugh, makes me cry, makes me sigh with pure pleasure."
—Susan Andersen, *New York Times* bestselling author

"A writer of fast-paced, edgy but realistic suspense . . . Fiercely evocative."
—*Booklist*

"Delightful . . . Jill Shalvis rules."
—*Midwest Book Review*

"Definitely a good way to spend a few hours with some sexy characters."
—*USA Today*

"Jill Shalvis has become one of my go-to authors for contemporary romance."
—*The Romance Dish*

"Shalvis excels at writing charming characters that leap right off the pages and into your heart."
—*Book Binge*

P9-CSV-882

Slow Heat

JILL SHALVIS

BERKLEY BOOKS, NEW YORK

THE BERKLEY PUBLISHING GROUP
Published by the Penguin Group
Penguin Group (USA) LLC
375 Hudson Street, New York, New York 10014

USA • Canada • UK • Ireland • Australia • New Zealand • India • South Africa • China

penguin.com

A Penguin Random House Company

SLOW HEAT

A Berkley Book / published by arrangement with the author

Berkley Books are published by The Berkley Publishing Group.
BERKLEY® is a registered trademark of Penguin Group (USA) LLC.
The "B" design is a trademark of Penguin Group (USA) LLC.

For information, address: The Berkley Publishing Group,
a division of Penguin Group (USA) LLC,
375 Hudson Street, New York, New York 10014.

ISBN: 978-0-425-27099-8

PUBLISHING HISTORY
Berkely Sensation mass-market edition / February 2010
Berkley mass-market edition / February 2014

PRINTED IN THE UNITED STATES OF AMERICA

10 9 8 7 6 5 4 3 2 1

Cover photographs: man © Shutterstock/Yuri Arcurs;
woman © Shutterstock/Elnur;
dugout © Getty/Flickr.
Cover design by Annette Fiore DeFex.

Acknowledgments

To my dear friend Gena, who when I said I was stuck, ever so sweetly told me to shut up and get writing, because she wanted something good to read.

And to Nicole, who is never afraid to tell me when I suck. The sign of a true friend.

Love you both bunches!

Chapter 1

Confucius say: "Baseball wrong—man with four balls cannot walk."

—Author Unknown

She'd read somewhere that the way to a man's heart was through his stomach, but Samantha McNead knew better than that—in certain men the stomach was aiming just a bit too high.

Wade O'Riley was one of them.

The best defensive catcher in Major League Baseball, he had women lining up to meet him wherever he went. And it wasn't home cooking that they wanted to give him either.

Not that Wade seemed to mind. Nope, even with all the constraints that went with the new big, fat, multimillion dollar contract he'd just signed for Santa Barbara's expansion team, the Heat, the guy seemed oblivious to pressure. Laid-back and easygoing, he took everything as it came, with a grain of salt and a slow, knowing smile that let everyone in on the joke.

Because life was one big funny joke to Wade.

Sam appreciated that, she just didn't live it the way he

did. Didn't know how. As the publicist for the Heat, as one of the few females in a man's world, her life tended to be more work than fun lately. Hence her mission today.

The limo pulled up in front of Wade's big, cottage-style beach house, perched on a bluff over the ocean. From the backseat she could see the waves froth and pitch.

Much like her stomach.

In the work aspect of her life, she was extremely comfortable. That was a given. She'd been raised by men: her father, her uncle, her brother, and her cousins were all tough, implacable, unforgiving alpha males. Failure had never been an option, which translated to being very good at whatever she tackled. Unfortunately for her more womanly parts, all she'd tackled lately was the job.

A job she loved with all her heart, but sometimes she yearned for more. Maybe one of these days a man would sweep her off her feet and then into bed, but it wouldn't be today, and it wouldn't be with the guy she'd been tasked with babysitting.

The Heat had played last night. It was the first week of April, and it'd been an exhibition game, a prelude to their season opener on Sunday. They'd played the Padres, and it'd turned out to be surprisingly down and dirty. Wade had hit a homer in the second inning, then been harshly walked in the third when the pitcher had hit him in the thigh with a throwaway pitch. The game had gone two extra innings, until past midnight, when the Heat had finally won on Wade's double, so Sam expected him to be exhausted and probably sore as hell. Maybe she'd even have to pull him out of bed.

The thought brought concern, and a secret tingle to those womanly parts she'd been neglecting.

Nice to know they still worked.

As she reached for the limo door handle, Wade's front

door opened, and six feet of rugged, lean, muscled male stepped out in Levi's and an untucked blue and white striped button-down. A gust of wind molded his clothes against the body that tended to make Sam's tongue stick to the roof of her mouth.

Wade stopped to slide on his sunglasses, the picture of a California surfer, all easygoing, laid-back charm.

He'd been a rock star in another life, Sam was convinced, and she purposely let out a breath and leaned back, reminding herself he was just a guy. A *flawed* guy at that, though certainly none of his flaws happened to be showing at the moment.

He moved across the lawn in an unhurried, sexy stride, all scruffy gorgeousness, and opened the limo door, letting in the chilly April afternoon air. With one hand on the roof, the other on the door, he bent down, peering in through his Prada sunglasses, merely arching a brow when he saw her.

Couldn't blame him. They weren't exactly on speaking terms.

His sun-kissed light brown hair was either styled messy today on purpose, or he hadn't bothered with a comb. His face sported at least a day-old beard so she was going with the no comb theory. He should have looked sloppy and unkempt but nothing about him ever looked anything less than God's gift. She'd seen him in uniform, in designer suits, in workout gear, in all sorts of things including absolutely nothing, and he always looked perfect.

Especially in the nothing.

"Hey," he said in that low, slightly raspy voice of his, the one that never failed to immediately put her back up.

And/or turn her on.

"Hey yourself." He hadn't limped, and he sure as hell didn't look exhausted. The opposite, she thought a little breathlessly as his deceptively lazy gaze raked her in from head to toe. Deceptively, because behind that beach bum front of his lay a sharp-as-hell wit.

Given their . . . tense relationship at the moment, she didn't smile.

And though he usually smiled at anything female, neither did he.

"Are you okay after last night's game?" she asked.

"Always. How about you, Princess?

She'd asked him a million times not to call her that. It drove her crazy, which was of course why he did it. "I'm fine. We need to talk."

"Sorry," he said with mock regret. "But we don't talk. We fight. And I'm not in the mood."

He hadn't been "in the mood" since what she called *The Mishap*.

The Mishap Never To Be Talked About.

Except . . . except Wade got along with the entire world, and she had to admit it was disturbing that they didn't. Couldn't. But there was nothing to be done about that now.

Nothing.

She had a job to do. *They* had a job to do. "I realize you probably don't want to go over the plan," she said, feeling at a disadvantage sitting while Wade still stood. "But I really think we should."

"I know the plan," he said. "One of the corporations endorsing the Heat has a new, conservative CEO who has high *family values*, and is upset with our PR troubles—"

"*Your* PR troubles," she corrected.

He let out a tight breath and bowed his head in agreement. "And you, the Skipper, the owners—hell *everyone but me*—believes that the world cares about one more ridiculous baseball scandal involving some woman claiming I've gotten her pregnant."

"You can't blame people for believing it; you do have a bit of a playboy reputation."

"I never slept with Tia."

"She produced pictures of you and her on the beach by your house."

He just looked at her.

"See," she pointed out. "*This* is why we have to talk about it."

"Look, I get what the powers-that-be want from me. From us. We pretend to be a couple in the eyes of the press so I look like a good boy, and our endorsements won't be pulled. How hard can it be?"

"I don't know," she replied cautiously. "How hard?"

His eyes heated. And a matching heat seared through her belly at the inadvertent double entrendre. "You know what I mean, Wade. The plan—"

"The plan is that I have to behave. And you're supposed to make me." He paused. "Though I am looking forward to the *make me* part."

Oh, God. "You know what? This isn't going to work." She was fun, dammit. Even lighthearted at times. Why the hell he made her sound so uptight and stuffy, she had no idea.

Wait. She did have an idea. *An exact idea.*

She'd slept with him.

Once.

On the one single night in her entire life when she'd had too much to drink. Except there'd been no sleeping involved. To make matters worse, it'd been one of the most erotic, sensual nights of her life. "Listen, I realize we've had our differences, but—"

"Differences?" He laughed, then shook his head, still amused.

"Fine, so *differences* doesn't quite cut it. We have to

get a move on." A friend of his was getting married. A close friend who just happened to be a big-time Hollywood producer, and Wade was one of the groomsmen. The wedding was an entire weekend extravaganza, where there was sure to be tons of press. If he attracted any of it—and just by being Wade, he most definitely would—he needed to attract *good* press.

By the end of the two-hour trip to the famed Orange County, specifically Laguna Beach, they needed to be in sync and looking like lovers. Willing to do her part, she practiced a smile on him, the smile that usually got her exactly what she wanted, which in this case was Wade's cooperation. Thing was, he didn't often feel the need to cooperate. "You getting in?"

He looked at her for a long beat, all big and built and completely inscrutable, during which time she held her breath. For as kicked back as he was, he was also tough as steel. He had to be. Catchers were known for their courage and toughness, having what was arguably the hardest position in baseball. And Wade was the best catcher behind the plate, period. He had to command the respect of all the players, make the calls on the field, have good sequences in those calls, and the ability to change it up and keep the hitters off balance. All of which meant he had to be smart, sharp, and strong in both mind and body.

Wade was all of those things and more, and clearly one of those things was decisive. He tossed his overnight bag into the limo and followed it in, dropping down next to her even though he could have had the opposite seat all to himself. Leaning back, he stretched out his long, long legs and looked around. "So. We have any food in here?"

"No. Are you hungry?"

"Starving."

He was always starving. Probably because he burned

God knew how many calories a day between his five-mile runs, weight training, and the game itself. "We can stop and get something to go. Rosa's?" she asked, naming the closest café. Look at that, she was getting the hang of taking care of him already.

"DQ is good."

She'd never met a grown man with such a love for fast food before. But whatever he wanted, she'd get. It would make him happy, and a happy Wade was a hopefully compliant one. With a nod from her, the driver started the engine and they began their trek, heading through town toward Dairy Queen.

Santa Barbara was a colorful blend of the Spanish history of California and beach living. Wade was looking out the window, taking it in, giving her his profile as they turned onto Highway 1, heading south. The sparkling Pacific was on their right, the green, craggily Santa Ynez peaks on their left, both breathtaking.

They stopped at Dairy Queen and quickly got back on the road. Wade was quiet as he ate, watching as they left the affluent homes and ranches, heading into the outlying county and the less privileged areas. She knew he'd been underprivileged himself. Despite his many faults, he was surprisingly humble and quick to laugh at himself, and often joked he'd grown up so far from the proverbial train tracks that he hadn't even been able to *see* the tracks.

And her?

Well, she'd grown up with a silver spoon in her mouth and everyone knew it. It was certainly all Wade knew about her, because it'd been the only thing she'd ever let him see. He had no idea that the two of them had a hell of a lot more in common that he'd ever guess.

He polished off two burgers and went to work on his fries. "So . . ." His green eyes were relaxed but assessing as they met hers. "When were you going to tell me they want us to do this boyfriend/girlfriend thing for a whole month?"

"You heard?" she asked in surprise. She'd been asked to talk him into it.

"I work with a bunch of women, Sam. They tell all."

"You work with a group of professional athletes, male."

"Who gossip more than a bunch of teenage girls after cheerleading practice. Pace heard it from Henry, who overheard Gage talking to you."

Pace being Wade's best friend and the Heat's pitcher. Henry was their shortstop. Gage, their team manager. And yes, the supposedly *professional* clubhouse really *was* similar in nature to a high school locker room.

Sprawled out, relaxed, Wade watched her with a half smile, looking far too appealing. She took a careful breath. "A month shows stability. It's more impressive than just a weekend wedding fling."

"So you're okay with being joined at the hip for a month?"

"If you are."

He considered this. "Are there benefits?"

"No."

He sighed. "So much for fun."

"Hey, I'm fun." He didn't say a word, which burned. "I am! And I just realized, there *are* benefits."

He cocked his head.

"Well . . . I can be a pretty convincing bitch when I want to be."

"Noooo," he said with feigned shock. "But how exactly is that a benefit?"

"I can scare away all the crazy women that chase you around, thereby giving you a break. And in return, you can relax knowing you won't have to take care of me like your usual fan-girl, clingy type who bores you within the span of one date."

He arched a brow.

"Just calling 'em like I see 'em."

He didn't say anything to that as he finished his fries, then tossed all the trash into the bag and set it aside. He rubbed a hand over his jaw and said another entire boat-load of nothing.

"It's just a role, Wade. And it could have been worse. We could have lost the endorsement entirely, or they could have traded you."

"They're that desperate for good press?" He shook his head in disbelief.

"Hey, baseball isn't exactly showing its best foot to the public lately. We need this. The Heat needs this."

"And your father's okay with it?" he asked carefully.

With good reason. Her father was one of the owners of the Heat. Her uncle owned their sister team, the South Carolina Charleston Bucks. The McNead brothers were famous for getting their way, or more accurately, infamous.

And they were baseball royalty.

Or had been until Samantha's brother Jeremy—her PR equivalent at the Bucks—had stepped over the ethics line, the moral line, and several other lines as well, and brought the wrath of the press down on the McNeads. It hadn't gone over well, and damage control was required. *Gee, guess who was in charge of damage control?* "Yes," she said quietly. "My father thinks it's a good idea."

"So they're willing to pimp out their princess when it suits them."

Ouch. But the answer was yes, a McNead was expected to stick to the pack. She'd known that by the time she could talk in full sentences. "It's just an illusion."

"It's an entire month."

The reminder made her stomach quiver. An entire month of being his girlfriend. "We're grown-ups."

"Really?" His stark green gaze was more genuine curiosity than sarcasm. "Because we've not spent more than two minutes together without snarling at each other."

God. So true.

"Well, except for the elevator," he said.

Also true, and her stomach executed a double gainer with a twist as the memory flew back, hot and sexy, resurrected by nothing more than the sound of his voice and the sudden sleepy look in his eyes.

It'd happened last season. The Heat had just lost, bad. The press had been ruthless, and her father had been pissed at her for somehow not being Super Woman. She'd been in desperate need of some alone time.

What she'd gotten instead was stuck in an elevator on the way to her hotel room with Wade and a couple little bottles of airplane Scotch, and her pity party for one had turned into a naked party for two. The erotic, alcohol-tinged memories came to her in slow-mo and as always, *always*, sent her spinning between total and complete humiliation and an even more devastating aching hunger and desire.

If she could just erase from her memory banks the picture of Wade taking her straight to heaven in under five minutes she would, but the pictures in her brain seemed to only strengthen with time instead of lessen. She darted a quick glance at their driver, who was currently sipping a seventy-two-ounce DQ soda and rocking his head to the radio as he beat the steering wheel like a drum. "I don't want to discuss that night."

Wade shrugged. No skin off his nose. Hell, he'd probably had lots of nights like that since. She concentrated on the view. Not a hardship. Santa Barbara wasn't called the American Riviera for nothing, and she watched as they passed four-thousand-foot peaks covered in unique and beautiful chaparral and sandstone outcrops. "So we're good?" she asked quietly.

Wade smiled. It was his professional smile, the one that could melt a woman's panties at fifty paces and make men wish that they had half his athletic prowess, and it was a charmer. She knew its potency, braced herself for it, and *still* felt her panties begin to melt. "What the hell." He stretched out even farther, his leg sliding to hers. "We're good. *Girlfriend*."

"*Fake* girlfriend," she corrected, shoving him over, telling herself she was absolutely not noticing the heat of him, the feel of his rock hard thigh . . .

He stretched some more, straightening his arms above him, briefly exposing a flash of washboard abs between the hem of his shirt and the waistband of his jeans. Jeans that were faded at all the stress points. He had some very fine stress points . . .

She saw more men in a day than the average woman dreamed of. Many of those men—if she was in the clubhouse before a game—in various stages of nakedness, leaving her utterly immune to tantalizing glimpses of male skin.

Which didn't explain why her mouth went dry.

"Maybe we should kiss on it," Wade suggested. "Seal the deal."

Her tummy quivered, a fact she firmly ignored. "What? No!"

"Spoilsport."

He'd probably have fallen over if she'd said yes, which she absolutely wouldn't do. Even if he was the kiss master.

Which he was . . .

His leg was touching hers again. He was hogging the backseat, albeit unintentionally. He was a big guy and he needed space. He also smelled good. He looked good, too, which really didn't seem fair at all. But he was here, not pitching a diva fit, and she owed him for that. "Thank you," she said. "For agreeing to this."

"You're welcome."

Well, that seemed surprisingly genuine, and she had to wonder if maybe she'd anticipated trouble with him simply because of their past. Maybe . . . maybe deep down he really was a good guy.

It was possible.

Maybe they could laugh about this, her having to keep up the pretense of being his lover, when they'd already done the deed.

That could possibly be fun. Maybe.

Sort of.

And maybe they could even become friends. It would be nice—

"You packing any Scotch today?" he asked, looking around the limo. "Should I be bracing myself for you to tear my clothes off again?"

With a sigh, she leaned back and closed her eyes. She could safely check both fun and friends off the list.

Chapter 2

Some people are born on third base and go through
life thinking they hit a triple.

—Barry Switzer

Wade didn't have a problem playing dress up with the
sexy, tough-as-nails Samantha McNead. Hell, he'd been
playing dress up in one form or another since birth, using
bravado, sheer grit, and a good amount of bullshit to get
to where he was today. His life was a virtual Mr. Cinder-
ella story.

Sometimes he still pinched himself.

So this pretend shit, whatever he and Sam were expected to do this weekend? Right up his alley, baby. But
he knew it wasn't up Sam's.

Her shoulders were back, spine stiff, the tension rolling
off her in waves. She was usually wound a little tight but
today she seemed to be setting new records for herself.
She wore her shoulder-length blond hair up in some complicated knot thing that had to be giving her a headache.
The fitted jacket of her business suit gave her the profes-
sionalism he knew she needed on her job. The narrow skirt
aimed to do the same thing, but instead emphasized the

greatest legs on this side of the Continental Divide. If they were less than a country mile, he'd eat his shorts. And her heels. Christ, those sexy heels. He had no idea how she could walk in them, but damn, he loved them.

She glanced over and caught him staring. With a sound that said she found his perusal unsettling, she crossed her legs away from him, bare skin sliding on bare skin.

Ah, man. He loved that sound. She had great skin. *Creamy and smooth and—*

His cell phone buzzed, interrupting the thought. Sam waved, gesturing that he should answer it, looking relieved to have him occupied.

"So," Pace said without a greeting when Wade opened his phone. "Is the rumor correct? Are you and Sam playing nice for an entire month?"

"Partially correct," Wade said.

"Which part?"

"The month part. Not necessarily the *play nice* part."

Sam had been looking at the water but that brought her attention back to him while in his ear Pace laughed softly. "Don't let her kill you before the wedding tomorrow," his bemused friend said. "Holly, Gage, and I will be there at noon. We want to see the show."

"You mean the wedding."

"That, too," Pace said with an obvious smirk.

"I'm sorry, exactly how is this so funny?"

"Well, you've never met a woman you couldn't conquer, and she's sure as hell never met a guy whose balls she couldn't crush. So who's going to survive? That's the million-dollar question."

Okay, so things were admittedly awkward between him and Sam, but whatever she wanted to believe, they *were* still attracted to each other. Wade had always been perfectly willing to follow through on their attraction, but she held back, leaving him unsure of what exactly her feelings were when it came to him. If he'd thought he had a snowball's chance in hell of winning her over, he'd have tried by now. "I didn't laugh at you when you had that sexy little reporter dogging your heels," he said to Pace. "The one you asked to marry you."

"Hell yeah, you did. You laughed your ass off. And what are you saying, that you're going to get engaged to Sam the way I did with Holly?"

Wade opened his mouth, then closed it *and* his phone.

"So," Sam murmured. "They think this is amusing."

"Yeah." He let out a breath. Not a lot got past his chill façade these days, but the reality of what they needed to pull off did. After a physically intense spring training, all he'd wanted was this weekend off before the crazy started again, a weekend of relaxation. Samantha McNead was nice on the eyes, very nice, but not much for relaxing. Letting out a low laugh, he rubbed his eyes with the heels of his hands. "So I get why I'm in this, but why you?"

"Gage."

The name was reason enough. Gage Pasquel was the youngest, toughest, most badass team manager in the MLB. He did whatever he felt necessary to run the Heat with winning efficiency, but in the end, he answered to the GM and the owners, one of which was her father. "You could have said no."

Sam slid him a long look. "And you could have behaved."

"I always behave."

She made a sound that said she thought he was full of shit. And she might be right. He did have a little authority problem, always had. "You have to admit," he said. "The press has been unfairly relentless."

"Yes, well, the probability of someone watching you at

any given moment is directly proportional to the level of stupidity of whatever it is you're doing."

"Are you suggesting I act stupidly?"

"No," she said. "That would be rude."

He laughed and shook his head.

She relaxed with a small smile. "As if you care what I think about you anyway."

He'd forgotten how pretty she was when she smiled, and seeing her good humor brought his own to the surface. Maybe there was hope for that stick-up-her-ass after all. "Admit it, Sam. You're already having fun."

"I'll have fun when this is over. And you're right, the press *is* relentless, especially with us, and you know why. We're a new team, a talented team, but we're young and we make young mistakes. We had those accusations of drug use last season, and—"

"I know." As a result of those accusations, they'd lost a promising pitcher and one of their coaches had retired early. Pace had briefly come under fire as well. Even Sam had inadvertently been dragged under when her brother Jeremy had confessed to leaking false stories to the press in order to make the Heat look bad.

Then to add insult to injury, Wade had attracted a bunch of press in the past few weeks when Tia Rodriquez, claiming to be pregnant with Wade's baby, had produced pictures of the two of them. As Tia wasn't exactly a credible source—after all, she'd stalked Pace just last year— management hadn't been overly concerned at first. But then she'd managed to get several national newspapers and blogs to take her seriously.

Baseball did love a scandal.

When the Heat's corporate sponsors had begun to make noise, management stepped in, getting a restraining order against Tia and slapping Wade's wrist at the same time.

He wasn't sure how he felt about pretending to be in a relationship to please some CEO he'd never even met. On one hand, it would be nice to have someone to share this weekend event with. On the other hand, it was Sam, who gave him a hard time about everything. Sam who'd argue with him about the sky being blue. Sam with whom he'd once spent those wild few hours in an Atlanta hotel elevator. Sam who'd rocked his world after he'd gotten his ass kicked two games in a row by the Braves.

The *Braves*.

He could still remember striking out and then missing a pop fly at home, letting in two runs. Gage had chewed his ass out. Hell, he'd chewed his own ass out. And then the coup de grace. He'd gone back to the hotel, gotten onto an elevator, and realized he was alone with Sam.

He'd expected it to be more hell, but it'd turned out to be the best two hours in his entire damn life. He'd never forget the sound she'd made as she'd come for him, as if she hadn't come in forever, as if he'd given her something no one else had.

And yet now . . . now she preferred to ignore him.

As if her thoughts were just as disturbing, Sam sighed and leaned her head back, exposing her neck as she closed her eyes.

"Well, one thing's for sure," he murmured, eyes on the spot where her pulse beat, a spot he'd once ravished and suddenly wanted to ravish again. "It's going to be an interesting month."

"Hmm."

Something about the doubt loaded into that single syllable made him want to push her buttons. "I'll be sure to carry around a flask in case you feel the need for another quickie."

Eyes still closed, her mouth tightened. "You can carry

an entire bar with you, I'm not interested in anything happening between us ever again."

"Ever?"

Opening her eyes, she leveled him with one single withering stare. "Ever."

"Yeah." He slid his sunglasses on and eased back. "Me either."

"Good," she said.

Better than good, he thought. Except for two small points. She was lying.

And so was he.

It took exactly two hours to make the drive from Santa Barbara to Laguna Beach. At the exclusive Laguna Rey Resort, there were already paparazzi in the lobby, looking to get shots of the famous wedding guests as they arrived for their weekend.

Until recently, Wade had always had a sort of live-and-let-live relationship with the press. He'd always understood that the more uptight he got about smiling for the cameras, the more houndlike the people behind the cameras got.

So he smiled as he reached back to offer Sam a hand out of the limo, carefully blocking the money shot with his body so that the paparazzi couldn't snap the view up her skirt.

And it was a glorious view.

Once she straightened, she sent him a thanks with her eyes, and for an odd second, he got snagged by the sky-blue depths. She seemed to do the same, then the beat was gone and she tried to step back, away from him.

He merely tightened his grip and reeled her in, dipping down to put his mouth to the sweet spot beneath her ear as the flashes went off all around them. "Mine," he whispered. "Remember?"

She shot him a look that made his whole afternoon. Someday he'd have to visit why the hell he loved to piss her off, but for now he'd just enjoy the effects. "Oh, and hey," he murmured. "My girlfriend would definitely be all over me. Hands, mouth, *everything*, so—"

"Yeah, yeah." But she softened her smile, and then blew his mind when she pressed her body to his.

Look at that, she was really going to do this. And he wondered with a little surge of sheer lust just how far she would be willing to take it.

At the resort doors, they were nearly bowled over by the crowd. There was a group of fans who wanted autographs, and several women who managed to write their phone numbers on Wade's hand before he pulled free.

Sam sent him an arched brow, but he just shrugged. He got numbers written on him a lot; he'd never figured out how to stop that from happening.

Then there were the photographers. One particularly zealous guy was standing in their way, trying to get their picture. "Who's your date, Wade?" he shouted.

Wade just smiled and tucked Sam in closer to his side. She squirmed against him, just a little, until he whispered "photo op" in her ear, and like magic she went still.

Yeah. This was going to be fun after all.

Chapter 3

Being with a woman all night never hurt no professional baseball player. It's staying up all night looking for a woman that does him in.

—Casey Stengel

Sam had spent much of her professional life being in charge: of crowd control, of taking care of the players, the staff, everyone, and yet she let Wade lead her through the lobby. He had her pulled in close to him, her hand firmly in his big, warm, callused one, relaxed and easy as he moved through the masses with ease.

It wasn't as hard as she'd thought. In fact, secretly it was nice to be taken care of for once instead of the other way around.

Even if it was pretend.

The press stuck to them like ants at a picnic. The same obnoxious photographer from outside managed to follow them in, and nearly clubbed her with his long lens, but a strong forearm suddenly blocked Sam's vision. Wade, pushing the lens away from her. "Watch it," he said to the photographer.

Not listening, or maybe just not caring, the guy lifted

the lens again, this time right in Sam's face. Wade shook his head, like he couldn't believe what an idiot he was, then solved the problem by stepping in front of the camera so that the lens bumped his chest.

The photographer, now looking straight up into the six feet of sheer muscle that made up Wade O'Riley, swallowed and backed up.

And stayed there.

That was the thing about Wade. First impression said lazy beach bum. Many didn't look closer than that, but if they did, they'd see a guy with a highly developed sense of ease with himself, but also a low tolerance for bullshit.

"I'm supposed to meet up with Mark at the lounge," he said to Sam as if nothing had happened, as if they were all alone. "You coming?"

Mark was Mark Lyons, the groom. He and Wade had been close friends ever since their wild college days at Cal State Long Beach. Sam should excuse herself and go to the room and get some work done, but this weekend was about getting the message out that Wade was off the market, so she nodded. She was going. She was going wherever he went. For a month.

Good Lord.

The magnitude of what she'd agreed to was starting to hit her. But her family had been through a rough time lately with the trouble her brother had caused. And although she'd rather *not* play Wade's girlfriend, she didn't want to let her dad down, or the team. Yes, she was still embarrassed about the elevator incident, but it was long over and done. There was nothing she could do about it other than give in as gracefully as she could, and work together with Wade to get past it. If he was willing, then so was she.

Wade drew her into an open, elegant lounge off the lobby, which was as upscale as the rest of the resort. They sat at a small table near the back so as to be as inconspicuous as possible. It was habit on Wade's part, she knew, self-preservation against getting recognized.

Not that he ever seemed to mind the obligatory and endless autograph signing, or even stopping to chat with fans. Unlike many players at his level, he never turned anyone away, or revealed anything but that easy charm and patience when stopped—pushy paparazzi aside—but he at least tried to fly under the radar when he could.

A pretty, young waitress made her way to them and immediately lit up at the sight of Wade. "Hey, gorgeous! I've got tickets to Sunday's game. You gonna kick some ass?"

He smiled. "Going to try."

She grinned. "God, you are *hawt*." She shifted a little closer, like they were alone in the world, "What can I get for ya?" she murmured throatily.

"Let me check with my girlfriend." Wade looked at Sam, the smile still playing about his lips, enjoying the game. "What would you like, Princess?"

What she would like was to smack him for calling her *princess*. "An iced tea," she started, then shook her head. She was going to need more than caffeine for this, she was going to need fortification. "No, make that a Corona."

Wade leaned in and waggled a brow. "Sure you don't want a Scotch?"

"I'm sure!"

He smiled at her, then at the waitress. "Two Coronas, please."

"Sure thing, baby. Anything for you."

As she sauntered away, hips swinging, Sam rolled her eyes so hard they nearly fell onto the table.

"Sorry about the press rush out there," Wade said. "You okay?"

"Sure thing, baby."

He grimaced at her imitation of the waitress. "Okay, keep in mind, not everything that happens with women is my fault."

"Uh-huh. How much of it would you say *is* your fault? Fifty percent?"

He scratched his chin. "That might be a little low."

The server came back with their beers and a Sharpie pen. "Can you sign me?" She turned, giving Wade her profile, and stuck her hip out. She was wearing a short white skirt and a matching polo shirt with a black apron.

Wade obligingly took the Sharpie. "On your skirt? This is permanent ink."

"Well," she said, eating him up with her eyes. "If you want to sign under it . . ."

Oh, for crissake. Sam leaned over and grabbed a beer from the tray. She was at a slow simmer, which made no sense. No sense at all. For four years she'd been privy to the way the public fell all over themselves for Wade, especially women. Hell, it was why she was here today. She needed to get over herself.

He signed on the skirt, and not beneath it, much to the waitress's obvious disappointment. When she was gone, Sam gave him a look. "Must suck to be you."

"My cross to bear," he agreed easily.

She nudged her chin in the direction of the two other waitresses behind the bar, staring at him, giggling. "Brace yourself."

And sure enough, not two minutes later, they sidled up to the table, holding out Sharpies as well.

Wade slid Sam a quick look, which she met drolly, only to find herself surprised at the apology in his eyes. He signed the autographs, then obligingly posed for their camera phone when they handed it to Sam and asked her to take their picture with Wade.

"Can we kiss you?" one of them asked him.

"No," Sam said.

Disappointed, they left.

Wade looked amused. And obnoxiously full of himself. "I've never seen this jealous streak in you before. I like it."

"You are so ridiculously spoiled. You have no idea."

"I think I do," he said mildly.

She laughed and reached for her beer. "Yeah, right."

"Hey, I wasn't born like this, you know. I had a childhood, and then the awkward teenage stage where no girl would even look at me—"

"*Pul-leeze.*"

"I'm serious." He studied her for a long moment. "I was small for my age, and scrawny. It was survival of the fittest, and I definitely wasn't anywhere close. I got beat up all the time."

She looked at him, not sure if he was pulling her leg, but he looked right back, eyes even and steady.

He was telling the truth. "So what happened?" she asked. "You magically got big and bad and sexy in college?"

He arched a brow.

"Come on, you have a mirror."

"What happened is I finally grew, and in college had access to a gym, so yeah on the big and bad." He flashed her a smile.

"What?"

"You think I'm sexy."

"Looks will fade."

He kept smiling.

"What *now*?"

"You want me."

"I do not." She did. God help her, she did.

"You want me bad, Princess. Admit it."

She was spared responding when a tall, dark, and handsome man came up to Wade and grabbed his beer. He downed it, slapped it back to the table, then wiped his mouth with the back of his hand. "You son of a bitch." And then he swung a punch at Wade's head.

Wade ducked the punch, then went low and hard, grabbing the guy around the middle and surging up with him to his feet.

Sam leapt to her feet as well, pulling out her cell phone to call the police, but Wade was laughing, and the guy he was holding on to grabbed him up in a great, big bear hug.

"Can you believe it?" he asked Wade with a wide grin as flashes went off all around them. "We're here for my *wedding*. Meg still hasn't run off and left my sorry ass— at least not yet." Built like a football linesman, with the smile of a real charmer, he finally let go of Wade and pulled back to look at Sam. "Well, hello there," he purred.

"Mark, I presume," Sam said drolly, putting away her phone since it appeared she didn't have to protect her multimillion dollar player.

"In the flesh," Mark said with a little bow.

"You two always greet each other like Neanderthals?"

Wade watched Mark laugh and shake Sam's hand, watched Sam smile back at Mark—and for the record, it was her real smile, too, not the fake ones she'd been pawning off on him all damn day.

"Samantha McNead," she said smoothly. "Publicist for the Heat—" She broke off, looking horrified as she clearly recognized her mistake.

She'd introduced herself as if she were here in a professional capacity.

But she wasn't.

She was here, pretending to be Wade's girlfriend.

Mark cocked his head and studied her. "Well, aren't you a serious thing?" He glanced at Wade. "Not your usual type, is she?"

Sam had frozen, so Wade opened his mouth to tell Mark the real deal between them, but before he could say a word, Mark laughed good and hard and pulled Sam up for the same bear hug he'd given Wade. "So maybe you'll actually stick."

Sam relaxed, and seeming relieved, she hugged Mark back as Wade looked on, a little surprised to find that her real smile completely softened her face.

Not that she wasn't gorgeous. Because she was. Willowy, stacked, and blond, she absolutely was, and she took his breath . . . But when she smiled from the heart, she was more than just beautiful. She seemed approachable.

Sweet.

Which had to be an optical illusion.

"I'm still blown away that we're actually here." Mark gestured to their luxurious surroundings, then slapped Wade's back. "Not bad considering how we started out, huh?"

"How did you start out?" Sam asked.

"Don't get him started," Wade told her, hoping to get a subject change pronto.

But of course Sam ignored him. "I'd love to hear it," she said to Mark with that sweet smile.

Wade groaned and Mark grinned as they all sat back down. He loved to tell this story every bit as much as Wade hated to hear it.

"Wade and I go way back," Mark started. "We met at orientation for Cal State Long Beach, just two punk street kids. We became roommates." He grinned in fond memory. "I think we lived off ramen noodles for the next four years, not a frigging penny to our names, either of us." He looked at Wade. "How many nights did we steal food out of the cafeteria while dreaming of Big Macs?"

"Too many," Wade said, giving in with a shake of his head. Mark found it all vastly amusing, but when Wade thought of those days, more than the long hours of studying to make up for his lack of such habits in high school, more than finding his love of baseball, he remembered the nights he'd gone to bed with his belly growling. Feeling Sam's eyes on him, he turned and looked into her baby blues, filled with a surprising warmth and compassion.

Great. Now she felt sorry for him.

Perfect.

"And now look at us," Mark marveled. "Me, a freaking Hollywood producer, and Wade a star pro ballplayer. Blows my mind every time." He grabbed Wade in another bone-crunching hug. "Love you, man."

"Okay," Wade said, good-naturedly hugging him back before gently shoving free. "Save it for the alcohol-soaked reception. We're going to check in."

"Good." Mark nodded. "I'll see you in a few."

Wade watched Mark walk off, well aware that Sam was still studying him, probably trying to figure out how he felt about Mark exposing such a personal time in his life, but the only thing he felt was relief that he no longer went to bed hungry, and an undeniable joy at the thought of the weekend ahead, spent with good friends.

"Oh, and don't forget Meg's schedule," Mark called back. "God help us all if we don't follow it."

"Schedule?" Sam murmured.

Wade slung a friendly arm over her shoulders and kissed the top of her head. "I'm all the schedule you need, baby."

With a short laugh, she eyed the bill for their drinks and reached for her purse.

Wade put a hand over hers and dropped some cash on the table.

"I don't expect you to pay for me this weekend, Wade."

"You're just worried you'll owe me."

The look that crossed her face told him he was right as they headed across the lobby toward the front desk. She walked quickly and efficiently, pulling ahead of him, her very professional business suit giving a serious back-off air to anyone who looked. Or maybe that was the way she walked, as if she owned her world and intended to own his as well, her narrow, fitted skirt hugging her very fine hips and ass, her heels clicking with authority.

Wade caught up with her, setting a hand on the small of her back, smiling with satisfaction when she gave a little jump.

"Just me," he murmured, liking the feel of her beneath his fingers. *Feminine. Curvy.*

Warm.

She was talking to the clerk, so he pulled out his phone to check for messages. He had a text from his father, which sucked some of the air out of him.

Hey, hot shot. Return a damn call sometime.
Thanks for the physical therapist slash babysitter,
but no thanks. You know what I want.

Yeah, what John O'Riley wanted was far harder to give than something Wade could write a check for. Forgiveness. But Wade had spent his entire childhood wanting something, too, and that something was to be more important to his father than the alcohol.

It hadn't happened then, and it wasn't likely to happen now, so Wade hit delete. Not the smartest or most efficient way to handle his father, but hell, he'd gotten his stubbornness from the gene pool, and as John himself was fond of saying, the apple hadn't fallen far from the tree.

"The name again?" the guy behind the counter asked Sam as his fingers worked the keyboard.

"McNead," Sam said.

"And O'Riley," Wade added, sliding his phone away. "I have a suite. Maybe we should get connecting—"

"Just McNead," Sam said, giving Wade a little nudge, trying to move him away.

Interesting. He nudged back, letting her leg bump his. Dipping his head so that his nose brushed her soft and silky hair, he murmured, "What are you up to?"

"Nothing." She smiled at the check-in clerk, who handed over two card keys.

Wade remained silent until they stood waiting for an elevator. "What was that?"

"What was what?"

"You hijacked my room."

She leaned forward and hit the elevator button three times in quick, irritated succession. "I didn't think you'd mind sharing with your girlfriend."

"I'd be excited, if I thought it meant that we were going to—"

"We're not." She punched the button again. "This was part of the mandate, okay? It has to look real. People are watching. I'm no more comfortable with this than you are, but we agreed to do it." The elevator opened and she shoved him inside, quickly smacking the close door button, even as one poor soul ran toward them yelling, "Hold that elevator!"

She didn't.

Wade turned to face her as the doors slid closed. "Wow."

"I know!" She covered her face. "Please, let's just *not* talk."

He studied her flaming ears. She was cute when she was flustered. "That's bad karma, you know, not holding the elevator."

"Thanks for not talking."

"And trust me, bad karma comes back around like a boomerang. That one's going to bite you right on your very nice ass, Sam."

"He'll get another elevator!" she exclaimed, tossing up her hands. "We needed privacy."

God, he loved it when she lost her cool and revealed the real Sam lurking beneath that princess exterior. "You're right. We need privacy. In fact, I should have done this in the limo and gotten it out of the way." He reached for the top button on his Levi's.

Her eyes nearly bugged right out of her head. "What are you doing?"

"Getting naked, which is how you wanted me the last time we were alone in an elevator."

"Oh my God." She pressed her hands to her head as if she couldn't quite believe it, then slapped one of those hands to his chest and shoved him back another step.

That, too. He loved that, too, when she got physical. He'd never told her, but when she was in the stands during a game screaming for him, he loved it.

"For the last time," she said urgently, almost desperately, as if trying to talk herself into believing it. "It's never going to happen again. *Never*, Wade."

"Never is a long time."

"Never. Ever. *Ever*. Which is even longer than never!"

Her eyes were dilated, which was fascinating. And he'd swear that the pulse at the base of her neck was fluttering faster than a hummingbird's wings, which was even more fascinating.

Yeah. This really was going to be fun.

Chapter 4

To have some idea what it's like [to be a MLB catcher], stand in the outside lane of a motorway, get your mate to drive his car at you at ninety-five mph and wait until he's twelve yards away before you decide which way to jump.

—Geoffrey Boycott

Samantha walked through the suite. It was beautiful and quiet, with a gorgeous view of the ocean.

It had only one bedroom.

And one bed.

Sure, it was a king and piled thick with luxurious bedding, and looked so comfortable that she could have lain on it forever, but the knowledge that when it came time to hit the sack later, she'd be hitting it with Wade sent butterflies straight to her stomach.

And other parts . . .

Her cell phone rang. It was Holly, Pace's fiancée. "Pace is working out, so I had a few minutes."

Holly and Sam had become good friends this past year, even more so now that Pace and Wade had become business partners as well as best friends, purchasing and renovating random parcels of land into parks for kids and creating sports clubs in those parks with coaching and organized league games.

Well, Pace had anyway.

Mostly Wade just wrote checks.

He was good at that, writing checks, Sam had noticed. He often solved problems by throwing money at them. She only wished this problem could be solved so easily.

"I'm eating popcorn and watching a *Friends* marathon," Holly said in her ear. "I thought I'd call and see how it's going."

Well aware of Wade checking out the suite behind her, Sam kept her voice down. "I'd rather be eating popcorn and watching a *Friends* marathon."

"Sam," Holly said very gently. "You need professional help."

"Why?"

"You'd actually pick *Friends* over one of the yummiest guys I've ever seen?"

"I'm going to tell Pace you said that."

"Just think about how long it's been since you've gotten laid," Holly said. "And then do yourself a favor and turn off your phone and look at Wade. Just look at all his yumminess and do what comes naturally."

"What comes naturally will get me twenty-five years to life."

"Don't kill him, honey. *Do* him."

Sam rolled her eyes and hung up on Holly's laugh, then turned and came face-to-face with the six-foot-tall, heart-stopping, annoying-as-hell catcher she'd arranged to "sleep" with.

Thanks to her job, the first thing that usually came to mind when she thought about any of the Heat players was their stats. And Wade had stats in spades. At the moment, he was the most celebrated catcher in the National League. His defensive prowess was more anecdotal than measured but his numbers were telling. Last year he'd picked twenty-eight runners off the bases, an astonishing fifty percent of the runners attempting to steal. He also had 32 HRs, a 120 RBI, a .355 BA, and had placed second in the MVP voting.

But that's not what she thought of when she looked at him. Nope, she was thinking Holly was right about one thing, he *was* pretty damn *yum*.

He began unbuttoning his shirt and tossed his bag to the bed to rifle through it. He shrugged out of the shirt—holy cow—and while she concentrated on not dragging her tongue down his chest clear to his low-slung Levi's, he replaced it with a light blue T-shirt advertising some surf shop in Mexico. He kicked off the clean running shoes he'd been wearing and pulled on a pair of battered Nikes instead.

"Casual wear for this kind of place," she noted, voice shockingly even, given that she watched as he bent to tie the Nikes, his jeans stretched tight across his perfect ass.

"There's a charity baseball game in thirty minutes," he said, straightening. "And God willing, food as well."

"You just ate. And there's a game?"

"I ate two hours ago. And yeah, there's a game. All the guys in the wedding party are playing. Thought you'd heard."

No, she hadn't, as he damn well knew. And since she'd had approximately fifteen minutes of advance warning about this whole weekend adventure, she'd grabbed only her usual daywear. Business suits, which she'd figured would cover both the wedding and any other parties they'd have to attend. "Good thing I'm not part of the wedding party then."

His smile changed, went a little secretive. "Yes, it's a good thing."

She paused, eyes narrowed. "I'm not playing in this charity game."

"No, unless you've grown a penis I don't know about."

"I mean it, Wade." She'd been watching baseball since before she could walk, but as a girlie-girl from Rochester, New York, one who'd gone to Princeton before joining the family obsession with baseball, she'd actually never played.

She could golf, she could play ping-pong, and she could bowl when she had to, but she could not throw, catch, or hit a baseball to save her life.

Wade pulled out his phone and looked at the time. "We have five minutes. You might want to change."

"I'm fine in this."

"Suit yourself." He grabbed his second duffle, an equipment bag, and opened it to check his glove and bat, then shouldered the bag. "Ready?"

Was she? She had no idea.

He opened the suite door and pushed Sam through ahead of him.

"So," she said as they headed toward the elevators. "There's only one bed."

"I noticed. You're the best girlfriend ever."

She let out a low laugh. "I meant for there to be two."

"Ah."

"We should probably talk about it now."

"Sure."

"Want to flip for the couch?"

"Nope." He smiled and slipped an arm around her. "Don't worry. I only want the bed, not you."

She looked up into his face. "Really?"

He grinned. "What do you think?"

She narrowed her eyes. "I think the couch has your name all over it."

"I'm too big."

Undoubtedly true. "I'll call up for a roll-away mattress."

He sighed. "I think I'm beginning to see why you have

to be the pretend girlfriend. You're not so good at the real thing."

Ouch. And okay, so she wasn't so good at the real thing; she tended to sabotage her own happiness for work, but hell if she'd admit that out loud.

They came up to the elevator, and once again unwelcome memories smacked into her unbidden; Wade's long, drugging kisses melting away her bones, how he'd looked at her from those sleepy, sexy eyes as he'd unbuttoned her jacket, his long, nimble fingers on her body. In her body . . .

Dammit. She got on elevators all the time. That she was having flashbacks now had to be *his* fault—

Wade crowded up behind her and reached around to push the button. "We don't have time for a quickie right now," he murmured soft and husky in her ear. "But if you behave, I'll let you seduce me on the way back."

She gritted her teeth. "Wade?"

"Yes, Princess?"

"Shut up."

He grinned and grabbed her hand when the doors opened at the lobby level.

"What are you doing?" she asked, trying to pull free.

"Pretending. Join me, won't you?"

He so messed with her head, she'd nearly forgotten. He was smiling, talking to her, looking perfectly at ease as they walked across the lobby, and her head was spinning, from his easy touch, his smile . . .

He tugged her closer. "My girlfriends think I'm adorable and sexy as hell, so you should be all over me. And smile at me a lot."

She choked. "Adorable?"

He thought about that. "You're right, adorable might be a stretch. Okay, we'll stick with the sexy-as-hell part. Photo op, three o'clock."

Oh, God. "This is such a bad idea."

"A spectacularly bad one." He turned her in the right direction. "But I've learned to always make the best of a situation." With a grin, he leaned in and gave her one smacking kiss on the lips, and flashes went off all around them.

Her lips tingled as he pulled back. His hand was big and warm in hers, and rough with calluses. That should have turned her off, but instead, it sent a flicker of heat straight through her. Because she didn't have to wonder how his palm would feel against her skin, not when the memory of it was imprinted in her mind, that hand gliding over her breasts, up her legs. Beneath her skirt.

Goose bumps broke out across her body as he pulled her out the fancy side doors of the resort, onto the lush grounds. There were gardens and a huge pool, beyond which was a big grassy field. And in the center of it, a baseball diamond had been set up, as well as spectator stands running from third base to home, a sight that made Sam relax.

She could easily spend a couple of hours watching a game anytime. It was like comfort food.

A sign told her that tickets were fifty bucks a pop and all proceeds were going to the Children's Hospital, which made her happy. She herself ran the 4 The Kids charity for the Heat and loved that the game would raise money for kids.

"Meg—Mark's fiancée—works at the Children's Hospital," Wade said. "You'll like her."

The press was there in force, of course, and Wade took her past them to the gate and pulled two tickets from his pocket.

On the field, Mark was talking to a guy who was pulling on catcher's gear. "You're not catching?" she asked Wade in surprise.

"They wouldn't let me." He flashed a grin. "No one liked the odds of playing against me."

She could well imagine. No one in the MLB liked the odds of playing against him either. He was known for being a human vacuum behind the plate. Pitchers loved him because he caught whatever they threw.

He was still holding her hand, and at the bottom of the stands, in plain sight of anyone and everyone standing around, he pulled her to him.

For a minute she went still, discombobulated and shocked to find herself pressed up against his hard, warm chest. "Um . . ."

"Give me a kiss for good luck, Princess."

She tilted her head to look up into his face, her mouth opening to tell him hell-to-the-no was she going to kiss him, but he had an oddly soft look in his eyes, and then his hand came up to cup her face, his thumb caressing her jaw.

Don't. The word echoed between her ears. *Don't touch me like I mean something to you . . .*

But his mouth took hers before she could get out a single syllable of protest, and then the only syllable that did escape was an inarticulate but undeniable sound of pleasure. She'd almost forgotten that kissing him was the equivalent of an entire fudge brownie with warm chocolate sauce poured over the top, and her hands stroked up his steel biceps before she could help herself because she needed an anchor and he was all she had.

Far before she was ready, he broke off the kiss, his mouth remaining a breath from hers for a long beat, as if maybe she wasn't the only one knocked completely off guard.

Slowly his eyes opened, and when they did, the corners of his mouth hinted at a smile. "I'll be listening for you to scream my name when I hit a homer."

"I've never screamed your name."

His smile let loose. "Sure, you have. There was that time we played Arizona last year in the playoffs and I hit that double. You screamed my name when I made it home."

Oh, God. She had.

"And then when we played China in that exhibition game during spring training and I got slammed into at the plate and nearly cracked my rib."

"You didn't get right up," she said in her defense, remembering clearly the terror she'd felt at seeing him crumpled on the ground, not moving. "You have to get right up or we *all* worry."

His knowing smirk told her he knew exactly who'd worried herself sick from the stands. Then he lowered his voice to a soft whisper. "And then there was that other time."

"No." She shook her head. There'd been no third time, she was sure of it.

"In the elevator, when I—"

Oh, God. She shoved him, and laughing, he staggered back a step. "Aw. Love you, too, Princess." With a wink, he turned and walked off, leaving her standing there remembering . . .

Remembering being sandwiched between the mirror in the elevator and his long, hard body, which had been completely supporting hers, her legs wrapped around his waist, his hands cupping her bottom as he effortlessly held her against the glass, holding her on the very edge until she'd begged softly, "Wade, please."

He'd pleased all right, he'd flexed his hips and thrust into her one last time and she'd come.

With a little scream.

Heat flooded her face, and she was very glad he'd

walked away, the ass. She climbed the stands, found a seat and plopped down, and only because several people were looking at her did she smooth the frown from her face and force a smile.

"So you're the one," said a pretty brunette.

Sam looked down at the woman sitting in front of her. "Excuse me?"

"I'm Tess. Mark's sister." The woman leaned up, offering her hand. "I take it you're the new girlfriend."

"Very new," Sam said, and swallowed the irony.

"Wade doesn't usually do the relationship thing." Clearly fishing, Tess scooted up a row to sit right next to Sam. She was twentysomething, with a sweet smile and warm, brown eyes. She wore jeans and a long-sleeved T-shirt, and as Sam took in most of the crowd, she realized just about everyone was casually dressed.

Except her.

"We were all wondering what kind of a woman could snare him," Tess said. "Mark had guessed a movie star. You look like one, but—"

"I'm a publicist. For the Heat." She'd known there'd be plenty of talk this weekend about who Wade had brought with him, which had been the point. It was what had gotten him into trouble in the first place, the parade of women in and out of his life, none sticking. Because beneath the surfer beauty and athletic glory beat a fiercely protected, loyal heart, making him about as easy to crack open as a brick wall.

Sam understood the appeal, she really did. He was gorgeous and yet approachable, both cocky and discreet, a paradox since those deep sea-green eyes of his promised he was an open book.

In truth, she was discovering that he was anything but.

"A publicist," Tess said, and nodded. "Sounds like a

fun job, getting to be around all those sexy ball players for a living."

"That much testosterone isn't as much fun as you might think."

"Probably not, but the view has *got* to be nice—" Tess broke off, standing up and whistling as some of the guys took the field, jogging out to their various positions. "Woo hoo!" she yelled. "Let's kick some ass." She grinned at Sam. "You know who's out there, right? Two TV stars, one movie star, and three world-class athletes, including your boyfriend."

Sam looked at the diamond and saw Wade at right field. Mark was standing on the mound. The guy at third plate did look familiar, and then she realized he played a cop in one of her favorite TV shows.

"There's my dream boyfriend," Tess said, nodding to the batter. "Isn't he hot? He snowboarded for gold at last year's X Games . . . uh oh—"

He'd swung at Mark's first pitch and connected.

"Yeah, baby!" Tess yelled.

The pop ball went straight to . . .

Right field.

Wade shoved his sunglasses to the top of his head and kept his eyes on the fly ball as it . . .

Landed right in his glove. She supposed he couldn't help but play like the superstar he was, and it made her a little squirmy to watch him.

Squirmy as in turned-on.

The crowd booed as Wade threw the ball to second in time to get the snowboarder out. "They're booing him?" Sam asked in shock.

"Just our little way of keeping his ego in check." Tess laughed as out in the field Wade took a bow. The boos turned to cheers. "We all love him, and he knows it."

Indeed, the guys playing second and center field ran up to Wade. One slapped his back and fist bumped him. The other grabbed him around the middle and swung him around. In the next inning, she watched him throw back his head and roar with laughter when the groom tripped over his own two feet running for home. And in the inning after that, he purposely struck out.

Sam had viewed countless baseball games in her life. She'd watched every single one of the Heat's games over the past three years.

Every.

Single.

One.

But as she leaned back and soaked up the sun and the laughter and joy around her, she realized she'd never viewed one like this, where both teams were more interested in the beer and snacks on the sidelines, in taunting each other with private jokes and easy laughter, where the outcome wasn't nearly as important as the game itself.

She watched Wade thoroughly enjoy himself, watched as he became unbearably human in her eyes, and when the game ended, as she stood up with everyone else to cheer, she told herself it was a damn good thing that this was pretend because she was feeling squirmy again.

And yeah, her body was definitely sending mayday signals to her brain. The *oh-please-can-we-have-him* signals.

Bad body.

Very bad body.

After the game, Wade walked to the stands. His "girlfriend" was sitting there in her elegant and sophisticated suit, revealing those knock-'em dead legs that went on for days, looking for all the world like a princess on a Nord-strom's budget.

God, she was something. And if he wasn't careful, she'd make him lose his head. Good thing he was careful.

Very careful. "Hey, woman," he called up to her. "Where's my victory kiss?"

Tess laughed and cleared the stands to give him room as he made his way to her. Sam narrowed her eyes, giving him the don't-you-dare death-glare. Ignoring the look, he pulled her to her feet and leaned in, enjoying the scent of her, the feel of her, letting his eyes drift closed as he headed for her mouth—

She slapped a hand to his chest, and with a sigh, he opened his eyes. "Can I call management and get an ex-change on the girlfriend thing? Cuz this one's uncoopera-tive."

"Our turn, Sam," Tess told her, climbing down, waving at her to hurry and follow. "We're up first."

"We're up first?" Sam repeated, turning to Wade. "What does she mean?"

"Powder-puff time."

"Powder puff? What's a powder puff?"

"They're doing an extra inning so the women get a chance to play, too. You're catcher."

She just stared at him, mouth open.

He smiled, gently tapped his finger beneath her chin until her mouth closed, and sank to the seat she'd just vacated. "Don't worry, I'll cheer you on."

"But I'm in heels."

Tess came running up the stands and grabbed Sam's hand, pulling her down toward the field. "Come on, it'll be fun."

"B-but I'm not dressed for this," she protested as Tess left her no choice but to run alongside her, which she did like a pro in spite of the four-inch heels. "I don't know how to play . . ."

Wade watched her go, grinning from ear to ear. *Oh, hell, yeah.* This was exactly what he'd needed, a weekend of entertainment. And it *was* greatly entertaining, watching Sam get handed over the catcher's gear. Watching her stare at the equipment in her hands, making him realize that she truly had no idea what she was doing. He took in the sheer panic on her face and sighed as he rose to his feet, then made his way down to her.

"Problem?" he asked.

"Yes." She fisted his shirt and held on, eyes wide. "I don't know what I'm doing."

And she hated that, he knew. His Sam thrived on knowing exactly what she was doing, at all times. "It's called winging it, Princess. In the name of fun."

She tugged harder, bringing him nose to nose with her. "You have no idea how much I hate to admit this, but *I need your help.*"

He let out a slow smile. "It's going to cost you."

"I don't care."

"Oh, Sam." His hands went to her hips and squeezed gently. "You're going to care."

She let out a breath. "You're getting a kick out of this."

"Seeing you out of your element?" His full grin escaped. "You can bet your sweet ass on it."

Chapter 5

It's a funny kind of month, October. For the really keen baseball fan it's when you discover that your wife left you in May.

—Denis Norden

"Hold the mitt up a little higher," Wade instructed Sam, and then stepped behind her, putting one hand on her hip, the other guiding her arm a little higher.

If she hadn't been so terrified, so aware of the full stands and everyone around her readying for the powder-puff inning, she might have enjoyed the feeling of his big, hard, warm body behind hers.

"Open the mitt more," he told her. "It'll align with the ball."

"It will?" she asked doubtfully. "Even if you're not a natural athlete?"

"You're a natural."

Her tummy quivered. "How do you know?"

"I know."

She wanted to believe that.

"Once the ball's in your glove, throw it quickly and as straight as possible."

"Straight," she said faintly. "Sure thing." It was a cool

day, with a lovely breeze coming in off the ocean and yet she was sweating. She yanked off her jacket and tossed it aside.

Wade abruptly stopped talking. When she turned her head to look at him, he was staring at her white silky knit tank. "It's a top, Wade."

"It's a sexy little top that just made me forget what the hell I was telling you."

"You were telling me how to be a catcher."

"Right." He gave himself a visible shake. "Be sure not to hit the pitcher. They hate that."

She closed her eyes and tried not to panic.

He laughed softly and ran a finger over the narrow strap on her shoulder. "Don't worry, a good pitcher will get out of your way when he sees you get ready to throw down."

"Is Tess a good pitcher?"

"We'll find out."

She swallowed hard.

"And don't get yourself hit either."

"Oh, God."

"Don't worry. Probably Tess can't get a ball over home plate to save her life. Which means you're going to be running after it, not catching it. But if you do catch it, keep your chin down."

"Why?"

"Keeps the ball from bouncing up and hitting you in the throat."

Okay. So she'd keep her chin down.

He turned her to face him and tightened her face mask, then bent his knees a little to look into her eyes. "Ready?"

"Sure thing."

He smiled again. "Go get 'em, Tiger."

Then he was gone before she could kill him.

But he'd been right about her spending far more time

running after the pitches than catching them. She'd ditched her heels, kicking them to the grass a few feet away, dirt clinging to the soles. But that wasn't her biggest problem. Somehow her team managed to get three outs, which was a miracle considering the pitching and catching efforts. But then came the real terror.

She was up at bat.

She looked into the eyes of the pretty brunette who was pitching. It was Meg, the bride-to-be, and Sam watched Mark walk out to the mound to coach his future wife, ending with a sweet kiss that turned into a very long, sloppy wet one that might have never ended except that Tess ran out and shoved Mark off the mound.

Now Meg was grinning dreamily as she pitched to Sam, giving her a sweet slow ball—

Sam hit it.

Even with her eyes closed and a startled little squeak coming out of her as she swung, she hit it right up the center of the field.

Meg, still dazed from Mark's kiss, missed it.

"Run, Sam, run!"

This came from the sidelines, and she realized it was Wade yelling at her. She'd been standing there like an idiot. Dropping the bat she headed for first in her bare feet and business suit. The skirt was too damn tight for this, so she tugged it up, freeing her legs so that she could move faster.

She got to first and looked back.

Wade had leapt off the stands and was standing there on edge of the field, practically doubled over with laughter as he waved her on to second.

So she ran to second just as the center fielder missed the ball. Which meant that Sam kept running, all the way home, where she finally came to a breathless stop and realized people were cheering wildly.

For her.

She stood there bowled over by an entire stand full of perfect strangers cheering her on. It was the oddest thing, and the most flattering thing, and she found herself standing there grinning like an idiot as a pair of hard, warm arms pulled her back against an even harder, warmer chest.

"Nicely done, Princess." Wade pressed his mouth to her neck. "You can thank me later."

"For what?" she asked, still breathless and getting more so with his mouth on her.

He tugged her skirt back down for her. "For teaching you everything you know."

After the game, Sam showered to get the dirt off her feet and legs. Nothing was going to help the suit though, so she started over with a different one.

Wade had gone to the wedding rehearsal, and then straight to the restaurant to help set up for the rehearsal dinner, leaving Sam alone for a few hours. She spent the time on her laptop in the suite doing some work.

With the season starting up, her e-mail box was full. First up, Henry. Henry Weston was the Heat's shortstop. He was young, talented, and shy as hell, so when a group of female fans had chased him through a mall, he'd panicked on his way out and rear-ended a delivery truck, leaving her with some damage control to do there. After that, she organized a few interviews and wrote press releases on some bull pen trades. She was working on a press packet for two upcoming charity events the Heat was sponsoring, a carnival and an auction, when her cell phone rang. Her brother Jeremy. Temper warred with blood ties, but in the end, she let out a long breath and let temper win. He could leave a message because she was done being bullied by the McNeads in the guise of family love, thank you very much.

But when he called three more times in a row, she began having flashbacks to being little, to all the times it'd been her and Jeremy against the world. Though she was only one year older, she'd spent much of their childhood protecting him from her other brothers and cousins, all older and meaner.

That age-old responsibility was hitting her now, and she caved. "Jeremy."

"Don't hang up," he said quickly. "Please, don't, Sam."

"Tell me why I shouldn't." Maybe it'd been them against the world as kids. But even then, he'd always been competitive with her. It was elevated now by the nature of their jobs, a competitive nature he'd taken way too far when he'd jeopardized her job and the Heat's good public track record by logging into her computer and gathering private information, which he'd then leaked to the press. He'd done this to give the Heat a bad name with their faithful fans, hoping to elevate his Bucks to the same favored pitch the Heat had enjoyed.

He'd betrayed her. He'd betrayed several close friends of hers. And when he'd attempted to sell that information, he'd also come horrifyingly close to getting his ass thrown in jail.

She hadn't spoken to him in spite of the heavy leaning from her father and uncle, both of whom believed she should forgive Jeremy as they had.

"I just wanted to tell you how sorry I am," Jeremy said quietly. "I never got a chance to tell you that."

"You weren't sorry until you got caught."

"True." He sighed, then said perhaps the last thing she could have imagined he'd say, "I'm hitting rehab, Sam."

"What?"

"Obviously my personal habits have gotten out of control, and are affecting the way I handle myself."

She hated that her first response was suspicion, but she'd bet her last dollar that he was full of shit and only wanted her sympathy. Or something. "What are you addicted to?"

"It's complicated."

"Complicated?" she asked warily. "Or a lie?"

He sighed. "I'm suffering from exhaustion, okay? I joined a ninety-day program here in South Carolina."

"Exhaustion? Come on, Jeremy. That's a total celebrity cop-out."

"Okay, and maybe prescription pain meds from my knee surgery last year."

She sighed. "You were a snake. Own up to it."

"I was a snake and I'll be back in ninety days. Minus the snake part, and better behaved, I promise."

"Jeremy." She rubbed her temples. "I don't know what to say."

"Say that even though I know I have no right to ask you, you'll take care of . . . something for me."

Ah, there it was. "Something?"

"You're the only one I can trust with this—" He broke off, and Sam heard someone telling him to hang up.

"Jeremy?" she said. "Who's that?"

"Just say yes, Sam," he said quickly now, low and urgent. "I'm going in and I'm not allowed any phone calls or any contact with the outside world for two weeks minimum. I need an answer. Please, Sam."

Ah, hell. He sounded scared, and one thing Jeremy had never been was scared. "Fine. But so help me God, if it's something illegal, I'll—"

Click.

"Jeremy?"

Nothing. When her cell rang immediately, she snatched it open. "Jeremy? Stop being vague. Just tell me what you need me to do."

"Not Jeremy," said a familiar low, husky voice. "It's your boyfriend."

She sighed and felt the beginning of a headache. "Wade."

"Oh, good, you do remember me. Now if you could remember that you were supposed to be my date about fifteen minutes ago and get your pretty ass up to the restaurant, that'd be fantastic. I'm starving."

Shaking her head, she put her brother and his troubles out of her mind, and headed out to meet her "boyfriend" for the rehearsal dinner.

The restaurant was on the rooftop, and as it was a glorious evening in perpetually sunny SoCal, the weather couldn't be more accommodating. It was a fantastic seventy-two degrees, with the setting sun casting the sky into an orange and red and purple extravaganza over a group of people who genuinely seemed to care about each other. As Sam got off the elevator, her eyes went immediately to the man standing at the entrance, waiting.

Her date.

Tall, built, and amazing. He'd changed somewhere, into a dark charcoal suit with a French blue silk shirt, the combination pretty much taking her breath away. He'd even combed his unruly sun-kissed hair and shaved, and as he moved toward her in that easygoing, almost lazy stride that was in complete contrast with his intense eyes, she actually felt her knees wobble and her tongue stick to the roof of her mouth.

He was the most gorgeous man in the room and he was heading right for her. Resolutely, she locked her knees.

Sure he looked good. Sure he kissed even better. But this was just a gig to keep him out of trouble.

Part of her job, nothing more. "Not your type," she reminded herself. "Not even close."

He lifted her hand to his mouth and eyed her over their entwined fingers. "How am I not your type?"

"You're nice on the eyes, but you're a player."

He pulled her in and put his mouth to her ear. "Yeah?"

"Yeah." His lips had touched her earlobe as he spoke, and dammit, her eyes drifted shut. "You go out with one woman for a night or two, and granted, you make her feel like the only woman on earth, but then you're on to the next flavor of the month. Nothing serious, nothing long-lasting."

"Ah."

"You're funny," she granted him. "But everything's a joke, everything's lightweight. Until it isn't."

He pulled back enough to look into her face, looking amused. "You're trying to talk yourself out of me."

She blew out a breath. "Yeah."

"Is it working?"

"Yes," she lied.

"Good." He startled her by stroking a finger over her temple in the exact spot it ached. "Because you're right about all of it. Especially the part about me not being a keeper. Now tell me what's really wrong."

"Nothing. I'm fine."

"Well, then, please God, let's be fine inside. I need a steak." He turned her from him and nudged her inside. "Or a plate of burgers. Hell, I don't care what it is as long as it's red meat and no longer mooing. I hate being hungry."

They sat down just in time to be served appetizers: codfish mousse with fried plantain chips. It was fantastic, but after a minute, Sam realized she was the only one of them eating. Wade was pushing his around with his fork, a deep frown on his face.

"Problem?" she asked.

"It's *fish*."

"Uh-huh."

He wrinkled his nose.

She laughed. "You don't like fish?"

"Does a fish say *moo*?"

"Don't be a baby."

"A *baby*?" He slid her a brooding look. "I'm wasting away here from starvation."

The main course was a guava-glazed red snapper and Wade groaned. "You're fucking kidding me."

"Looks good."

A scowl had creased his forehead. "Mark didn't have a hand in this; he hates fish, too." He looked around for the groom, spotting him sitting across the room with Meg in his lap, who was kissing his face all over. "Well, that explains it. He's getting laid out of this deal, so he doesn't care what he eats."

"It's really delicious." She took another bite. "Maybe if you just try it."

"It's *fish,* Sam." He pulled his napkin from his lap and stood. "I'll be back."

She watched his tall, rangy form make its way to the doors and vanish. When he didn't immediately return, she figured he was checking out the vending machine in the hotel lobby in search of a candy bar.

Mark plopped down next to her. "Let me guess. Wade got his lucky ass out of this fancy joint and is out seeking real food."

"I'm thinking yeah."

He sighed wistfully. "That guy always did have the best survival instincts. I'd kill for a burger."

"It's *your* dinner," she noted, amused. "Order one."

"Clearly you've never been the groom-to-be. And you've certainly never had to stand up to a bride." He looked over at Meg, sitting at a table surrounded by other women, positively glowing, and he smiled dopily. "God, she's amazing."

"Which is why you're willing to eat food you don't even like."

"Yeah." He grinned. "I let her have her way, and she . . ." His grin widened. "Well, let's just say it works to my favor."

She laughed. "A marriage made in heaven. You'll make a good family together."

"Thank you." He studied her a moment. "You know, I've never said this to one of Wade's girlfriends before, but I'm going to say it now. I hope you stick."

"Oh. Well—"

"If anyone could use more good family around, it's Wade. I mean he has me, of course, but we don't get to see each other much these days. There's his dad, but he doesn't really count. And he has his teammates, but a guy could use more, you know?"

Sam was stuck on the dad comment. She'd written the bio for every player on the team, Wade's included, so she'd always figured she knew most everything there was to know about them. "His dad is alive?"

A funny looked crossed Mark's face, and he set his drink down. "Wow, Meg was right. I *should* have quit two drinks ago." He paused. "Look, he's a bit touchy about his past, which is silly given how much money he sends home, but still, he'd hate that I brought it up." Mark caught Meg waving at him and stood up. "Gotta go pretend I love the seafood. Tell Wade he's a lucky bastard."

"Oh, I will." As Mark walked away, Sam looked around for Wade. It'd been ten minutes since he'd vanished on her.

She waited five more, then left the table and made her way down to the lobby, thinking about Wade's father. Wade had always been open about growing up poor as dirt, about the fact that it'd been just his father and him in a single-wide in the woods in some tiny town in Oregon, and that it was just Wade now.

But it wasn't just Wade, not if his father was still alive. Was the man still in Oregon? Or here in California, maybe even in Santa Barbara somewhere? But if that was the case, why had she never heard about him? Or seen him at a game?

She checked the restaurant and bar, then stepped out of the resort's front double doors, onto a huge grassy area, lined with wild flowers in every conceivable color. And there, sitting on the grass in that beautiful suit was her multimillion dollar MLB catcher, eating a Big Mac.

Chapter 6

Love is the most important thing in the world, but
baseball is pretty good, too.

—Greg, age 8

Sitting on the perfectly manicured lawn, Wade slurped
down his soda and tried not to think about the message
he'd just retrieved from his voice mail. It'd been someone
from the senior center reporting that if his father didn't
stop handing out contraband—alcohol and cigars—to the
other residents, he'd be kicked out.

And then his father's message, the softly slurred, "Yo,
when are you going to get it? I don't want to be here, I
want to be with you."

There'd been a long pause, and Wade had thought maybe
his father had hung up.

He hadn't.

Because there was more—his dad's voice lowered, hoarse
and thick, but even so, still filled with the despair that had
coated most of Wade's childhood: "Need you, Wade. Not
your money. You."

Uh-huh. He'd heard that before. Shrugging it off, Wade
tilted the carton of fries up to his mouth, soaking up the

last of the sun as it sank into the horizon. French fries and sunsets were God's gift, he decided.

"I should have known."

He looked up.

And up.

And up the best set of legs he'd ever had the pleasure of having wrapped around him. Which made him amend his thought. French fries were definitely God's gift. But so were a woman's legs.

And what those legs led to . . .

"You look like you just had really great sex," Sam murmured, her eyes on his.

"You should know."

She shook her head. "Why do you always circle back to that one bad decision? It was a long time ago, it meant nothing, and it's never going to happen again."

"Come down here and say that."

She didn't, reminding him that she possessed an unusually strong survivor's instinct.

"How did you get to McDonald's?" she asked.

"One of the guys lent me his car." Leaning back, he dug into the bag for another carton of fries.

"How many of those have you had?"

"This is my second super-sized helping."

"Maybe we should get your cholesterol checked."

He laughed. "Are you worried about my weight?"

She slid her gaze down his body, and he could tell by the way she sucked her bottom lip into her mouth and how her eyes dilated that she liked what she saw.

"You know damn well you don't have a weight problem," she finally said. "You don't have an ounce of fat on you, you lucky bastard. Your body couldn't get more perfect."

It's an illusion, he nearly said. Instead, he popped more

fries in his mouth and moaned out loud. "Good Christ, these are amazing. Every single time." He offered up the carton. "How do you suppose they do it?"

"It's the salt." She sighed and stared at the fries, clearly wrestling with herself. After a moment, she grabbed the carton and dug in, and then let out a hum of pleasure that rocked through him.

He grinned. "Yeah?"

"Oh, yeah." She licked her fingers. "Almost as good as an orgasm."

He stared at her mouth. "Baby, nothing's as good as an orgasm."

"French fries are," she said firmly. "Well, mostly." She sighed. "Honestly, it's been so long I can't remember. French fries might actually be better."

"Aw, now you're just daring me to remind you how good it was in that Atlanta elevator."

She slid him an assessing gaze. "You're fishing."

He smiled. "Guilty."

"Are you that insecure about your manhood?"

"Yeah. Reassure me."

She just shook her head.

With a grin, he patted the grass next to him, wanting her to sit with him, to just relax. Be.

Make him laugh some more.

Her black suit was dressier than her earlier one, the skirt shorter, the heels higher and strappy and pretty much blowing his mind as she shook her head and gestured to her hem. "I can't get down there without flashing everybody."

Probably true. He eyed the few people wandering around, then got to his feet, took off his jacket, and held it around her.

She hesitated. "We should go back inside."

"Is there still fish in there?" he asked.

"Yes."

"Then not yet. Come on, sit."

"You have another phone number written on your hand."

"The server at McDonald's. You weren't there to protect me."

She rolled her eyes, then let him guide her down to the grass, cocking her head to look into his eyes. "Red meat agrees with you."

"I know it. Other things agree with me. Want to guess what any of them are?"

"Ha," she said. "And no. I don't need to guess. I already know."

"Well then?" he asked hopefully.

With a low laugh, she put her finger on a corner of his mouth.

The touch was like a bolt of lightning straight through his gut. As she lightly rubbed the pad of her finger over his lip, he had to make a correction. The bolt hadn't gone to his gut, but parts south.

"Ketchup," she murmured, then let out a throaty gasp when he sucked the tip of her finger into his mouth.

She closed her eyes as he lightly raked his teeth over the pad of her finger. "I'm not going to have sex with you, Wade," she said, her voice husky. "Not out here on the grass. Not inside. Not anywhere."

"Sam I am," he whispered, but he couldn't help it. He was feeling odd. Uneasy. Restless.

Aroused.

Slowly he pulled her in using the lapels of his jacket. She resisted but was little match for his strength, going into a controlled freefall against his chest.

"Don't make this into something it's not," she said very softly as she fit against him like she was made for him.

"It's just a moment. A weird sort of chemical attraction moment that can't really be explained."

"All chemistry can be explained. You plus me equals combustion."

She flashed a quick, tight smile. "Dangerous combustion, don't you think?"

"I'm not afraid of you." He lowered his head to see into her eyes. "Is that it, Sam? Are you afraid of me?"

"Don't flatter yourself."

But she didn't look sure, and he took mercy on the both of them and dropped the subject.

"I'm surprised at how long you've stayed out here," she said after a moment. "You're missing all kinds of photo ops at the rehearsal dinner."

"Can't have that."

"No."

She was practically in his lap, her hand on his chest, whether to keep him at bay or to hold on, he wasn't yet sure.

"Wade."

"Right here." He dipped his head, his lips a fraction from hers.

"There's no one around," she said shakily, gripping his bicep with one hand, his chest with the other, like he was her only anchor in a churning sea. "No paps, nothing."

"Then this one will have to be just for us." Leaning even closer, he stopped only a millimeter away from her lips when she tightened her fingers on his chest, getting a few chest hairs in the mix. "What now?"

"I didn't know your father was alive."

Like a cold bucket of water. With a sigh, he set her away from him. "Where did this come from?"

"Mark mentioned it."

"Mark has a big mouth."

"What's the secret?"

"There is no secret." There really wasn't. Wade had been born in a trailer and had nearly died that same day. Would have, if John O'Riley hadn't gathered his son in a towel and brought him to the closest doctor at an Urgent Care nearly an hour away. Wade had been cleaned up and fixed up and handed back over two days later to his father, who'd gone home and found his woman gone.

This had left the mild-tempered, easygoing John in a bit of a quandary. He'd been a small-bit character actor who'd traveled from tiny town theater to tiny town theater, not easy to do with a baby and no woman. So he'd adapted, as all O'Rileys were apt to do, and switched professions from acting to gambling, aka conning.

And had become a professional drunk while he was at it. He hadn't been a mean drunk, or even a particularly difficult one. Just quiet and sad and utterly clueless about everything, including raising a kid.

"Where does he live?" Sam asked.

"Oregon."

"Do you ever go back?"

Wade had few memories from his childhood worth revisiting, so no, he never went back. Not for sentimental reasons, and not for his father, who'd done far better with Wade a thousand miles away making enough money for the both of them. Wade had lost track of the number of times he'd tried to get his father to rehab, and in fact, no longer cared. Things had been fine, just fine, until recently when John'd had a medical problem. A weakened liver. Shock. His doctor had told him he could quit drinking or die. So suddenly John was looking his mortality right in the face, and fretting about his lack of a relationship with his son. "I don't want to talk about it." Wade gathered his trash and stood up, offering her a hand, watching from hooded eyes as she struggled not to flash him her goodies beneath that short skirt.

She wasn't entirely successful; he caught a quick glimpse of something black and lacy. "Pretty."

"You are such a guy."

"Guilty."

She stood before him, looking into his face for answers.

Answers he wasn't ready to give. "I'm going back to Mickey D's for a hot fudge sundae," he decided, pulling the borrowed keys out of his pocket. "Quiet people are welcome to come."

"Meaning no more questions, I suppose."

"Pretty *and* smart," he murmured. He was only partially surprised when she walked along at his side. He knew enough about her to know she'd do just about anything for ice cream.

"Won't the bride be upset that a member of the wedding party just up and left to eat somewhere else?"

"If it'd been anyone else but me, probably. Me, she likes." He had them at the McDonald's drive-thru in less than five minutes, and they were halfway back when he caught the red and blue lights flashing in his rearview mirror. "Shit."

Sam didn't slow down in her consumption of her hot fudge sundae, scooping a huge dollop into her mouth, licking her lips in a way that nearly made him forget to pull over. "Probably you shouldn't have been speeding," she said as he turned off his engine.

He slid her a look as the officer came to the window, one hand on his gun, the other wielding a flashlight.

"License and registration, please," he said. "Sir, do you know how fast you were going?"

"No," Wade said.

"Thirty-five-ish," Sam said helpfully from the passenger seat, "in a twenty-five zone."

Wade turned and gave her a long look.

She smiled, and he had to shake his head. *Now* she smiled at him like that. *Nice.*

"She's right," the officer told him. "Thirty-five in a twenty-five."

Sam gave Wade the I-told-you-so look.

"License and registration," the officer said again.

Wade blew out a breath. He'd left his wallet in the hotel room. He'd borrowed keys and a twenty from Matt's brother. This was not going to go well. He flashed a quick, apologetic smile to the cop. "You're not going to believe this, hell even *I* don't believe it, but I forgot my license back at my room at the Laguna Rey Resort."

The cop gave him an unimpressed look, then slowly narrowed his gaze. "Wait a minute. Do I know you?"

Wade smiled in relief. Once in a while fame really did pay.

"I do know you," the cop said. "Hey, you're big in my house."

Okay, so maybe this wasn't going to be so bad after all. Wade reached into the glove box for the registration and handed it over.

The officer glanced at it and then handed it back without going to his vehicle to run it. He was smiling now. "Ah, man, this is my lucky day. My wife was pissed at me this morning, but an autograph from you will make it all better."

"Absolutely." Wade was perfectly willing to sign his John Hancock on a piece of paper instead of at the bottom of a speeding violation. He searched the car and came up with a pad of paper and a pen in the console. "How should I sign it?"

"If you could say 'To Leslie,'" the cop said. "'With love, Matthew McConaughey.'"

Sam snorted softly as Wade went still.

"She loves you, man. You still play the bongos in the buff?"

Wade slid his eyes to Sam, who rolled her lips into her mouth to keep from bursting out with laughter. He gave her the death-glare and looked down at the paper in his hand. He'd written the "To Leslie with love" part. And with a sudden genuine smile, he signed "Matthew McConaughey" with a flourish. "I've cut back on the naked bongo playing."

"Cool," the officer said. "Thank you so much."

"My pleasure," Wade murmured as the officer walked away.

Sam gave him one beat of silence. Then she burst out laughing.

He stared at her. "I don't think I've ever seen you laugh like that."

She wiped a tear from her eyes and tried to collect herself. "I'm sorry. But Matthew McConaughey?"

"What? I look sort of like him."

She laughed again, and Wade shook his head and drove them back to the resort, feeling irritated all over again. When they were back on the grass, heading toward the hotel doors, Sam put a hand on his arm. "Can I ask a question now?"

"I've been mistaken for him before, you know."

"A different question."

"No," he said, knowing where she was going to go. "No other questions."

"Do you really never go home?"

"Jesus." He drew a deep breath. "Home? My home's in Santa Barbara, Sam."

"Are you in contact with him? Your dad?"

Yes. Monetary contact. Monetary payback for not being able to be the son John had apparently needed in order to not pickle his liver on a daily basis. "You're harshing my ice-cream-sundae buzz."

"I'm sure he's getting up there in years but maybe we could bring him out for a game some time. Give him the VIP treatment."

Uh-huh. Problem was, the old man would rather play cards than sit through a baseball game.

"He'd probably love it," she said.

What John would love was conning everyone Wade knew out of their pocket change. "Stop."

"But—"

"You know what, Sam? Mark puts up with nagging from Meg, but then again, she blows him every night, so . . ."

She narrowed her eyes at him. "I'm not nagging. I'm just saying that for the past three years we've done a special Father's Day event. This year we're having it at the Railroad Museum. Think of the positive, heart-warming press—"

"Jesus, Sam. Stop working and fucking drop it already. *Please.*"

And then, to be sure she did, he headed back inside.

Chapter 7

Slump? I ain't in no slump. I just ain't hitting.

—Yogi Berra

The rest of the rehearsal dinner passed without further provocation or argument, mostly because there were so many people who wanted to talk to Wade, many of them being gorgeous women, that Sam didn't get the opportunity to irritate him more.

She supposed that was a bonus.

Afterwards, she went back to the suite while Wade stayed behind to help clean up and carry the presents to Meg and Mark's suite. She offered to help, but he'd given her a quick "I've got it" and left her alone.

Which was fine. This was all just pretend, after all. And she had plenty to keep her occupied. She had work she could do. Hell, she always had work she could do, and calls to return. She'd missed a call from her father, her uncle, and her cousin, each of whom read her the riot act by the time she got back to them.

"Why the hell aren't you answering your phone?" her father demanded.

After years of trying, they had come to a tenuously decent relationship. He'd agreed to let her run her own life without his interference, and she'd agreed to work for the Heat. She wasn't sure why he stuck to his part of the deal, but for her, she worked for the Heat because she loved the job. And she'd like to think that her father got something out of it, too: the best publicist in the business—if she said so herself. She was happy there, or had been until the Jeremy bullshit last season. But lately she'd had a little seed of discontent in the back of her mind, and she found herself wondering if she'd be happier running her own PR firm when her contract with the Heat was over at the end of this season.

Her father had sensed her discontent and had commented several times that she needed to get over herself. To keep the peace, they rarely spoke. They got together at holidays, birthdays, and the occasional Heat team meeting that he made it to, but for the most part, he stayed on the other side of the country running the rest of his vast business empire. "Well, hello to you, Dad."

"Sorry," he said gruffly. "I didn't mean to bark."

Yes, he had, but she could forgive him since he'd apologized. Another relatively new thing with him, which she knew he'd gotten from Wife Number Five. Or was it six? If he didn't apologize quickly and sweetly, it cost him. Usually in diamonds, and not the kind on the baseball field. "I didn't answer my phone," she told him, "because I was at the rehearsal dinner."

"Well, do me a damn favor, and be more available for the next few days. We need you to—"

"Wait. Stop right there," she said firmly. One had to be firm with her father, or risk getting walked all over. "I'm still in the middle of the *last* favor you asked me to do. One thing at a time. Is it business-related? Because Gage is—"

"It's not business-related."

"Dad," she said as gently as possible, "you need to go to your wife for the other stuff. It's what she wants from you, remember? Didn't you have to go to counseling last year to learn just that?"

"Christ, don't remind me. Listen, Sam—"

The suite door opened and in walked Wade. She braced for a continuation of their earlier fight, but he didn't look like he was in a fighting mood. He'd shed his jacket, which was carelessly slung over one shoulder. His tie had been loosened, his shirt unbuttoned, the sleeves shoved up. His hair was a little ruffled and he had a new phone number on his forearm.

He looked at her and grinned.

Oh, boy. He was clearly inebriated, which was interesting given that in the four years she'd known him, she'd only seen him in that condition once.

That night in the Atlanta elevator. "I have to go, Dad."

"Not yet, Sam. I—"

"I'll talk to you on Sunday, when I'm back in Santa Barbara for the opening game."

"Samantha Ann McNead—"

She winced as he middle-named her and shut her phone.

Wade tossed his jacket to a chair. His tie went the same route. "Not very nice to hang up on him."

"At least I call him."

He sighed and walked very carefully over to the bed. "You have Daddy issues."

"I think you have that backwards."

He sank to the bed and put his hands on the mattress at his side as if he were on a moving boat and unsure of his balance. "Come here, little girl." He grinned. "I'll be your daddy tonight."

"You're drunk."

"Yes. Yes, I am." He kicked off one shoe, but had some trouble with the other.

Watching him fight the laces, she sighed and went to him. Kneeling, she untied his shoe and pulled it off. Then she rose up a little and looked into his eyes. "I think you should go to bed."

"I do, too." He reached out and ran a finger over the stress spot between her eyes. "Tell me what's wrong, Princess. Tell Daddy all your troubles."

She nudged him in the chest and he fell back onto the mattress, just over six feet of sprawled-out limbs. "Whoa," he said.

Rolling her eyes, she moved away from the bed over to the small desk. She picked up the phone, dialing housekeeping for a roll-away bed. While the phone was ringing in her ear, two big, warm hands settled on her shoulders and started kneading, and before she could stop herself, she'd let out a low, heartfelt moan.

"You've got an entire rock quarry in here," he murmured, going right for her tight, tension knots and digging in as his mouth settled on the nape of her neck.

Oh God, she was melting. "Stop. I can't talk when you do that—"

"Then don't." Reaching around her, he took the phone from her fingers and hung it up.

"I was trying to get a roll-away bed."

"Roll-aways are pieces of shit."

"But—"

"Shhh."

His fingers were long and strong and firm, and knew exactly where to press to turn her limbs into overcooked noodles. Unable to stop herself, she sank to the chair, closing her eyes at his soft, knowing laugh.

"I make you weak in the knees," he said silkily.

"No, your *hands* make me weak in the knees."

He laughed again. "I might be buzzed, but not too buzzed to know that you are *such* a liar."

And then he pulled his hands free.

She nearly cried at the loss, but got herself together. When she turned to look at him, he was headed for the bathroom, unbuttoning his shirt, which he shrugged off halfway there.

She told herself not to stare but he truly had the most glorious physique. His back was all sleek, smooth, bronzed flesh, sinew rippling as he moved— "Hey!" she said as his pants dropped. He kicked free and kept walking, in nothing but black knit boxers. "What are you doing?" she squeaked, even as her gaze soaked up the fact that he had a tan line, and that the waistband of his boxers had slipped past it, revealing a tantalizing strip of paler, smooth, tight skin. "We're not doing this, Wade O'Riley. Do you hear me? This is all pretend, remember?"

"I remember. The question is, do you?" He sent her a cheeky grin over his shoulder.

"Put your clothes back on!"

"Taking a shower."

And then he dropped his boxers.

Oh, sweet baby Jesus. "Don't drown," she murmured, watching the most excellent ass in all the land vanish behind the door. She heard the shower go on and leaned back in the chair, letting out a long, shaky breath.

She was in big trouble.

All the way around.

Wade sobered up a bit in the shower. The nice alcohol daze couldn't stand up to the pressing thoughts bumping around in his brain like bumper cars.

Mark getting married.

His father drunk-dialing him . . .

There was also a disturbing ache in his bones, suggesting his body was damn tired, and maybe, just maybe at age thirty-two, also damn old. With Opening Day less than forty-eight hours away, that couldn't be good, but that problem would have to get in line.

He hadn't meant to get toasted tonight, but Mark had been so goddamned happy and over the moon, and looking at him had made Wade feel just a little envious.

Mark had a life. A real life, one that went deeper than nights out with the guys and the occasional hot woman in his bed, one that went past what ESPN had to say about his athletic prowess.

One that wasn't defined by what he did for a living.

Feeling a little off his game, he got out of the shower, wrapped a towel around his hips, and opened the bathroom door.

Complete darkness greeted him.

"Sam?" He wondered if she ever felt off herself. Probably not. She had her shit together. She was cool as ice, baby, ice, and never doubted herself.

And she sure as hell didn't want a guy like him. Because what was it she'd said? He wasn't keeper material. "Princess?"

"Shh. She's sleeping."

He padded toward the voice, tripped over something, and hit the floor. Reaching out, he realized he'd fallen over his own shoes. "Marco . . ."

"Polo," she said on a sigh. "Are you all right?"

"Yeah." He followed the voice to the small, narrow couch and stood above her, blinking through the dark. "What are you doing there?"

"Trying to sleep. You should try it."

"Okay." But he didn't move. "Sam?"

"Yeah?"

"You being here with me, it's really just pretend, right?"

"Take the bed, Wade."

"Yeah. Just pretend," he said, nodding. He'd known it, but he seemed to keep forgetting.

"You're still wet. You're dripping on me."

"Sorry." He crouched at her side and put out a hand, which settled on her belly. She was warm and soft and wearing something silky smooth. He bent his head and nuzzled his face against her throat. "You smell good," he whispered. "You always smell good."

A small, inarticulate sound escaped her, and for a beat he went still as it reverberated through him. Then he pressed his mouth to the sweet spot right beneath her ear, listening as she made the sound again.

It wasn't annoyance, not that breathy little sigh. Nope, even drunk, he knew it was arousal. To make sure, he used his teeth this time, a light grazing over her flesh and she shivered. She moaned, too, though she did her best to suck it back in, but it was too late. "I heard that," he said.

"I didn't say anything."

"You moaned."

"I did not."

God, she was so soft. He flicked his tongue at her earlobe, and then sucked it into his mouth, giving it a little nip, too, one that had her hissing in a breath as she lifted a hand, running it down his bare back as if she needed to touch him.

It did him in, and he shifted, kissing his way to the very corner of her mouth. "Admit it, Sam. You want me."

She admitted exactly nothing, but dug her fingers into the small of his back.

"I want you," he confessed, and nipped her jaw. "Bad enough to be getting rug burns already."

"Then stop."

He could. He should. But her breathing had accelerated, and beneath his hand, her abs quivered, softening for him now in a way she never did.

And he got it. "This in the dark thing, it's right up your alley."

"What's all that alcohol in your brain talking about?"

He kissed her jaw, loving how she arched her neck to give him more room, and that her breathing had become the loudest thing in the room. "You like this because it's anonymous." He kissed her. "Nothing too deep."

Another shaky breath escaped her and her hands finally came up to cup his face. "You're one to talk."

"Admit it. You want me as bad as I want you." His mouth was so close to hers that his lips lightly brushed hers, barely touching until, with a hungry little sound, she tightened her grip, gliding her fingers into his hair, pulling his mouth down to hers.

The kiss went from sweet to wild in less than two seconds, egged on by her frustration and his own inexplicable loneliness and the way she held on to him, letting out the sexiest little murmur, as if there was nothing, absolutely nothing better than his mouth on hers.

But he had a point, and he was trying to make it. Sure the alcohol had slowed him down some, as well as the utter sexiness wrapped around him now, which went by the name of Samantha McNead—but he managed to get it together and slowly pull back.

Her mouth tried to follow his, and he groaned, his thumbs stroking over her jaw. "Just admit you're into this little game, Princess. And then we can have our fun."

"There is no game. This is just our job, what we both as consenting adults agreed to do." She sat up, nearly bumping heads with him in the dark. "But I didn't agree to *this*. I'm sorry, Wade, but it ends here. It has to. Our last fun took me a year to get over." And with that shockingly revealing statement, she rose, and then he heard her flop onto the bed.

"You lose," she muttered, and tossed him a blanket, which hit him in the face.

He sighed as he fell back onto the couch. Hard as a rock.

And all alone.

Chapter 8

The tradition of professional baseball always has been agreeably free of chivalry. The rule is, "Do anything you can get away with."

—Heywood Hale Broun

Sam woke up to the sound of rustling and squinted at the clock. One in the morning. The rustling was Wade. She could see his tall, built outline walking to the door. "What are you doing?"

"I'm hungry."

Of course he was.

"I ordered a pizza and I hear the guy coming."

Sure enough, a soft knock came at the door. The room service waiter handed Wade a box of pizza and Wade handed him some cash.

Sam sat up, nose wriggling at the scent of melted cheese and sauce, and, if she wasn't mistaken, pepperoni. Her stomach rumbled. "Smells good."

Wade switched the light on in the bathroom, which bathed the room with a soft glow. His broad shadow gleamed in the pale light, his hair rumpled from sleep. In nothing but dark blue knit boxers, he slouched on the couch, opened the box, and sank his teeth into a big piece. Moaning, he closed his eyes. "Oh, yeah."

Sam's mouth watered.

He took another bite and she couldn't take it. "Um, hi."

He looked up and took in her cream spaghetti-strapped silk nightie. His eyes darkened. "Hi."

"You going to share?"

"If you are."

She weighed the danger of letting him into the bed with the promise of the mouth-watering pizza. She wasn't afraid Wade would push himself on her. Rather she was afraid she'd push herself on him. But then her stomach told her brain to shut up, and she scooted over. With a grin, he joined her, fluffing the pillows against the headboard to make them both comfortable before offering the box with an innocent smile that didn't fool her one little bit. "You were going to share before I made room for you," she said.

"Maybe." He made sure that they were skin to skin as he polished off his first piece and looked at her. "Hope you haven't forgotten that you owe me."

"For . . . ?"

"Coaching you at the game."

"Let me guess," she said dryly. "Monkey sex?"

He arched a brow. "Is that on the table?"

His boxers had slid disturbingly low on his hips. His body was perfection, hard and deliciously warm, and she wanted it on hers, pushing her down into the mattress, sinking into her . . . "No."

"Something else then."

"What?" she asked warily.

"Truth or dare."

A game? "Truth," she said, thinking she'd gotten off easy.

"Atlanta. The elevator. Just an alcohol-induced fuck, or more?"

She set down her pizza. *Okay, maybe not so easy.* Wade nudged her with his arm and she met his gaze. "Truth," he reminded her softly.

"More," she said, just as softly. "But I really *wanted* it to be just an alcohol-induced fuck."

He absorbed that. "Did it really take you all year to get over it?"

"That's two questions." She reached for her slice again, licking cheese off her finger. "My turn. Truth or dare?"

"Truth," he said, eyes locked on her mouth.

"Why did you ask me that?"

He paused and met her gaze. "I don't know."

She gave him a long look, but decided he wasn't being evasive, he either honestly didn't know or couldn't put words to his need to know.

"Truth or dare?" he asked.

"Truth."

"You could have any guy you crooked your little finger at, but you hold yourself back. Why?"

"I don't know," she said, giving him a taste of his own medicine.

He wasn't as accepting as she'd been. "Maybe you're afraid."

"Of what?"

"You tell me. You grew up stifled by alpha males. I didn't think you were afraid of anything."

She paused at that shockingly accurate and insightful statement. "Maybe I'm happy to be my own woman. Maybe I don't want to lose myself again." She broke off, a little unnerved at what had come out of her mouth. "Okay, that sounded—"

"Honest." He took her hand and pressed his mouth to

her palm. "One of the most honest things I've ever heard you say."

Pulling her hand free, she took another bite of pizza and chewed on it.

"The right man won't hold you back, Sam."

"Truth or dare?" she asked, needing a subject change.

"Truth."

"Your most embarrassing moment."

He winced and she laughed. "That bad?"

He didn't say anything for a long moment as he inhaled another piece of pizza. "Would you buy the I-don't-know excuse again?"

"No."

He sighed.

"It can't be that bad."

He met her gaze. "It's you thinking I slept with Tia."

She gaped at him, shocked to her core that he would even give this a second thought. It was nearly as revealing about him as what she'd admitted only a moment before about never wanting to lose herself in another man again. "You've slept with half the women in Santa Barbara county, why would that bother you?"

"Because I haven't slept with anyone in months." He paused. "And months."

She gave him a get-real look. "There were pictures of you with Tia, Wade."

"Last month we had a three-day break in the middle of spring training. I flew home from Arizona and spent the first day sleeping on my beach. My private beach. The only thing I can figure is that she found me there, dead to the world, and posed next to me, taking the shots herself." He hesitated. "I haven't slept with anyone since you, Sam. Truth or dare."

"Dare," she whispered around the bombshell he'd just

dropped, not trusting herself with another intimate question. She braced for the dare to be something outrageously sexual. She had no idea how she'd get out of it.

Or if she even wanted to.

But he didn't make a move toward her, just looked at her with those stark green eyes. "I dare you to believe it," he whispered, and in her stunned silence, he took the empty pizza box, tossed it to the desk, rolled off the bed, and went back to the couch.

In the morning, the first sound Sam heard was someone singing in the bathroom.

Off key.

The bathroom door was open. She could see Wade brushing his teeth as he sang. He wore tux pants and an unbuttoned white tuxedo shirt that revealed a wide strip of broad, hard chest and washboard abs. His hair was wet and silky straight, falling over his forehead.

Holy cow.

He lifted his head and took in her undoubtedly bed-head hair and dazed expression, and smiled.

He hadn't taken advantage of her last night, which meant that in spite of his smart-ass mouth and smart-ass *everything*, he was a good guy.

Unfortunately turned on and not sure what to do with that, she grabbed her last remaining suit and kicked his sexy ass out of the bathroom. By the time she finished getting ready, he was seated on the bed next to her open suitcase, flicking through the channels with the remote. "Daytime TV sucks."

His shirt was still open, his feet bare, and yet in spite of it, or maybe because of it, he looked worth every penny of the multimillion dollar guy he was. He took in her carefully tamed hair, makeup, and her pale blue silk suit and smiled. "I love it when my date is smoking hot. I'm starving." He rubbed his belly. "You have anything to eat?"

"I have a breakfast bar in my purse."

"Is it a nuts and berries number, or something good?"

"Nuts and berries."

"No, thanks. I'd prefer cardboard." His hair was still damp, and because he was on the wrong side of a haircut, it lay against the nape of his neck. He smelled like himself, which was to say *amazing*, and his opened shirt kept giving her a peek-a-boo glimpse of those rock-hard pecs and eight-pack abs that could make a grown woman weep with wanting. The muscles bunched as he reached out to tug on her hand.

Though she wanted to remain far, far away so that she didn't actually fall to her knees and try to lick him like a lollipop, she allowed him to pull her down next to him.

And then she saw what was in his other hand, the antique pearl pin she always had on her. "That's mine."

"I know. I've seen it on you. It's pretty. Soft and pretty." He cocked his head to look at her, and she knew what he was thinking.

"And I'm not soft," she said. "I know. It was my mother's." Who had been soft and pretty.

At least in photographs.

"I think you're soft," he said quietly. "When it counts."

She ran her finger over the pearls that had once belonged to her great-grandmother, his words meaning far more than they should. The pin was the only thing Sam had of her maternal side of the family. "I wear it because it makes me feel like she's with me." She shook her head. "And I have no idea why I just told you that." She went to move away, but Wade leaned in and held her gaze, then kissed her softly, a kiss that made no sense at all and yet made her ache from the depths of her soul.

He pulled back, looking as thrown as she felt, so she broke eye contact and pinned the broach to her lapel.

"She died when you were young," Wade said quietly.

"Yes. In fact, my brother killed her." As his mouth fell open in shock, she stood, turning to the mirror to check herself over. "She died in childbirth. Sorry, my father always found that an amusing way to horrify people."

Wade came up behind her. He slipped an arm around her waist and hugged her back against him, and met her gaze in the mirror. "No offense, Sam, but your father is an insensitive ass."

"Yes, he can be." She let out a breath and tilted her head to look up at him. "How about yours? Is he an ass, too? Is that why—"

He set a finger to her lips. "Still not going there." He let go of her, watching as she applied lip gloss. "While you were in the shower, your phone rang."

"I had the ringer off."

"Okay, so it lit up silently. You smell good enough to eat, Sam. Is that peach-flavored gloss?"

"What?" She turned to stare at him. "Why did you answer my phone?"

"Because it was The Man. Your father himself." The world-class athlete who caught balls whipping toward his face at ninety-plus miles per hour shuddered. "Christ, he's scary."

She had to laugh. "You're not scared of anything, not even him."

"Not true. I'm scared of plenty."

"Like?"

"Like not getting food. Hungry, Sam."

She rolled her eyes. "What did you tell him?"

"*Not* that you keep kissing me. Or that you slept in my bed. And sure as hell not that you were in my shower. Naked. Wet. Glistening. All soapy . . ." His eyes glazed over and he gave himself a shake. "Sorry, but that's a really great image."

She narrowed her eyes at him as he sat on the bed and pulled on a pair of socks. He shrugged his massive shoulders. "Standard-issue male fantasy. Hot girl in the shower." He stood and began to button his shirt.

"So what *did* you tell my father?"

"It was what he wanted to tell you." The good humor drained from his eyes as he tucked in his shirt and fastened his pants. "Jeremy's in a ninety-day rehab program for prescription drugs. He's—"

"Yeah. I already know." She headed for the closet to get the strappy heels that would give her height and power. She was going to need both today. Too bad there wasn't a closet where she could grab some extra common sense because she sure as hell needed some of that.

"Nice," he said about the heels. "So you know about the rehab? You're okay?"

"When are you going to learn? I'm always okay." But since that was a big, fat lie, and she knew her eyes would give her away in a heartbeat, she grabbed her purse, keeping her face averted. "You coming, or what?"

He caught her at the door. "Hey. *Hey*," he murmured when she tried to shrug him off. He merely tightened his grip and turned her around to face him.

She studied his chest. Not a hardship. "Wade, you're hungry, remember?"

"Not going to distract me." He tipped up her chin with a finger and looked her over. "Well, unless you're ready to admit how bad you want me."

"I admit nothing. Finish buttoning your damn shirt. Get your damn shoes. We're out of here."

And to make sure of it, she pushed past him and let herself out, leaving him to swear and scramble to catch up.

Chapter 9

Swing hard, in case they throw the ball where you're swinging.

—Duke Snider

Later, Samantha sat in the gloriously decorated resort garden with the other wedding guests, watching the bridal party take their places. Watching as, along with the rest of the groomsmen, Wade escorted grandmothers and elderly aunts down the aisle with that long-legged grace and easy hello, his smile turning a little misty along with the rest of the party as the vows were spoken.

And afterwards, at the open, beautiful, lovely reception, she was still watching as he danced with a little girl who had sweetly asked him, helped serve when they were short-handed, and gave a moving toast to the bride and groom.

Sam was seated at a table with the other Heat players who'd been invited, and right next to the Heat's manager, Gage. She and Gage had a longtime ease with each other, and had been having a good time. It was hard not to have a good time with Gage. He was a mix of his Latino father and supermodel mother, and within the confines of baseball, possessed a will of sheer steel that served him well. Outside the sport, like today, he let loose a little bit, and attracted nearly as many women as his players did.

On her other side was Pace, no slouch in the catching-women department himself, though the Heat's ace pitcher had eyes only for his fiancée these days, as proven when Pace slipped his arms around Holly and kissed her with a soft smile.

And when a slow song came on, Pace led Holly to the dance floor. Soon as his seat was empty, Wade moved in. He kicked the chair even closer to Sam and dropped into it, stretching out his tux-covered legs with a sigh.

"Tired?" she asked.

"Whipped. All this flowers and hearts and love-love-love is pretty exhausting work. Hope Mark knows what he's getting into."

Sam looked over at Mark, dancing with his new bride, wearing a wide dopey grin. "I think he knows."

Wade looked at them and shook his head. "One woman for the rest of his life. No more quickies. No more un-knowns. Just a ball and chain."

She laughed. "Is that what you really think of love?"

He flashed her a quick grin. "Nah. Just figured it's what you think of it and I wanted to be agreeable today."

"Why today?"

His grin widened and he slung an arm around her. He'd removed his jacket. The white shirt stretched across his broad chest and shoulders. She lifted her eyes to his, and found him looking at her. "So," she asked, suddenly need-ing to know. "What do you really think of love?"

He didn't hesitate. "I think it's great as long as it's fun. No stress, no anxiety, no worries. Light and easy required."

"Yeah, I don't think love always works that way."

"Really?" His fingers brushed the nape of her neck, bringing a tingle to her entire body. "So you've been in love then?"

"No," she had to admit. "But nothing with such deep emotion can ever be fun and stress-free all the time."

"Well, then, maybe that's why I'm not in it. Because if it's not light and easy, preferably with lots of sex, then forget-about-it."

She knew by the little smile on his face he was messing with her. "You really like to perpetuate this whole laid-back, dumb jock thing, don't you? But I'm on to you, Wade. I know you go deeper."

"No, I don't."

"No," Pace agreed, coming back from the dance floor, leaning over Wade's shoulder. "He really doesn't."

Wade put his hand to Pace's face and pushed. Pace laughed and turned his back on them to cuddle with Holly, then walked with her to the open bar.

"You go deeper," Sam said to Wade. "I've seen you. With Pace, with the other guys. And Mark told me you send money to your father every month. A ton of money."

"A ton is relative."

"You work with kids. You build ballparks for them to have a place to play. You and Pace create clubs that provide coaching, something positive to do after school."

He shrugged. "Money's meant for spending."

"Don't do that," she said quietly. "Don't underrate what you do."

"Okay, as long as you don't overrate it. Look, I have money, more than I need. So I give it. The end."

She sighed and shook her head. So she wasn't going to get him to admit he had more substance to him than a rock, fine. What did she care?

"And you're one to talk, Princess. You haven't exactly

been doing the deep thing either. Or the love thing, for that matter. Why not, if you're all for it?"

"Because if I'm going to let someone into my life, it's going to be for the long haul. And yet I'm surrounded by players. Literally and figuratively."

"Ah." Amused, he nodded. "Because if you're going to go for it, the ball and chain and all, you want someone serious, like you. Good plan, I'm sure you'll laugh a lot. And hey, the sex should be perfunctory."

"We'll laugh," she said, a little defensive.

"Yeah?"

"Yeah. And we'll have *great* sex."

"Are you sure?" he asked. "Won't you both be too busy reading the manuals to make sure you're doing it right?"

Even knowing he was baiting her, she couldn't keep her quiet. "You *know* that I do it right. You had a damn good time in that elevator, too. I remember. You—" He'd come hard with her, holding her through it, pressing his pelvis to hers for long moments afterwards as if to savor the last of their pleasure, and remembering it had a blush creep up her face. "You had a good time, too," she finished softly, unable to stop from meeting his gaze for the confirmation.

He played with a strand of her hair, twirling that strand on a finger, reeling her in until they were nose to nose, as if they were lovers for real. "Is it your turn for fishing now?" he murmured.

Dammit. Yes. She lifted a hand to push him away, but remembered that they were out in public, and therefore a couple, and left it on his chest. "I don't need to fish. I know it was good for you. Just as you know . . ." She broke off, deciding to let it pass.

But did he ever let an awkward moment go? Hell, no.

He jumped on it with both feet. "Just as I know it was good for you," he murmured, eyes heated and sparkling as he paused meaningfully. "*Twice*."

More heat flooded her cheeks and she sat back, ignoring his soft laugh. In the end, when he'd still been buried inside her, he'd dropped his forehead to hers, and in perhaps the sweetest memory she had of him, he'd let out a low breath, kissed her jaw, and whispered, "Going to be hard to walk away from you, Sam."

Granted, she'd been supremely plowed at the time, but she could remember clinging to him, having to bite back the urge to ask why he'd have to walk away at all.

And then, in the name of self protection, *she'd* walked away first.

She'd made herself, to avoid thinking about it too much, to avoid the wondering, but mostly to squelch that secret little hope that they could make something work between the two of them.

In the haze of the next morning's hangover, she'd been able to admit that had been the alcohol talking. They could never make anything between them work, not when at their core, they were two totally different people, with two totally and completely different sets of hopes and dreams.

"Sam?"

She looked at him.

"It *was* good for me," he said softly. He paused a moment, watching his fingers play with her hair. "I'm just not sure that a repeat wouldn't kill me."

"What does that mean?"

"You were like a freight truck, Princess. Hot and fast and too much for me to handle."

Yeah, right. He couldn't possibly mean that. Unless he meant . . . "Are you saying I'm high maintenance?"

"On the contrary." With that enigmatic statement, he lifted

two fresh flutes of champagne from a passing waiter, handed her one and gently knocked his to hers in an unspoken toast.

"You confuse me," she said.

"Ditto."

They both sat back now, eyeing each other like two formidable boxers in the ring, deciding on their next strategy. By all rights, they would probably kill each other if they ever were insane enough to try for round two. So why a secret part of her was still tempted, she had no idea.

She chalked it up to the sentimentality of being at a wedding, to the fact that she'd been in close quarters with him for over twenty-four hours now, and the forced intimacy had gone straight to her head.

And to the fact that she couldn't stop looking at him in that tux, and wondering how long it would take her to get it off of him.

A flash went off right in their faces, and Sam nearly jumped out of her skin.

Wade didn't react, except to soothe her by running a hand up her arm.

"Sorry." The wedding photographer smiled. "Can you two scoot closer to each other?"

No. Closer was a major league bad idea all the way around. If she scooted closer, she'd possibly jump him.

"Just shift into each other a little," the photographer coaxed, gesturing to them with his hands. "Come on, give me a romantic shot."

Sam looked into Wade's face questioningly but she should have known better. Always game, he tugged her in. He wrapped an arm around her waist, then tugged a surprised gasp out of her when he bowed her back, low and deep. Leaning over her, he gave her a kiss.

For show, she reminded herself as her fingers ran up

his strong, warm arms, past rock-hard biceps to his hard chest, which she held on to. *For show*, she had to remind herself yet again when he nibbled at the corner of her mouth, encouraging her to open to him. And when she did, he slid his tongue to hers in a lazy, sexy, fiery, *perfect* kiss that made it difficult to keep her balance.

Luckily he was fully supporting her. Far before she was ready, he pulled back, straightened her up, and shot a quick grin at the photog. "You get it?"

The photog winked and backed off, and by the time Wade looked down into Sam's face she'd managed to collect herself.

"They're going to be serving soon," Wade said with clear relief, eyeing the servers bustling around, getting ready. "Mark promised me steak."

Sam managed to find her brain. He wasn't affected by that kiss, and so she refused to be. "Good to know you won't be needing a Mickey D's run."

"Yeah, though I haven't ruled it out for later."

The music changed, quickened, and the dance floor began to fill up. He stood up, stripped off his tux jacket, and held out a hand.

She stared at his long fingers and felt her stomach tighten. "What?"

"Let's dance."

No. Hell, no. "Pass."

"Why?"

"Uh, because I don't want to?"

"You like to dance," he said. "I've seen you at lots of Heat functions."

He was right. She liked to dance. Not that she was necessarily any good at it, but she liked the feeling of letting go. Of not having a phone to her ear or an event in her head or a situation to make the best of.

But dancing with Wade would be a mistake. It was hard to fake anything on the dance floor. She'd forget that she was having a hell of a hard time remembering why she needed to guard her heart around him.

"You like to dance," he said again slowly, understanding dawning. "But you're afraid you can't control yourself with me." He grinned.

She rolled her eyes. Yeah, so she was worried that with her luck, a slow song would come on and then she'd have to be all pressed up against that body that already knew how to take her to heaven and back, and they were at a *wedding*, in a very romantic setting, and well . . . bad idea all around.

"This was all your idea," he reminded her, tauntingly. "Your game."

"Well, it was a bad idea. A stupid game."

"Granted. But you have to see it through now." He glanced beyond her, to where the wedding photographers were snapping pictures, and beyond that, to the waist-high white fence blocking the garden area off from the gawkers, which included paparazzi.

And their cameras.

With a grim sigh, she rose to her feet, took his hand, ignored his smirk, and followed him to the dance floor. "This is such a mistake," she said.

"Since when has that ever stopped us?"

For Wade, dancing with Sam was more like a forbidden treat. She felt good against him, too good, making him forget certain basics—that he'd purposely lived his adult life fun and carefree, without worry and anxiety, and he couldn't, wouldn't, go back there. Not for anything, or anyone.

Sam included.

Life was meant to be fun and light. Period. Preferably
with lots of sex and little depth. And that's what this weekend should have been. Hell, the music was nice, the beat
fast, and when she moved to it and smiled at him, he smiled
back. And yet at the same time, he felt something tighten
in his chest. Which wasn't good.

Not one little bit.

Neither was the way he automatically held out a hand
for her when the song slowed, when everyone around them
stepped into their partner.

Sam stared at his hand for a long moment, and he honestly expected that she'd turn away and walk back to the
table. Maybe even leave the reception.

It would have been the smart thing to do, after all he
was exactly what she'd labeled him—a player. But here was
the problem. For two incredibly smart people when they
were on their own, they'd never seemed to be able to fully
access their IQs when it came to each other.

"I can do this," she finally said, as if she needed to believe it, and she stepped into him.

He pulled her in closer, and could tell that she tried to
lose herself in the music, but he'd seen her slow dance before and she'd been a whole lot less stiff. "What's the
matter?"

"Nothing."

"It's something."

"You can move," she said so begrudgingly that she made
him laugh.

"Yeah?"

She let out a small smile. "Yeah."

"How's that a problem?"

She didn't answer, and he returned her smile and pressed
his mouth to her ear. "You want me bad. One of these days
you're going to admit it."

"Just because you look damn fine on the dance floor doesn't mean I want you."

"But you do."

She had no response to that. Nor did she protest when he drew her in even closer so that she was flush against him.

"Smooth," she managed. "For a jock."

He laughed softly against her temple, because cool as she sounded, her body trembled. "How about this?"

"What?"

He pulled her in even closer, still moving to the beat, a different one now, one that matched the same beat of his pulse and the blood pounding through his veins as he slid a hand nice and slow up her slim spine.

"Oh, boy," she whispered, telling him she was in as much trouble as he.

"Tell the truth, Sam. This feels good."

She paused. "It's okay."

"You are such a liar. A gorgeous one though, I'll give you that." His hand skimmed down again, just beneath the hem of her short, fitted jacket, low on her back, against the silk of her blouse. He slid a finger just beneath the waistband of her skirt and got bare skin.

In his arms, she shivered.

God, he wanted to be alone with her. He wanted that more than anything. "Maybe the elevator will get stuck again—"

"Wade." She shook her head. "I . . ."

"I know." Beneath her jacket, low on her spine, his fingers continued to play with her warm, and getting warmer, skin. "Bad idea, right?"

"The worst."

"The paps are watching."

"I think we've given them plenty," she said, and when

the song ended, she pulled free, met his gaze, her own hooded. "I'm sorry, Wade. I'm maxed out on the pretending. Excuse me a minute, okay?" And with a shaky smile, she walked off the floor. She passed by their table, grabbed her purse, then headed toward the building.

Don't do it, he told himself. *Don't follow her. The food is coming . . .*

Shit.

He followed Sam through the back door, into the huge, upscale kitchen area where the servers were quickly and efficiently—and frantically—working to get the food out to the guests. Wade looked at all the delicious steak, then to Sam's quickly retreating back. *Dammit.* "Sam—"

She didn't slow, leaving him with a life-altering decision. *Steak or the woman?*

With a grim sigh, he went after her, through a maze of kitchen areas and stopped, momentarily stymied by a restroom door clearly labeled *Women* as it swung shut in his face. *Well, hell.* He shoved his hands in his pockets, thought forlornly of the steak probably heading to his table right this second and sighed. "Sam."

He got the big nothing, and put a hand on the door. "Is there anyone in there with you?"

A server ducked past him, then skidded to a stop, clearly recognizing him. "Wow," she said breathless. She wiped her hands on her apron and grinned. "Wade O'Riley."

"Hey," he said. "How's it going?"

She watched him take his hand off the door. "It's a single stall," she told him. "You don't have to knock to go in, if it's unlocked, it's unoccupied. Help yourself, though the men's restroom is just around the corner. Hey, did you know you're even cuter in person?"

He was never quite sure what to say to stuff like that, but she didn't seem to need a response.

"I got to see game two of the playoffs last year," she said. "You guys were robbed, but my boyfriend says you'll take it this year. I think so, too. Your position is my favorite. Catchers are tough, real badass." She grinned. "You fit that bill, don't you?"

Again, no idea what to say to that.

"Will you sign an autograph for me?"

Finally, something he had an answer for. "Sure." He patted down his pockets but he didn't have a pen.

"Here." She pulled a ballpoint from her apron, and then turned her back, exposing the clean white cotton back of her server uniform. "Be sure to write 'Love, Wade' real big cuz it'll drive my boyfriend bonkers."

He'd had far odder requests, so he dutifully signed the back of her shirt, and with a happy wave at him, she was off.

Alone, he eyed the restroom door. *Fuck it,* he thought, and let himself in.

The server had been right, it was indeed a single stall, which was open and empty because Sam stood in front of the sink staring at herself in the mirror.

The restroom was as luxurious and elegant as the rest of the hotel, the walls painted in muted beachy colors, the tile floors and counter as sparkling and clean as the kitchens he'd just walked through to get here. "You owe me a steak," he said, and came up behind her to meet her eyes in the mirror's reflection. "Medium rare. Actually, make it two, with a baked potato, loaded. No veggies required."

"This is the women's restroom."

"I know." He looked around. "Not nearly as mysterious as I'd have thought. Where's the lesbian party?"

She choked out a laugh that had him taking a second, longer look at her. She was seriously unnerved, and he had an idea that he was a fairly big part of that unnerving.

He knew she had a lot going on: the high-powered job, a demanding family that, given the phone call he'd taken for her earlier, was about to become a lot more demanding.

But his tough-on-the-outside Sam was holding on to a surprisingly soft, tender, bruised heart on the inside, and it did something odd to his own heart. Setting his hands on her hips, he stepped close so that her back brushed his chest. He pressed his mouth to her neck, a motion that tugged a surprised breath out of her, just a little hum of helpless arousal that turned him upside down.

But though he was a lot of things, he wasn't stupid, and he raised his head to meet her gaze in the mirror. "So. What are we doing in here?"

"I don't know about you," she said. "But I'm running a poll with my bad and good side."

On whether to give into this attraction. "Do I get a vote?" he asked.

She didn't so much as blink, and taking that as a yes, he reached out and hit the lock on the restroom, because his vote was for the bad side, every time.

Chapter 10

[A knuckleball is] a curve ball that doesn't give a damn.

—Jimmy Cannon

Sam listened to the bolt on the bathroom slide home and resisted the urge to let out a half hysterical laugh. "Wade—"

"Do you remember what I said last night?" he asked. "What I need to hear from you?"

"Y-yes." *God, listen to her stutter.* With a low laugh, she tossed up her hands and faced the truth. "I want you. *Dammit.* I don't want to, but I do." She blew out a breath. "There are a thousand reasons why this is stupid, a *million*, but—"

He whipped her around, cupped her face and kissed her—probably to shut her up.

It worked. *Oh, good Lord, did it work.* She'd been standing there staring in the mirror at a woman she didn't recognize because she'd buried herself so deep behind the professional image that just a simple dance with a sexy guy, a guy who most definitely wanted to strip her out of her professional image, had terrified her.

So where was the ice princess now? Because she couldn't find her, not when she'd been standing in here alone wondering where the hell the good parts of her life had gone, and sure as hell not now that she was hauled up against the very warm, very hard body of the man she'd been fantasizing about for months.

"God, Sam," he murmured huskily against her mouth. "God. Kiss me back."

In that very beat it all tumbled together, her fear, her restlessness, her loneliness, and it turned into something else entirely.

Sheer, unadulterated need.

So much that she shook with it, and she dropped her purse to wrap her arms around his neck, for the first time in her life, doing as he asked.

She kissed him back.

It wrenched a rough groan from deep in his throat and this time he whipped them both around, pinning her to the wall as he kissed her, kissed her like he'd never kissed her before, as if she was so much more than the woman he'd happened to get caught on an elevator with, or a woman he was merely pretending to care for.

He kissed her as if she meant something to him, and it wrenched her heart wide open as she gave him the same back, what she'd never given before, which was to say *everything*.

He pressed into her, using the wall as leverage to free up his hands, which made great use of their liberation as he slid his fingers into her hair, angling her head to better suit him while he continued to devour her. Then suddenly he lifted his head, looking deep into her eyes, his dark and slumberous and sexy as he stared at her.

"What?" she whispered.

"Nothing. I just wanted to see you, see if you're half as gone as I am." His gaze swept her face and softened. "You are."

"I'm—" She closed her mouth on the lie, instead giving out a miserable nod. He let out a low sympathetic laugh before he came at her again, settling his mouth firmly over hers while she sank her fingers into his hair and clutched at him.

Yes. Yes, she was just as gone as he was, crazy as that seemed. She had no idea how long they went at each other, all she knew was that her toes were curling, her hips rocking to his, and she'd never, ever, felt as far "gone" as she did in that moment, like if he so much as touched her skin to skin she was going to burst into an instantaneous orgasm.

As if he read her mind, he slid his hands down her arms to her hips, and then up again, over her ribs, then higher, to her shoulders, where from the inside of her jacket, he nudged it off, down to her elbows. With her arms caught, his palms swept down again, covering her breasts, his thumbs rasping over her nipples, which wrenched a gasp from her and another heartfelt groan from him.

"Not enough," he muttered. "Not. Even. Close." He worked open the buttons of her blouse, murmured a wordless thanks when he found a front hook on her bra, and flicked it open. With an inarticulate sound of hunger, he bent his head, nibbling the full curve of a breast as he crushed the hem of her skirt in his fingers.

"Wade."

He looked up, eyes bright and intense.

She took a deep breath and searched her mind for a single coherent sentence. She had nothing. Less than nothing. "I forgot what I was going to say."

Face still serious, he pulled her skirt up. "Let me know when you remember."

And up . . .

When her skirt was bunched to her waist, he tilted his head down to take in her boy-cut panties and let out a rough breath. "God, look at you." He ran a finger over her hip, then beneath the silk, his other hand joining the fray, and then he was cupping her bare bottom in those big, warm, callused hands, hauling her up so that her legs could wrap around his hips.

"I don't—" She broke off as he rocked his hips, nudging his sex right up against the already damp crux of hers so that she cradled him between her thighs. "Oh, God," she managed on a rough exhale of breath as he tightened his grip on her and rocked again, his tongue tangling with hers.

She really had no idea what she'd been about to say, none. Maybe that this quick, aggressive, possessive style of his was over the line, that he was pushing her too hard too fast, taking her where she hadn't wanted to go again, but the truth was that it had a thrill rushing through her, exciting her to the very tips of her curling toes.

And she did want to go there with him. So very much.

He had his big body pressing her to the wall as he rocked to her, and she clung to him, breathing like she'd just run a mile. She didn't know how she could want him like this, but she did, and every shift of his hips brought her closer to the edge, and that edge was in sight. Gasping, she gripped the front of his shirt. "Wade—"

"I know. Christ, I know . . ."

Suddenly terrified with the depths of what he was wrenching from her, she tried to shake it off, tried to hold back, but he kissed her hard, bringing her focus back to him. "Oh, no you don't," he said against her mouth. "Don't pretend you don't feel anything, when I can see that you do." His fingers slid down, finding her hot and wet, and he tore his mouth from hers to groan as he dipped into that heat. "When I can *feel* you." Lowering his head, he watched as he stroked her right where she needed him, right there with her.

"*Wade*."

"Good?"

She gripped him tight, hips oscillating. "Don't stop . . . Please, don't stop—"

"I won't. I've got you, Sam, I've got you." He kissed his way to her ear, then sucked her lobe into his mouth, still working her with his fingers.

She pressed her head back hard against the wall as her muscles quivered, tightened. She gripped his biceps, tightening when he gently outlined her, then scrapped a callused thumb over her with exactly the right pressure, making her gasp and cry out. "Omigod, I need . . . I—"

"I know," he whispered hoarsely against her mouth, his own breathing coming hard and fast. "Let go. I want to feel you."

Her gaze flew to his. He was watching her, his eyes dark and tightly in focus.

On her.

He wanted her to come, wanted to see it, feel it, because it turned him on to watch her, and though it shouldn't have, that knowledge turned her on as well.

Let go, he'd said. And she did. Her muscles still rippling and quivering when he reached between them to unbutton his pants.

"Condom," she managed to say.

He went still, the "Oh, shit" look in his eyes unmistakable. During their elevator tryst, she'd admitted to being on the pill. But he'd also had his bag and had been able to access a condom, which they'd also used. She shook her head in disbelief. "Are you telling me that you came to a wedding without a condom? You?"

He groaned. "Contrary to what you might think, I don't get laid every damn weekend. Not anymore."

She stared at him for a moment. "I'm still on the pill."

He stared right back. "I know you're going to laugh your ass off, but I've never had sex without a condom. Ever."

And he'd just had a full physical. She knew this because all the guys had, as they always did before spring training.

The sound of his zipper rasped loudly. Apparently it was full speed ahead.

He gave her a beat to disagree with the chain of events. When she didn't, he bent his head and licked, sucked, and kissed his way over her collarbone to her breasts, paying special care and homage to her nipples until she was practically whimpering for more, which he had no problem giving. One shove and his pants slid down enough to free him. She stroked his hard, impressive length, reacquainting herself with what had for a few glorious hours in Atlanta been her favorite part of him.

He sucked some air in through his teeth, and with a quick scrape of his fingers slid her panties to the side, ripping another appreciative growl from his throat at the view he gave himself. "Wrap your legs around me, Sam—God, yeah, like that."

And then, with his eyes burning, holding hers prisoner, he pushed into her, big and thick and so perfect she cried out, the sound so dark and needy she bit his throat to keep herself quiet.

"Oh, Jesus." His breath hissed harshly in her ear. "You feel good. So damn good."

She'd have thought herself spent, but one stroke and she was right back on that perilous edge. It was shocking, disturbingly so, how he did this to her, how he turned her inside out, exposing her like no one else ever had or could, but in that moment, she didn't care. She wrapped her arms around his neck and held on. "*Wade*."

"Right here, I'm right here, Sam, right with you."

She could feel it, feel him, and every time he pulled back and thrust into her, grinding his hips to hers, she whimpered for more, so filled by him, stretched so tight she could hardly stand it.

"Again," he whispered, bending his knees to better align them as he surged into her. Lowering his head, he set his open mouth on her shoulder, kissing his way back to her ear, using his tongue and teeth as he moved within her, murmuring something wordless, the low, hoarse tone conveying the emotion, and that was it for her.

It came from deep within her this time, his name ripped from her throat as the sensations crashed over her. From far, far away she heard him follow her over, a guttural groan tearing from his throat as he slapped a hand on the wall behind her to keep them both from sinking to the floor in a tangled heap.

It took her a moment to realize he was completely supporting her with muscles that were still trembling, and she opened her eyes and met his.

He ran the tip of his nose along her jaw as he let her legs slide down his body, holding her until her feet hit the floor and she nodded that she was okay.

When she wasn't.

Turning from him, she tried to put herself back together, but her bra was hopelessly tangled in her blouse and she had to pull both off to start over.

The knock at the door galvanized her. "Um . . . just a second!" Horrified, she skipped the bra, dropping it to the counter to yank back on her blouse and her jacket, figuring it would have to do. She slipped into her heels, straightened her hair, and with a breath to fortify herself, turned to grab her bra.

Wade had rebuttoned and zipped, and was standing there silent, studying her.

"My bra," she murmured, moving close to him again because he had his hand in his pocket and she could see the little piece of lace peeking out.

The knock came again, stopping her in her tracks.

"Hello?" a female voice called through the door. "I really need to get in there."

"I'm nearly done," Sam said and held out her hand to Wade.

"It's really amazing, how you do that," he murmured softly. "How you pull yourself together in the blink of an eye."

"What choice do we have?" Taking a deep breath, she gave up on her bra and pulled open the door.

A woman stood there with a little girl, both of whom stared up at Sam and Wade, mouths open.

"I'm sorry," Sam said. "I—"

"It's fine." The woman tightened her lips in disapproval at her and Wade as they moved out of the bathroom.

"Mommy? Isn't this the women's bathroom?"

"Yes, baby, it is," the woman assured the little girl, shutting the door hard.

Wade reached for Sam's hand.

"Don't," she said very quietly. "Please, don't." She backed away. "I need a minute."

"Sam."

"Please," she whispered.

He studied her for a long beat, then with a reluctant nod, let her walk away.

Wade made his way back to the reception. That Sam needed a minute didn't surprise him. She wasn't one to let go of her famed control without a fight, and though she'd put up a good one, she *had* let go.

He pulled out a chair at the Heat table, turning it around to straddle it. Pace and Gage were using the silverware to create a makeshift diamond. A wadded napkin was the mound. "Seventh inning," Gage said.

"Henry's homer tied the game at the top." Pace shook his head. "But we couldn't go ahead because the Phillies threw me out at the plate to end the frame."

"Then the rain halted the damn game," Gage said in disgust. "It wasn't even that bad, they should have let the game go. When we finally got back to it, you didn't blow the save, you locked down the eighth."

"But then they got a tying run in scoring position, and Wade fucking popped out—"

"Hey," Wade said, grabbing Pace's beer for himself.

"Well, you did," Gage told him with a shake of his head. "You sucked."

"Again. *Hey*." Wade propped his elbows on the back of the chair, dropping his heavy head into his hands. "We won that game. I came back in the ninth, broke my bat on a base hit to right field. Henry stole home, and I followed, locking down the win, thank you very much." He sighed and lifted his head to find both Pace and Gage staring at him. "What? I did."

"I remember," Gage said. "Everyone dived on you at the plate and you cracked a rib. What's up?"

"Nothing."

Pace raised a brow. "You disappear with Sam for an hour, then only you come back, and nothing's up?"

Wade scrubbed a hand over his face. "I don't know what you're talking about. And it wasn't an hour."

"Forty-five minutes." Gage looked him over. "Your shirt is half untucked, your tie's gone, and probably you want to lift your collar to hide that bite mark on your neck. Either you got jumped by some fan girls, or you just got laid."

Wade tucked the rest of his shirt in. There was nothing to be done about the tie. It was wadded up in his pocket along with Sam's bra. He lifted a spoon from the table to use as a mirror to check his neck. *Yep.* He had a doozy of a hickey going.

Gage shook his head.

Pace grinned. "Nice."

Wade sighed. "Don't you have a fiancée to worry about? And you," he said to Gage. "Where's your date?"

"They've gone on a little girls' room run. They seem to do that in pairs."

Yeah. Most women did.

Not Sam.

She'd been in there all alone until he'd come along, though he had to say, they'd made a nice pair. Speaking of, where the hell was she? He craned his neck and looked around—

"Lose something?" Pace asked with mock politeness.

Wade ignored him, still searching through the wedding revelers for Sam.

"You know, I was going to keep my nose out of this one," Gage said. "But—"

"Oh, Christ," Wade groaned. "Not the but."

"*But*," Gage continued undeterred. "I don't think you two are a good idea."

"We're not a two," Wade said. "You more than anyone know that this whole weekend is pretend. Make-believe. A complete fallacy. Hell, it was *your* idea."

"And a bad one," Pace muttered.

"No shit," Wade muttered back.

"But only because you *are* a two," Pace said patiently. "And have been ever since Atlanta."

"Atlanta?" Gage asked, eyes narrowing. "What happened in Atlanta?"

"Nothing." Wade shook his head and glared at Pace. "*Nothing.*"

Pace leaned in close to Wade. "You remember right before the playoffs, when I fell hard for Holly and couldn't admit it? You made me face it."

"Yeah? So? You were being an idiot and needed a friendly shove."

"Consider this . . ." Pace gave Wade a good, hard shove on his shoulder, nearly knocking him off the chair. "The same."

"Don't encourage him," Gage told Pace. "He'll just fuck with her head."

"Sitting right here," Wade said, feeling more than a little tense.

"I'm sorry, man. But that's what you do. Fuck 'em and leave 'em."

"Not always."

"Always," Gage said firmly.

Wade opened his mouth to refute that and Gage just gave him a long, even look. "Name one time *you've* been ditched, Wade. One time."

Wade said nothing, but he counted in his head. His mother. His father.

Sam.

Not that he'd say so.

"She deserves better," Gage said.

Wade looked at Pace. "You think so, too?"

"She deserves to be more than the *pretend* girlfriend, I'll give you that. Because it's Sam, you know?"

Yeah. He knew. Sam, who they all cared about. Sam, who gave so much of herself to the team. Sam, who'd just given herself to him, and he had a feeling it was far more than she'd intended.

As it had been for him.

He sat there with a headache brewing and the certainty that he'd already fucked it up without even knowing exactly how. "Well, this has been fun, but I've got to go." He pushed away from the table and strode through the reception one more time, but he was certain.

Sam wasn't here.

He headed inside the main lobby and headed straight for the elevators, punching the button, suddenly afraid he was already too late.

The elevator didn't come. He hit the button again, swore, then headed for the stairs. He made it to their eighth floor suite three minutes later, running on adrenaline as he burst into their room. "Sam."

But he knew even before he called her name that she was gone. The note on the bathroom mirror confirmed it.

Take the limo back, I grabbed a cab.

Yep. He'd been ditched. "Well, hell," he said out loud, pulling the note down. As he did, something on the counter grabbed his attention.

Her bathroom bag.

It was stuffed with makeup and brushes and bottles of stuff—the mysteries of a woman.

It smelled like her.

And just next to the bag lay her mother's antique pearl pin.

"You *were* in a hurry," he murmured, and suddenly he didn't feel quite as bad. She hadn't run out on him because she was done with the pretense.

Nope.

She'd run because that pretense had turned into a few moments of . . . real.

Something neither of them had intended.

It'd been so real it'd scared her.

"Chicken," he said softly, surprised at this unexpected chink in her armor, while being equally surprised at something else.

He was afraid, too. Which meant it was a good thing she'd gone, a really good thing. And palming the pin, gently running his thumb over it, he willed himself to get over it before he saw her again, before she saw that she wasn't the only one with a chink in her armor.

Chapter 11

Baseball statistics are like a girl in a bikini. They show a lot, but not everything.

—Toby Harrah

Wade got back to Santa Barbara late, and hit the sack. He woke in his own bed, which was infinitely better than the couch had been in the hotel but somehow it was not nearly as much fun.

He got dressed and wondered what his pretend girl-friend was doing. Certainly *not* returning any of his calls . . .

Telling himself he was ready for the opening game of season four against the Padres, he drove to the Heat's facilities with the music cranking, walked into the club-house and felt adrenaline kick in. Adrenaline was good. It meant he wasn't thinking about Sam, or how she'd felt with her legs wrapped around his waist as he'd plunged into her.

Much.

The clubhouse was filled and noisy. Most MLB base-ball clubhouses gravitated toward a specific identity. The Yankees were corporate. The Rockies were religious. The Heat? *Rollicking.*

Today was no different. The air was excited and jubilant, just the way Wade liked it. They had an unusually tight, close-knit team, and almost everyone arrived within minutes of each other.

Food was set out, and they ate together: Wade, Pace, Joe Pickler, the Heat's second baseman, Henry Weston, their left-fielder-turned-shortstop, who was sporting a black eye from his fender bender two days ago, and Mason Rictor. Mason was their first baseman who was currently battling knee problems from a spring training incident involving not a ball but a woman, a stolen night, and her husband coming home early, which had forced Mason out a third-story window.

Gage was still barely speaking to him.

As they sat around inhaling a pile of sandwiches, Mike, their third baseman, and Kyle, their right-fielder, joined them. "Heard you had quite the weekend," Kyle said to Wade, and tossed down a stack of newspapers to the table.

Wade opened one up and stared at the picture of himself and Sam at the reception. They were locked together on the dance floor. Her arms were around his neck. He had one hand in her hair, the other on her ass.

"Looks like mission accomplished on the tame-Wade thing," Kyle said, heavy on the irony. "So was this before or after the quickie in the bathroom?"

Wade slid a death-glare at Pace.

Pace lifted his hands. "Hey, I didn't tell."

Henry choked on his drink. "You mean it's true? You and Sam had a quickie in the bathroom? *Our* Sam?"

All eyes swiveled to Wade.

"We're boyfriend and girlfriend," he said.

"*Pretend* boyfriend and girlfriend," Mike reminded him.

"Yeah," Wade said. "Right. *Pretend.*"

"Wait." Mike took a closer look at Wade, then glanced

at everyone else. "Am I the only one who heard that?" he demanded to know.

"Heard what?" Wade asked.

"Nope," Kyle said. "I heard it, too."

"Heard *what*?" Wade repeated through his teeth.

"That you don't want it to be pretend," Kyle told him.

Wade stared at him. "Shut up."

"You should tell her," Kyle said, unperturbed. "She's always telling us that she needs to know everything, and this is definitely need-to-know."

"Christ! Don't tell her," Mike said. "Are you kidding? She'll kill you. You can't get dead now, it's opening day."

"Maybe she likes me alive," Wade said, frowning when everyone laughed. Okay, so his and Sam's tension was legendary. Whatever. They'd gotten past it now.

Or so he hoped.

Gage walked in and as always, the room quieted. He was their age and yet his demeanor was such that everyone deferred to him as . . . well, God. He grabbed a soda and then slowly took each of them in and narrowed his gaze. "What's going on?"

"Nothing," Wade said, and gathered all the papers and threw them in the recycling bin next to the trash can.

"Hey, good job on those, by the way," Gage said, proving that nothing got past him, ever. "Our sponsors are happy."

"Good for them." Not wanting to hear more about how the ruse was working, Wade took off, moving toward the locker area to change for field practice. And yeah, maybe he was also keeping his eyes peeled for a glimpse of Sam . . .

The Heat's facilities were now four years old, with everything in it being the best of the best, including the clubhouse around him. Back before the economy had taken a nosedive, the Santa Barbara taxpayers had been ecstatic to put money into a new MLB expansion team. The Heat had returned the love. Last season they'd worked their asses off, and even with bad odds, rough press, and unfair disadvantages—they'd lost a good bull pen pitcher and a great pitching coach midseason—they'd gone to the playoffs.

This season, they wanted to go even further, all the way to the World Series. For a guy who'd been born in the gutter and then survived his childhood to scrape his way through college, Wade had been lucky enough to be drafted straight to an MLB contract. After a few years in Denver, the Heat had signed him, giving him a lucrative deal he'd been more than happy to accept. He'd moved to Santa Barbara, bought himself a big, new house on the beach, and he'd never been more content.

He pulled off his shirt and shoved it into his locker as the others made their way in to change as well. As was typical, he spent more time in these rooms with the team than he did anywhere else, and it'd been designed for comfort. Right here within reach was just about anything anyone could ever want: food, flat-screen TVs, video games, work-out equipment, massages, whirlpools, anything. He took in the guys all around, guys that were like his brothers as they talked, laughed, dressed, played, hung out, and he had to face one fact—the one thing he wanted hadn't showed up.

It was unlike Sam not to be around pre-game, especially today. She liked to be involved in everything, hustling reporters in and out of the area, putting her nose in, bossing them all around with a sweet smile that barely covered the unbendable sheer steel will just beneath the surface.

He looked at his cell phone, registering that she still hadn't returned a single one of his five phone calls. Shaking his head at her, at himself, he pulled on his uniform, nodding at Pace, who'd come up next to him and was doing the same.

The usual adrenaline was beginning to pound through his system as he dressed. Henry was on his other side now, pulling out his trusty headband, the same one he wore to every game. Mike pulled out his St. Christopher's Cross and kissed it, just as he did every time he jogged out to third base.

Superstitions.

The caveat of the game, and a habit that had actually brought Pace and Holly together. Wade turned his head and watched as Holly came into the clubhouse, heading straight for her fiancée with a secret smile on her face.

Pace's expression went just a little goofy. Taking Holly's hand, he pulled her into the shower room, where Wade knew—hell, everyone knew—that Pace would press her back against the tile wall of the showers and kiss her stupid.

That was Pace's superstition. If he kissed Holly, he'd pitch well.

They'd win.

Hell, even if it only worked in Pace's mind, it worked for Wade. He wanted to win today, wanted that badly. So badly he had to wonder if he wasn't putting some of his frustrations into the wrong avenue.

And then he felt it, the prickle of awareness on the back of his neck, and he turned to the door as Samantha McNead walked in.

She wore one of her power suits, red, snug in the jacket, short in the skirt. She and her mile-long legs strode through like she owned her world.

She'd sure as hell rocked his.

She smiled at Gage, who slipped an arm around her,

soft with Sam where he was never soft with his players. He murmured something into her ear, and though her easy smile never wavered, her eyes flickered as if a painful memory had presented itself, but it vanished so fast he couldn't be sure.

She hugged Gage, nodded as if reassuring him of something, and moved on. She smiled at Mason, bumped fists with Joe, and nodded at some of the other players nearby.

And then she glanced Wade's way, telling him that she was as aware of him as he was of her. Just a quick peek, nothing more, but it was enough.

She wanted to be cool, calm, and collected, and she needed distance to accomplish that.

So did he.

Desperately. He wasn't planning on pushing for anything more. That wasn't him. He never pushed. He'd never had to. Luckily for him, most of the women in his life had fallen for his easy charm with little to no effort on his part. And when this month was over, he'd go right back to that.

Pace and Holly reappeared from the shower rooms. Holly's lip gloss had been eaten off and she had a glow about her.

Pace had the predictable satisfied grin plastered on him.

Wade shook his head, then ignored everything he'd just told himself and came up behind Sam, who'd made her way to the table of drinks and was choosing between two different brands of iced tea. "Hey," he said. "How are you?"

"Hey, yourself. I'm fine, thanks."

"You left in a hurry yesterday."

"Things to do," she said.

Uh-huh. Like regroup. He leaned in. "Maybe we should come up with a ritual before each game, like Pace and Holly. There might be something to their superstition."

"Pace isn't superstitious," she said. "You know it's everyone *else* who thinks that their kisses work. Pace and Holly only go along with it because . . . well, because they're in love."

Wade looked into her eyes, searching for the warm, soft, sweet woman who'd been wrapped around him like a pretzel only yesterday afternoon, wrapped around him and panted his name like a mantra as he'd thrust into her welcoming body. But that woman was nowhere to be found. "Okay," he said quietly, turning her to fully face him. "Let's try this again. Hi. How are you really?"

She blew out a breath, and for a moment let herself lean into him. "I'm sorry I ran out on you."

"It's okay. I was tempted to do the same," he admitted, waiting until she looked up in surprise. He smiled ruefully. "Got a little too real there, didn't it?"

"Yeah." She sighed again. "Probably the whole losing our clothes thing was a real bad idea. We need to watch that."

"That's my favorite part."

She smiled but it faded quick. "I don't mind the pretend-relationship thing, Wade. But the getting naked thing is really hard for me to do so casually."

Yeah. He got that. He also had nothing to say in response, which was just as well since she was already gone.

Pace came up beside him. "Want some advice?"

"No."

"Yeah, didn't think so." He slung an arm around Wade. "Too bad I'm going to give it to you anyway. Remember when you told me to go get myself a life outside of MLB, a life with Holly?"

"I have *plenty* of life outside of it. And a good part of that is with you and the parks we're building for kids, or have you forgotten that big fat check I just wrote you? Or the two days we spent last week coaching spring camps for those kids?"

"I'm talking about you and Sam."

"There is no me and Sam. It's pretend, remember? We're just making the sponsors happy." His cell phone buzzed. He pulled it out of his pocket, saw the area code that signaled Oregon, and swore. His father. John had left Wade a message earlier, telling him that he'd gotten in trouble for running a poker game and he needed bribe money for the caretaker. Not needing another call like that, Wade hit *Ignore*.

Pace was watching him. "You're good at that, hitting *Ignore*."

"I've already sent money today to get him out of trouble for gambling. I think he can wait until after the game for anything else."

"Maybe it's not money he needs. Maybe writing a check, either to the kids, to your father, to whoever asks, isn't always the answer. And you're missing my point on purpose. Stop ignoring, Wade. Make a commitment, somewhere, with someone."

Wade just shook his head. He had a damn hard time with commitment, cliché or not. He'd been let down by commitment before, by people bound to him by blood even. It wasn't in the cards for him. Besides, even if he wanted to, he couldn't act on his growing feelings for Sam because in spite of her toughness, he sensed that *she* wanted to commit, and he refused to let her down. And he *would* eventually let her down.

"Look," Pace said. "You told me I had a real chance at a great life, with Holly. You told me to go for it."

"Yeah, and you told me I was full of shit."

"I was wrong. You were right. And now I'm right." He squeezed Wade's shoulder in commiseration. "Just as I also know you'd like to kick my ass for saying so, but you can't because Gage is looking at us right now, trying to decide if he needs to come intervene."

Wade looked up and met Gage's narrowed, carefully observant eyes. The team manager, aka Skipper, had broken up more fights between his players than he had fingers and toes. One more wouldn't be a problem, but Wade let out a rough breath. "I could kick your ass before he even got over here."

"Keep dreaming," Pace said in a mock soothing voice that really did make Wade want to smash his face in, best friend or not. "But if you tried, Sam would really be pissed."

Wade shoved away and stalked off to Pace's low, knowing laugh as he grabbed his gear and headed out for practice.

Chapter 12

Baseball is a ballet without music. Drama without words.

—Ernie Harwell

Feeling all mixed-up and churned-up and more confused than ever, Sam walked to her seat in the stands and found her usual seatmate waiting for her.

"Hiya," Holly said.

"I need sugar."

Without missing a beat, Holly handed over her lemonade, then pulled out a bag of M&M's to go with it.

Sam sighed in sheer pleasure as she ripped into them. "You're a good friend."

"I am." Holly looked at her speculatively. "I know why *I* usually need sugar. Either Pace has pissed me off, or I need to get me some."

"Some what?"

Holly waggled a brow.

Sam sighed.

"And," Holly said, "since I know you *just* got some—"

"I don't want to talk about it."

"Uh-huh. So that leaves pissed. Question is, are you pissed off at Wade, or yourself?"

Sam busied herself with the M&M's.

Holly snorted, then lifted a tray she'd stowed behind her feet. It held the bribes—two fully loaded hot dogs, peanuts, and cotton candy.

"I'm on a diet," Sam said in protest, but grabbed a dog. And then on second thought, the peanuts and cotton candy as well, hugging it all to her chest.

"Atta girl." Holly tore into her own hot dog. "So. How's that pretend thing going?"

Sam chewed a huge bite of hot dog. "I don't want to talk about that either."

"Okay."

"I mean there's really nothing to even talk about. We got into the papers over the weekend, got the word out, as planned. Sponsor's happy."

"Good."

"It's just playing a role." Sam sucked mustard off her finger. "Sure, maybe we got a little carried away for a minute." She grimaced. "Okay, for like an hour, but the man is . . . well. It wasn't my fault."

"Of course not."

"And anyway, he drives me batshit crazy," Sam said.

Holly made a soothing, understanding noise.

"And he's so easygoing and effortlessly sexy. He could reel in a damn nun."

"Good thing we're not talking about it."

Sam just sighed and stuffed her face, and Holly smiled. "Honey, admit it. You want to go for it. For real."

"No. If I'm going to let someone into my life, it's going to be a grown-up."

"That man is *allll* grown-up, and he is fine."

"I want a man who makes me laugh."

"*Hello—o—o*," Holly said. "Wade makes you laugh."

"It'll be someone who lights me up in the bedroom."

Holly just slid her a long look.

"Okay, so he lit me up like Fourth of July. But I want a guy in it for the long haul."

Holly sighed in defeat. "You have me there. He's not shown a lot of depth in relationships before. But that doesn't mean he wouldn't, for the right woman."

"Come on. It's Wade."

"Yeah, but he's the one who told Pace to get something else in his life besides baseball, and that the something should be me. He told Pace to let himself love me." She smiled at Sam's clear surprise. "So see? Maybe there's hope."

Sam didn't necessarily believe in hope. She believed in doing. In making one's own destiny. And though a part of her could admit she'd had a few fantasies about Wade being hers and only hers, she had to doubt it ever becoming a reality.

They ate their way through the first two tight innings, with Sam unable to tear her gaze off a completely oblivious Wade. At the top of the third, the guy behind Sam tapped her on the shoulder. "Excuse me."

She turned and looked at him. He was holding his iPhone open to a page from ESPN. It was a picture of her and Wade at the wedding. They were seated at a table, Wade sprawled out, his arm around the back of her chair, smiling into her face as his fingers played with her hair.

"Is this you?" the guy asked. "You Wade O'Riley's new girl?"

Holly looked at the picture, then to Sam, biting her lip to keep her smile back.

"Yes," Sam said on a barely there sigh. "That's me."

"Cool," the guy said, and leaned back.

"The press you two have gotten is fairly incredible," Holly whispered. "Nice to see it all positive for a change."

Which was the only reason she was still in this. Well that, and because her body was addicted to Wade's. She forced her mind off that problem and concentrated on the game. Wade was in his zone, running a good game. When a runner tried to steal third during a pitch, Wade made the catch, and without taking the time to wind up, shot the ball like a cannon at third to Mike, who made the pickoff. Mike pumped his fist and sent Wade a slow grin, which Wade returned.

And then he turned and looked right at her.

Okay, so maybe he wasn't completely clueless–and God, look at him. There was just something so innately sexy about him in his zone . . . .

"You're staring," Holly whispered.

"Am not."

"And you just let out a dreamy sigh, an I-wish-he-were-my-real-boyfriend sigh."

"For your information, I'm just noticing how the new hockey-style catcher's helmets really allow for superior side vision."

Holly laughed. "Look at you bullshit me."

At the top of the fifth inning, the Heat was down three-four, and tension was thick as the Heat took their field positions. Wade had all his gear on. Little of his face visible, and yet she knew what his expression would be.

Fun.

Easy.

Relaxed.

Chill.

Because that was Wade. He was all of those things. God, she envied that.

Pace was still pitching, and he was in fine form today,

but she still couldn't take her eyes off Wade. A runner tried to steal as Pace let out an unusually slow pitch. Wade was standing up almost before the ball hit his mitt, tossing off his mask to throw the ball down the line to Mason, who caught it.

Runner out.

She let out a low, appreciative breath and sank back to her seat. The runner should have known better. Wade had the best record in the league of picking off runners stealing bases. No one got past him.

In the bottom of the next inning, Wade hit a line drive and she involuntarily leapt to her feet. "Go, go, go!"

Wade made it to second.

Sam *woo-hoo*ed and jumped up and down.

Holly was grinning.

"What? I like to cheer."

"Uh-huh."

"Shut up." Sam held her breath during the next pitch, when Wade stole third. Sam gripped Holly's hand hard when Mike hit a pop fly and Wade headed home, sliding into the catcher a beat ahead of the ball.

The crowd went wild while Sam stared at the pile of entangled limbs over the home plate, "Get up," she whispered. "Get up, get up—"

Wade pushed to his feet, then reached a hand down to help the Padres player, taking a moment to look him in the eye and say something. The other player nodded and Wade headed back to his dugout.

But not before taking a quick and direct glance right at Sam.

Her breath stuttered in her throat and she lifted her hand at him before she could stop herself.

His lips curved.

"Aw," Holly said. "Look at you, all aquiver."

Sam sighed and sank to her chair. "It's ridiculous."

"It's sweet."

Sam closed her eyes against the bright sun and shook her head. "It's not sweet. Does he look sweet to you?"

"No, he looks big and sexy, and like a whole lot of fun."

Sam sighed. *Yeah. Yeah, he was big and sexy and a whole lot of fun.*

And a whole lot of heartache waiting to happen.

They went into the ninth inning up by one. The Heat came out ready to hold the Padres to that score. Wade crouched behind the plate and gave a sign to Pace, who shook his head. Wade gave him something else, and this time Pace nodded. He threw, but the hitter got a piece of it and the fly ball went straight up into the air.

Wade rose to his feet and shoved off his mask, squinting up into the sun, relaxed as the ball flew . . . right into his mitt.

Out. Game won.

Wade straightened just as Pace slammed into him, picking him up in a bear hug to spin him around.

Wade grinned and hugged him back.

And Sam never took her eyes off him. Playing the game for real or for fun, even living his life, little got to him. Not the pressure of the game that was his livelihood, not the responsibilities that came with the level of fame and fortune he dealt with on a daily basis, and not her.

And wasn't that just the crux.

Oh, he wanted her again. She knew it. It was there in the heat of his eyes as he once again turned and from twenty-five yards away met her gaze. A gaze which happened to melt her bones every time she found it leveled on her.

But it was lust. Nothing more. Because Wade didn't do more.

And she didn't do less.

After the game, the players signed autographs for an hour, during which time Sam stayed on scene as she always did, helping out with both crowd control and merchandise give-aways.

Wade was sitting at the table with the other players, signing autographs, completely oblivious to the fact that she'd just had security drag Tia—the woman who'd sent pictures of her and Wade to the press—off the premises and to the police station since she'd violated the restraining order.

It was Sam's job to shield the players where she could, and she did a good job, but she'd had to remind herself this time that it wasn't her job to want to punch a stalker for trying to get close to Wade.

It'd gotten personal, *waaay* too personal, but she had no idea what to do about it.

Wade had people in front of him but he was watching Sam with a little knowing look that heated her from the inside out. Could he read her inappropriate jealousy?

Halfway through the signing, three women tried to climb the table to get to him. With a sigh, she moved through the crowd and around the table, beating security there by two seconds, but not quite fast enough to stop one of the women from writing her phone number on Wade's hand. Sam leaned over Wade and put her face between his and the women's. "You ladies need to back up."

"Aw, we just want to give him a kiss," one of them said with a pout.

"No," Sam said.

"Why not?"

"Sorry." This from a grinning Wade. "She's not much on sharing." He turned his head, which was now only a few inches from Sam's, and gave her a warm, just-for-her smile that for a moment cut off the oxygen to her brain.

The women obligingly backed off.

Mouth curved, eyes warm, Wade tugged on a strand of her hair. "Makes me hot seeing you get all possessive like that."

Yeah, he read her. Like a well-thumbed book. She rolled her eyes and he caught her wrist, tugging her in so their mouths were close.

"Are you going to kiss me?" she whispered, half panicked and yet half hopeful at the same time.

"Only if you say please."

She tugged free and moved back to her real duties, which absolutely did not include falling for his effortless charm.

Afterwards, at the team meeting, Wade came up to her. "Thanks for protecting me out there."

She just gave him a long look, which crumpled completely when he slung an arm around her neck and pulled her in, pressing a lingering but friendly kiss on her temple. Her heart fluttered. "What are you doing?"

"Being your boyfriend."

"The signing's over, Wade. There's no need to pretend back here."

"Huh. Guess you're right." But it took him an extra long beat to remove his hands from her.

And another even longer beat for her to step back from him.

When the meeting was over, the team scattered, everyone off to celebrate. Sam turned to get the hell out of there before she did something stupid. Like offer to be Wade's celebration.

"Sam."

Dammit. She quickened her pace, escaping him and making her way through the facility. She got to her office, grabbed her purse, flicked off the lights, and turned to leave . . .

And slammed into the warm, hard wall of Wade's chest.

His hands came up to her arms to steady her. "In a hurry?" he asked in that same voice that had urged her to orgasm only yesterday.

God. "Yes, actually. A big hurry."

Not releasing her, he nodded, nothing more than a shadow in the doorway. "Avoiding anyone in particular?"

"You."

He laughed softly, his breath ruffling the hair at her temple, which meant he was entirely too close. She stepped back into her dark office, but he merely followed her in.

"Oh, no," she said. "I'm not getting into another room alone with you."

He hit the light switch. He was fresh from the shower he'd grabbed before the meeting, his hair wet and wavy, falling over his forehead and curling around his ears, hitting the collar of his black polo shirt, which was untucked over a pair of cargoes. She had no idea how he looked so damn fine all the time but he did, and she met his gaze, knowing hers was filled with frustration to his amusement. "My clothes are staying on," she said firmly.

"You trying to convince me, or yourself?"

She refused to answer on the grounds she might incriminate herself. He smelled good, all warm and sexy, and that frustrated her because she wanted to go up on her tiptoes and press her face into his throat and just breathe him in. She wanted to have him inside her again, but she also wanted more. She wanted to be with him, just be . . . and that terrified her because she was alone in that. "No one's here. We're offline."

"Sam—"

"I mean it, Wade." She put her hand to her heart but she couldn't rub the ache away. "You can't just waltz in here with that low, husky voice and those bedroom eyes, okay? We don't have to play until the next public outing, and as I've already told you, we're not going to play like we did this weekend."

"Sam—"

"No. Listen, Wade, please? We had our fun, *and* it was fun," she told him, softening, unable to keep the wistfulness out of her voice. "But now I need to be far, far away from you." *Before I rip off your clothes.*

His eyes were dark, and had gone serious. "I understand."

His easy acceptance derailed her. "You do?"

"Yeah. Actually, I just wanted to give you something." He held out his hand, fisted. Slowly he turned it over and opened his fingers, revealing what he held on his palm.

Oh, God. Her mother's pin. She took it and brought it to her heart. "Okay, now I feel like a mean, bitchy idiot."

Wade shook his head. "Definitely not mean. And definitely not an idiot either."

And as he walked off, he actually left her with a laugh. Because he was right. She *was* bitchy.

Dammit.

Chapter 13

Progress always involves risks. You can't steal second base and keep your foot on first.

—Frederick B. Wilcox

Wade walked away from Sam's office, through the Heat's huge facility, telling himself to just go home and hit the sack and sleep off this odd sense of restlessness.

It wasn't his usual MO after a game, especially after a win, but though he was stopped by Joe and Henry, and then Mason, each of them inviting him to several different parties, he didn't feel like partying.

He didn't know exactly what he did feel like doing . . .

Okay, lie. A big, fat lie. He knew exactly what he wanted to be doing, or more correctly, *who* he wanted to be doing.

One sweet and fiery and sexy Samantha McNead.

He thumbed through his iPhone as he walked the hall, heading out. A hundred and thirty-five unread e-mails. Ignoring most of them, he went straight to the few that mattered. Pace had sent him more pictures from Mark's wedding, including a different one of Wade and Sam slow dancing. Her back was to the camera. He couldn't see her expression but her head was cocked up at him, a little tilted.

He most definitely had her attention. He was smiling down into her face, his expression a little too open for his own comfort. He saved the e-mail and moved on to the next, from his father.

I'm breaking out, and thinking of heading south.

His father was free to do whatever the hell he wanted. He wasn't a prisoner and never had been. But Wade sighed and called the center to check on him and he was promptly assured that John O'Riley was fine and well and still on site, though he had somehow sneaked in a fifth and had gotten the guys on his floor bombed, then proceeded to win more loot from them at poker.

Nothing about this surprised Wade. He apologized to the nurse and hung up, shaking his head.

But it was the next e-mail that really grabbed him— from Sam dated very late last night. Which meant she'd written it after the wedding and he'd somehow missed it earlier. She typed formally as if they hadn't had each other up against the bathroom wall.

Wade—I need your assistance for the carnival. I'm putting your name on the ticket. If you have a problem with this, please respond. Otherwise I'll assume you're on-board.

Samantha McNead, Heat Publicist

He shook his head with a grim smile. Look at her, all professional, being a pain-in-his-ass.
Good strategy. Hell, it was an excellent strategy.
And if he hadn't watched her come for him, multiple

times now, thank you very much, each of those times panting his name like he was the be-all-of-the-end-all, he might have even bought the ploy. "But I'm on to you," he murmured, and forwarded the picture of the two of them dancing to her. He thumbed in a message to go with it.

> Had a great weekend, Sam, pretend or otherwise. I still have your bathroom bag and a sexy little lace bra. You can come get them, or I'll bring them to you. Oh, and if you have a problem with this, please respond. Otherwise I'll assume you're onboard.

With a small smile, he slid his phone away. Yeah, that was going to chap her sweet ass but good. In the main hall now, he walked past huge boards plastered with press from the past three years of the Heat's existence, pictures of the team members, their bios, and some of the available merchandise.

He came face-to-face with his own publicity photo blown up to life-size. In six-foot-plus full-color print, he wore his Heat jersey. He was holding his mitt and bat, smiling easily and confidently into the camera, like he didn't have a worry in the world.

Wade looked at himself and suddenly wondered who the hell that was, because he wasn't feeling so easily confident. Despite the very satisfying win, he was feeling a little off his game.

Okay, a lot off his game, and it had nothing to do with baseball and everything to do with—

"Sam." He stopped in surprise at the sight of her ahead of him. She'd clearly come down the opposite end of the hallway, probably having taken the elevator, not the stairs as he had. She was staring at a kid, who was in turn staring at her, both of them looking like they were watching a horror flick, braced for the psycho villain to pop out any second.

Sam's job as publicist often brought her in close contact with kids. Hell, half the Heat's fans were underage, and Sam had always made a point to cater to them, using child-oriented events to make the Heat's players accessible to them. On top of that, she pretty much single-handedly ran the 4 The Kids charity that the Heat sponsored, and by all accounts, she loved both the work *and* the kids.

So this was odd. It'd only been five minutes max since Wade had seen her in her office, since he'd gathered his stuff, said good-bye to the guys, and walked through the facility. But Sam's expression said it'd been a rough five minutes. Really rough.

"Hey," he said, coming up to her side, sliding a hand to the small of her back. "You okay?"

She jumped a mile. "Yes." She nodded wildly. "Absolutely. Yes. Yes I am."

He looked into her wide eyes. "That was a couple too many yeses."

"I'm fine."

She didn't look fine. She looked . . . panicked. Ditto for the kid. Wade tossed an easy smile at him, but he didn't respond. He looked to be around ten and had wheat-colored hair that fell over his eyes. His jeans were new but too long, frayed at the cuffs over a set of brand spanking new Nikes. His T-shirt was standard kid-issued and had X-Men splayed across the front. "Hey, man," Wade said to him. "Gotta name?"

"Tag."

"You watch the game today?"

"No." Tag paused, then spoke quietly but with a little defiance in his tone, as if he was scared to death but hell if he was going to show it. "Dad says we only watch the Heat if they're getting their asses kicked."

Sam let out a choked laugh.

Wade eyeballed her, then turned back to Tag. "So you what, kept your eyes closed during the game?"

Tag shoved his hands into his pockets and looked at the floor. "I sat in the car with the babysitter on accounta *she* didn't answer her phone."

No doubt as to who the *she* was, and above him, Sam made a sound of distress.

"My phone was off during the game," she said quietly. "I'm very sorry, Tag. I didn't know you were coming."

Tag jerked a shoulder, doing his best impression of someone who could give a shit.

But his eyes, big and full of hurt, gave him away.

"Are you here to meet the players?" Wade asked him.

"No," Sam said. "He's—"

"My dad went to rehab," Tag muttered, again to his shoes. "I have to stay with my Aunt Sam."

Aunt Sam. So Tag was Jeremy's kid.

"Tag." Sam put her hand on his shoulders, the kid who was in that awkward stage between child and teen. "We're going to be fine," she said, not sounding like she really believed that.

Tag executed another jerk of his narrow shoulders that dislodged Sam's hand and tugged hard at Wade. God, he'd been there, right there where this kid was, pissed at the world, with parents who could give a shit, feeling about alone as one could get.

Tag turned his back on the both of them and stared out the ceiling-to-floor windows to the front parking lot, his fingers resting on the glass, his breath leaving a foggy circle, his shoulders sagged.

"I'm sorry I wasn't there when you landed," Sam told

him, at a loss in a way Wade had never seen from her before.

"My dad told you I was coming."

Sam closed her eyes, then opened them, looking at Wade with a slow shake of her head, helpless.

She hadn't known. For whatever reason, she honestly hadn't known Tag was to be in her care, but she didn't try to defend herself.

"I wanna go home now," Tag said, then added a quiet, "please" as an afterthought, as though he knew it was expected of him.

A polite delinquent.

"I'm sorry, Tag," Sam said. "I know this isn't what you want. But until I figure out exactly why you're here, and for how long . . ."

Tag set his head on the glass, the picture of dejected resolve.

Sam rubbed her forehead, appearing uncharacteristically stymied, and Wade could tell she needed a minute. "Wanna see the equipment room?" he asked Tag. "I bet we could find you some gear in there."

Tag lifted his head. "The Bucks' gear?"

Wade arched a brow. "The Heat's."

"Tag," Sam said. "This man is Wade O'Riley, our catcher."

Tag met Wade's gaze, not seeming all that impressed.

"Even though we're not the Bucks," Wade told him. "Maybe you'll find something you like."

Tag didn't answer, but his expression said he sincerely doubted that.

"I need to call my father." Sam smoothed down her skirt, which was longer today, meaning Wade could only see a mile of gorgeous leg instead of five miles. *A damn shame.* "It should only take a minute."

"To the goodie room then," Wade said to Tag, and put his hand on Tag's neck to steer him in the right direction.

Tag stiffened.

"I don't bite," Wade promised mildly, but removed his hand.

Tag relaxed, made a little sound, a kid sound, one that managed to convey both utter disdain and buckets of false bravado all in one, and right then and there, Wade lost a piece of his heart to him.

Sam watched Wade lead the reluctant but silent Tag away as she waited for her father to answer his phone. As unbelievable as it seemed, apparently Tag had been the "something" Jeremy had needed Sam to take care of for him, and at the thought, a cold fury twisted in her heart. She could have strangled her brother. A child. *His* child. And he'd treated Tag like little more than a piece of luggage.

"McNead here," boomed her father's voice in her ear.

Sam gripped her cell phone tight. "I have Tag? Dad, why do I have Tag?"

"Because Jeremy can't bring a ten-year-old to rehab, Samantha."

"I meant why am I in charge of him? Why not Brett or Michael?" she asked tightly, naming her two older brothers. "And where's Lynn?" Tag's mother had certainly not been any of the McNead's favorites, as she'd dumped Jeremy shortly after Tag's birth, taking half of everything Jeremy owned, but still. She was the mother!

"Lynn's been in Europe for several months modeling and there's no sign of her returning anytime soon. Plus she's not exactly up to the job."

"What does that mean?"

"She's not good with kids. That leaves us McNeads."

"Okay, but poor Tag barely knows me. He's not happy, and I don't blame him."

"You're the logical choice, Sam."

"Why, because I have the vagina?"

Her father sounded annoyed. "I'm busy right now. It's a bad time."

Yes. Yes, she knew exactly how busy he was. He'd been busy all her life, far too busy for her unless it was work-related. And suddenly—or maybe not so suddenly at all—starting up her own PR firm, away from all this McNead drama, was starting to look better and better. "It's just odd that Jeremy would ask this of me after his attempt to destroy my life and career."

"Jesus, Samantha. He fucked up, and he's paying the price. It's time to get over your grudge."

"Get over it?" she asked incredulously. "He sneaked into my locked work files to use my knowledge and privileged information on the Heat against us. He sold information, *privileged* information, to the press. He set it up to look like I was sabotaging my own team. I think I'm entitled to a little grudge."

"Fine. Just hold it on your own time."

"But—" But nothing, her father was gone. Sam pinched the bridge of her nose and tried deep breathing. It didn't work. Jeremy and Lynn had been together for about fifteen minutes, and when Lynn left, Jeremy and Tag had stayed in South Carolina. It was where Jeremy now worked—as Sam's equivalent—at the Buck's home facilities. Sam hadn't even met Tag until he'd turned four, and that was only because Jeremy had flown him to California for Christmas one year.

She had seen him at a few family gatherings since, for a grand total of three times.

Three.

Which would mean *nothing* to a frightened, lonely boy. *God.* This wasn't her fault but guilt swamped her all the same. There'd been plenty of family events she could have attended: birthdays, weddings . . . But she'd skipped them. She'd skipped them because she'd always been working.

Which meant she was just as bad as the rest of the McNeads. Discovering she was more like her father than she could possibly have imagined was a bitter pill. Yes, she'd been distant because they weren't a close family. After all, her brothers and father had their own lives and she had hers. But surely if she'd had a kid, her own kid, she wouldn't have worked as much as she had over the years.

She'd have . . .

What?

Would she have given up the job, the career she loved with all her heart?

Dammit.

Not happy with herself, she headed down the hall after Wade and Tag, wondering how she'd survive the next ninety days. She knew as much about little boys as she knew about . . .

Big boys.

Which wasn't all that much, as evidenced by the complete lack of boys in her life. Well, with the exception of one, big, bad, sexy-as-hell boy who wasn't a boy at all, but a man. Though honestly, she considered Wade more of a problem than a man. Which meant that she had her biggest problem leading her next biggest problem by the proverbial hand, and she could do little else but follow.

Chapter 14

It ain't nothin' till I call it.

—Bill Klem, umpire

Sam entered the vast equipment storage room. It was lined with rows of metal shelving units holding the stuff of any sports lover's fantasy: bats, gloves, mitts, uniforms, athletic shoes, sweats, medical equipment, even bottled water with the Heat label.

Sam had taken grown men through here and seen them actually well up at the sheer joy and awe. She didn't feel the pull of the room as someone with a penis might, but could understand it. After all, she loved the game, loved almost everything about it: the way it felt to sit in the stands on a steamy, hot summer night with a hot dog in one hand and a soda in the other, the scent of freshly cut grass on the air as the sun sank, the sound of the bat hitting the ball just right.

Walking down the main aisle, different scents assaulted her. Clean, untried leather. Ace bandages. Fresh wood bats. She inhaled and found herself relaxing as if she'd been at home.

Until she heard the soft, male voices, one higher in tenor—Tag. The sound of him made her stomach hurt.

The other voice was low and calm and just a little bit raspy—Wade.

The sound of him made her nipples go hard.

She took a deep, fortifying breath, assured herself she could handle this—hell, she could handle anything—and moved forward.

Wade led Tag down the aisles of the equipment room. Tag was trying to play it cool but the inherent boy in him couldn't seem to resist the goods all around them. He'd widened his eyes at first but then checked himself, reaching out to touch a jersey, then pulling back his hand like he was too cool to be excited.

"You've seen a room like this before, right?" Wade asked. "You've been to the Bucks's facility?"

"Yeah, but you have way more stuff." Tag stuffed his hand into his pocket, which suddenly bulged suspiciously.

"What's that?" Wade asked.

"Nothing."

Nothing his ass. "Let me see."

With a soft exhale of sheer bravado, Tag shoved his hand into his pocket, then opened his fingers, revealing a deck of trading cards.

Unopened.

"You have sticky fingers."

Tag studied the tops of his shoes.

"Thought you didn't like the Heat."

More studying of the shoes.

Wade sighed, handing the cards back to him.

Tag lifted his head and stared at him like, *What's the catch?*

"If you don't attempt another five-fingered discount, you can keep them," Wade said. "And next time, just ask."

"I was gonna." Tag shoved the cards back in his pocket.

"Uh-huh. What else did you snag?"

"Nothing."

From Tag's his other pocket came a pack of Sugarlicious bubblegum, half eaten. "See?" He popped a huge piece of gum in his mouth, started chewing, drooled a little bit, and swiped his mouth with his sleeve. When he saw Wade watching him, he paused. "Want a piece?"

"Sure." Wade popped a piece in his mouth and strawberry flavor burst over his tongue. "How long are you staying?"

"Dunno. My mom's in Europe. She doesn't make it home very often."

Wade remembered that feeling all too vividly. "That sucks."

Tag slid him a surprised look. Most likely people had been glossing over it all his short life. Wade didn't believe in glossing.

"My dad's going to be gone for three months." Tag said this nonchalantly, but the undercurrent of grief was apparent. "I guess rehab takes a while."

"Do you understand what rehab is?"

Tag didn't look up. "Not really."

Anger welled within Wade for the kid, who should have been told so much more than he had been. "It's a place to go when you need help to try to get better." *Try* being the operative word here. Wade hoped like hell it worked better for Jeremy than it'd ever worked for Wade's dad. "In the meantime, you have your Aunt Sam looking out for you." She was already on the job, he could hear her heels clicking along with efficient authority. "She's pretty great."

Tag looked at Wade, eyes suddenly sharp. "You like her or something?"

"We're . . . friends."

"You *like* her."

Wade studied Tag. "How are you at keeping secrets?"

"Real good."

Wade didn't believe that for a minute but he answered anyway. "You're right. I like her."

Tag studied Wade with all the scrutiny a frustrated, angry ten-year-old could muster. "When my dad likes a girl, they sleep over and I have to stay upstairs."

While Wade wrestled with his sudden urge to hurt Jeremy, Tag turned his attention to the jerseys hanging over his head. Wade pulled one down. "This is Pace Martin's."

"Your pitcher."

"Yes."

Tag was quiet a moment, but Wade could see that he wanted something. "You can say anything to me. We're in the cone of silence here."

Tag worried his lower lip between his teeth a moment. He looked at his shoes, clearly his favorite delay tactic. "Can I have your jersey instead?"

Wade turned to exchange the jersey just as Sam came around the last corner, heading toward them. She'd gotten herself together. The panic was gone, as was the fear. Wade had no doubt she was still wrestling with both, but she'd successfully hidden them.

She was nothing if not a master multitasker.

At the sight of them, her lips curved slightly in relief, making Wade wonder what the hell she'd expected to find. The two of them sharing a beer? She put her hand on Tag's arm. "You ready to go?"

Tag clutched Wade's jersey in a tight fist and gave her the silent treatment.

A McNead specialty.

Sam took in the jersey, caught Wade's number, and shot Wade a look he couldn't interpret. If he had to guess, he'd go with gratitude that he'd been able to break through to Tag, along with the envy. He'd broken through when she hadn't a clue how to do so.

Wade made a barely there gesture with his chin toward the shelves, signaling that she should try his tactic. Taking the hint, she grabbed a baseball cap. "How about this to go with the jersey?" she asked Tag.

He shrugged casually, even indifferently, but couldn't hide the excitement in his eyes. "'Kay."

Wade dropped the jersey over Tag's head, then put the baseball cap in place, gently taping the bill. "All set then."

Tag looked up at him. "Can I stay here instead?"

A direct hit, given the flash of emotion in Sam's eyes. Feeling like the biggest of all the shitheads and not even sure why, Wade reluctantly shook his head. "I'd love to have you, but that's not the plan right now."

"Plans change," Tag told him. "My dad says that all the time."

Above him, Sam was clearly grappling with the unaccustomed vulnerability, and killing Wade while she was at it. "It's the way things are," he said softly. "But you should know, I think you're lucky."

"Lucky?"

"Uh-huh." He slid a look at Sam. "I'd give just about anything to get to stay at your Aunt Sam's."

"Aunt Sam" narrowed her eyes at him.

"I'd rather sleep here," Tag insisted.

"They don't let people sleep here," Sam said.

Which, technically, wasn't quite true. The guys occasionally crashed out in the clubhouse when they'd had a late-night game and were too exhausted to get up and go home, or maybe if their wife or girlfriend had given them explicit instructions *not* to come home.

Wade had slept here a few times himself, but he didn't say so. This was Sam's gig. He expected her to give the kid an ultimatum; a fair one, but an ultimatum nevertheless.

She surprised him.

"I have ice cream," she said.

Tag lifted his head and looked at her, his eyes wary.

"Double fudge chocolate. And I have chocolate syrup to pour all over the top of it. And marshmallows. Not the little ones either."

Wade let out a low whistle. "You had me at ice cream." Hell, she'd had him at the fuck-you look the minute those Atlanta elevator doors had closed on them, but best not to go there.

Tag nodded, looking a little defeated, as if he knew a bribe when he saw one, and Wade felt another hard tug of empathy. "Do you have a cell phone?"

When Tag handed it over, Wade programmed himself into it. "There. Now you can call me anytime, day or night. 'Kay?"

"'Kay." Tag stuffed his hands back in his pocket, which now bulged even farther out, and Wade narrowed his eyes.

Tag pretended not to see, and Wade leaned close and spoke in his ear. "Do you remember what I said before?"

"That you *like* Aunt Sam?"

Sam's brow arched so far it vanished into her long side-swept bangs.

"After that," Wade said dryly, with a heavy dose of "thanks a lot, buddy" mixed in. "About taking whatever you want without asking."

Tag's cheeks pinkened, but he played mute, keeping his gaze down yet again.

Wade waited until Tag couldn't stand it and caved, meeting his eyes. Wade held out his hand, palm up.

Tag sighed and pulled out a can of tobacco.

Sam sucked in a breath. "What do you need with that?"

"My dad lets me chew sometimes."

"He does not," she said certainly.

"I can call him. Can I?"

Sam removed the tobacco from Tag's hands and set it back on the shelf. "I'm sorry, but I don't think he can talk right now."

Trying to be tough but failing, Tag nodded.

Wade bent and looked into his eyes. "Don't forget. Call me anytime." He straightened and exchanged a look with Sam, whose eyes softened, surprising him. Warming him.

"Tag," she said quietly. "We'll figure it all out, I promise. Say good-bye to your partner-in-crime here."

"Bye," Tag said to Wade. "I hope you get traded to the Bucks."

Wade raised an amused brow as Sam started to lead Tag away. He caught Sam and reeled her in, putting his mouth to her ear. "That goes for you, too, Princess. Call me anytime, day or night."

She started to roll her eyes, then went stock-still when, with his back blocking her from view, he very lightly scraped his teeth over her earlobe. He wasn't sure why except he couldn't help himself. Her breath hitched, a very satisfying response, and he then kissed the spot before letting go of her. He watched her hurry to catch up with Tag, picturing the next few hours in her world, wondering as he did who he felt the most sorry for: her, or the kid . . .

Chapter 15

It ain't over till it's over.

—Yogi Berra

Sam glanced over at Tag as they hit Highway 1. He was eyeing the interior of her car with surprise.

She drove a standard Honda Accord, which she liked for its value and gas mileage, plus the sunroof always made her feel like she was doing more to enjoy herself than she really was. "What?" she asked him.

"Is your real car in the shop or something?"

"No, why?"

"I thought when you were in the big show, you got whatever you want."

"I'm not in the big show. I just work for the big show."

"Grandpa and dad have Beemers."

Sam slid him a look. "I like this car."

"It's just like Grandma's."

"Your mom's mom? You see her a lot?"

"Just at Christmas. She makes me kiss her." He shuddered.

"This can't be an old lady's car, if that's what you're inferring. I'm only twenty-nine." *Thirty in three weeks, but who was counting?*

His mouth hung open. "Does dad know how old you are?"

"Hey, he's only one year younger than me."

"His girlfriend is twenty-two. He says twenty-two is perfect."

She sighed, and Tag fell back into silence. She glanced at him. "You still want ice cream?"

He lifted a shoulder indifferently. "If you do."

"What do *you* want?"

"To go home."

A one-two kidney shot. Sam exited the highway and drove through downtown. It was evening now, which meant that the streets were loaded with UCSB students looking for fun, tourists looking for bars, and the occasional poor schmuck like her just trying to get home from a long day at the office.

They passed outdoor paseos, beautifully landscaped plazas, brick-lined sidewalks in front of local specialty shops, and world-class shopping. She turned off the main drag and down one of the myriad multi-use avenues. Here there were sidewalk cafes mixed with little boutiques, bookstores, and unique specialty shops. She lived in one of four refurbished condos over an art gallery. Parking was always a bitch but today, since karma had already laughed at her, she was rewarded with a spot only one block down. "Okay," she said to Tag, turning off the engine, reaching for his bag. "We're here."

He took his bag from her, either to be a little gentleman, or because he didn't want her to touch his stuff any more than he seemed to want her to touch him. He eyed the little Italian restaurant on the corner. The chef was in the window tossing a large round of dough in the air. "You live at a pizza joint?"

"Nope."

"Oh," he said with disappointment.

Because she figured he was hungry, she led him inside to put in an order.

The place was filled to overflowing with a crowd ranging from starving college students all sharing one pie and one check to the upscale, ritzy shoppers with their fancy shopping bags at their feet.

Ernie was behind the counter. Rumor had it he was good in both the kitchen and the bedroom, but Sam could only attest to the kitchen part. He made the best Italian food anywhere, he and his dark hair and matching dark, dreamy eyes, with the smile that could melt bones at a hundred feet. He was her age, a few inches taller than her five foot six, and built like a boxer. They spent several evenings together a month, but unfortunately he wasn't her type.

Actually, more accurately, she wasn't his type, in that she didn't have a penis.

"Hey, gorgeous," he said, smiling at her. "What'll it be tonight?"

Sam turned to Tag. "What'll it be?"

Tag looked startled to be asked, and he played with the baseball cap on his head uneasily. "What do *you* want?" he asked Sam.

Did no one ever ask his opinion? "I'd love to have your favorite tonight, whatever that is."

He gave that some very serious thought, his brow furrowed like an old man. "Pepperoni, extra cheese."

"Nice choice," Ernie said.

Sam thought about the calories and mentally groaned

but smiled at Tag, who was still looking like he was thinking too hard. "Is your bag heavy? Let me—"

"Girls aren't supposed to carry stuff for boys."

So Jeremy had taught his son how to treat a woman, but not how to be a kid. Sam looked into Tag's far too solemn eyes and damn if she didn't see past the delinquent-in-the-making and completely melt. She arranged for delivery, then led Tag out of the place. On the crowded sidewalk, a group of college students passed by them. Five females, all dressed like it was Halloween at Victoria's Secret.

Tag's neck nearly snapped as he tried to keep them in his sight. "Holy cow," he whispered. "Do they walk around like that all the time?"

"It's a college town," she said, barely suppressing the urge to cover his eyes. She led him across the street to the art gallery. By sheer bad timing, the window display had changed from the gorgeous oils of the different seasons of Yosemite to a series of nude sculptures.

"You live *here*?" he asked in awe.

"On the second floor."

Tag blinked at the nudes but didn't voice his thoughts, which Sam figured was just as well. They climbed the open stairs to the second floor and walked along a balcony to the third door. She fished through her purse for her keys while Tag leaned on the railing, watching the goings-on below, running his fingers over Wade's number on his chest.

She opened her door and let him in. He paused before stepping inside, all ten-year-old bravado combined with a heartbreaking smile and assessing eyes that reminded her of someone that she couldn't quite put her finger on. "Make yourself at home."

Tag carefully set his bag on the floor and stood in the foyer, not moving.

Sam loved her condo. It was surprisingly big and airy,

with high ceilings and big picture windows. But she hadn't done much with the place. The walls were the same cream they'd been when she'd moved in three years ago, and mostly bare, but she'd decided she liked the clean, efficient look. Her furniture came in earth tones and was sparse but soothing.

It definitely wasn't set up for kids.

Hell, it was barely set up for her, given how much she traveled with the Heat seven months out of the year. "Are you thirsty?"

"No, thank you."

They looked at each other in awkward silence. "Is there anything you'd like to ask me, Tag?"

"When am I going home?"

Her heart tightened. "Not for a while."

She watched the hope die in his eyes and she wished she had a road map on how to handle this. "How about a tour?" She pointed to the other end of the living room, which spilled into the kitchen and a dining area. "Food's in there. I'm probably not stocked for your palate but we can fix that." In the kitchen, she opened the refrigerator. "You can help yourself . . ."

Tag stared into the fridge with absolutely no expression. Sam looked from his face into the refrigerator as well. Water. Apples. Coffee beans.

No kid food.

Feeling like she was failing, she sighed. "Okay, so during the season I eat out a lot. We'll get you stuff tomorrow, okay? What constitutes kid food these days?"

He lifted a shoulder.

"Come on. Give me a hint."

Nothing.

"Spinach?" she teased gently. "Liver and onions?"

His eyes cut to hers, caught her smile, and then it

happened. His lips twitched. He caught himself before he allowed a full-blown smile though, so it wasn't complete success, but she was going to win him over. Any minute now.

"Maybe quesadillas," he finally said.

"Great." Tortillas and cheese, easy enough. "What else?"

"Mac and cheese."

"Okay."

"And pizza."

She smiled. "So anything with cheese."

He did the almost smile thing again.

"I have a secret Cheez Doodle stash," she admitted, and opened the shelf above the refrigerator.

Tag eyed the bag. "My dad never lets me have Cheez Doodles. I leave orange handprints everywhere."

"Then you're not eating them right. The trick is to lick your fingers clean."

Again with the almost smile. She showed him her spare bedroom, which had a bed and an exercise bike that she'd used exactly twice. The spread on the bed was a pale yellow down comforter, with a pile of pillows. Probably a little girly. "This can be your room," she said. "We can get you different bedding. Maybe send for some more of your things."

Tag was quiet a moment. "Am I going to be here that long then?"

Her heart squeezed, but he'd asked several times now and she knew she had to be as honest as she could. "Maybe three months."

He let out a barely heard sigh.

She wanted to promise him Cheez Doodles for the rest of his life if he'd stop looking like she'd just handed him a death sentence. "What are we going to do about school?" she asked.

"I'm homeschooled. Or I was. But last week my teacher chucked the coffeepot at dad's head and didn't come back."

"Let me guess. The twenty-two-year-old?"

"Yeah."

Sam opened her mouth, then closed it. Seemed she'd be hiring a tutor. They watched TV while sharing the pizza, and she offered him the remote, interested in what he'd pick.

A *SpongeBob SquarePants* repeat.

He ate three pieces of pizza when it came, and shocked her by taking her plate away and cleaning up afterwards without being asked.

She was beginning to realize that in his household, he'd been the grown-up.

"Maybe we should go to bed," she said. "It's already nine-thirty. What's your bedtime?"

"I don't have a bedtime."

"You do now. Come on. Shower first." She brought him to the bathroom and pulled out fresh towels for him.

When he emerged a few minutes later, his hair was standing straight up and he still had a smudge of something near his ear. "Did you use soap?" she asked.

"No."

"Why not?"

"You didn't say I had to use soap."

She stared at him. "For the record, from now on when you take a shower, I'll want you to use soap. And shampoo. You know, actually clean yourself."

"'Kay."

"How about toothpaste?"

He tossed up his arms like *who knew?* and disappeared back into the bathroom.

When he came back out, she decided not to mention

that he'd also need to use a comb regularly. One battle at a time. "Ready for bed?"

"I'm not tired."

His eyes were drooping and he was yawning even as he said this. "Humor me," she said.

"Can I make a call first?"

She'd like to save him the disappointment of calling his dad and not having him answer but she didn't want to say no to such a simple request. "Sure."

He pulled out his cell. "Hey," he said. "You said I could call any time, day or night. Can I come over?" Tag's gaze slid to Sam. "Yeah, she's here. Hang on." He handed the phone out to Sam.

"Having trouble, Princess?" came Wade's low, husky voice.

"No." At least nothing she wanted to admit to. Sam looked at Tag. "No trouble at all."

Wade let out a soft laugh that scraped at her belly. "You're as talkative as he is. And you sound like you're a woman on the edge."

"No. There's no edge." Only a huge gaping black hole swirling, waiting to gobble her up.

"Want me to come save you and take him for the night?"

Yes to the coming over. But that was certain parts of her body talking, and they didn't get a vote. "No."

"You sure? I have ways to tame kids."

And women . . . "We're fine." She shut the phone and tossed it back to Tag. "Sorry, but it's you and me, Tag. We can do this."

Tag sighed and nodded.

Not exactly a vote of confidence.

Chapter 16

The great thing about baseball is that there's a crisis every day.

—Gabe Paul

The blogs and newspapers continued to buzz with the fact that a woman had tamed Wade, and the Heat's likeability improved daily. The sponsors were happy. Gage was happy.

Then the Heat took the Padres at home on game two and the fans were happy, too.

Sam wasn't sure what she was, but it didn't matter. She was too busy to think about it. She had pre-game interviews, post-game interviews, and everything promotion-related in between, which included lots of standing next to Wade and smiling for a camera.

He seemed to get a kick out of it, making sure to touch her as often as possible. Before the third Padres game, the reporter asked Wade to kiss her, and with a grin, he bent her over his arm and did.

He kissed her long and wet and deep.

Sam made sure to pretend to like it.

Except there wasn't much pretending involved.

Tag joined Sam and Holly in the stands, happy to dig into their standard tray of delicious junk food, but when she and Holly leapt to their feet to cheer Pace on during a tense third inning, he remained seated.

Until the fifth inning, when it was Wade they were cheering for. Tag got up for Wade when he hit a triple. Sam stared at him, grinning broadly.

"What?" he asked.

"You cheered."

"It was a good hit." And he calmly sat back down and grabbed another hot dog, as he was apparently a bottomless pit masquerading as a kid. Or maybe he had a tapeworm. She knew he was still dealing with missing home, missing Jeremy, the only real family he'd ever had in his life, and she worried every minute of every day that he was leaving his childhood behind too soon, that he'd suffer long-term from abandonment issues.

Especially since Jeremy didn't call—either because he couldn't, or because it didn't occur to him. Either way, Samantha hated him for it. Tag deserved better. Hell, a dog deserved better. She'd managed to hire a tutor/nanny to travel with them—a guy, which seemed to please Tag. As did Wade, who took Tag with him to practices when he could, and also out to eat. He'd made Sam come, too, and she'd gone back to her office afterwards with her cheeks aching from laughing.

After the Padres series, they flew to San Francisco to play the Giants. Before the first game, Sam was working the clubhouse as she always did. She'd been worried about Tag being bored, but it turned out he wasn't any harder to take care of than any of the other men around her. At the moment, he was in the guest clubhouse on a couch with a control box in his lap, playing a video game. His head was tilted back, his eyes glazed and locked on the TV, his mouth open as he worked the controls. He was decked out in Wade's jersey, with someone's far too large Adidas on his feet. He had a huge wad of bubblegum in his mouth, which was probably why it hung open.

And just looking at him squeezed her heart. How one little kid could worm his way into her life so damn fast, she had no idea. She brought him an apple juice and ruffled his hair, barely managing to resist hugging him because she knew he'd just squirm free. "Want a sandwich?"

He didn't respond.

"Tag?"

He grunted, then shook his head.

Good Lord. He was already a guy through and through. Shaking her head, she moved past him. As always, the players arrived at least five hours early for the game, and even though they had a clubbie—a guy paid to make sure they had everything they needed—she always walked through to check on them as well. She'd been doing so since the beginning of time, so she no longer even noticed the half-naked men wandering back and forth from showers to lockers, or the behavior such testosterone brought out. In one corner Mason and Kyle were sparring with their gloves on for no discernable reason. She'd discovered guys didn't need a reason for aggression, so she'd long ago ceased looking for one.

"Cool it," Gage told them.

Joe walked out of the shower completely butt-ass naked. Mike snapped his ass with a towel and in return, Joe shoved him into a wall and kept walking, a big welt now blooming on one butt cheek.

Sam registered it all and saw none of it.

She turned to get herself a bottle of water just as one more player walked out of the shower room.

Wade.

He wore a towel and nothing else except drops of water and those lean, hard muscles. And unlike with the other guys, her mind went there, to him in the shower, all naked and soapy, and she felt heat slash through her belly. She opened her bottle of water and took a sip for her suddenly parched throat.

Wade was in his zone, his game face on, heading for his locker. When their eyes connected, some of the intensity left his face, softening his eyes and softening her insides, and for a moment, she wished that he wanted more, more of her and from her.

He was still looking at her, too gorgeous for words, and without her permission, a ridiculously helpless smile curved her lips.

In return, he let loose a smile, too, the warm, intimate one that he always gave her after kissing her stupid. They were staring at each other like idiots, surrounded by people. Uncharacteristically flustered, she turned away first, and plowed directly into Gage with her opened water bottle.

He was tall and built like the players. Solid muscle. Bumping into him was like bumping into a brick wall, but he absorbed the impact and caught her, holding her up as water splashed down the front of him. "I'm sorry," she gasped.

He pulled his shirt away from his skin, his dark features twisting into a grimace. "Me, too. Where's the fire?" He looked behind her to see what she'd been running from.

Wade was in front of his locker. He'd pulled on his compression shorts and was reaching for his jersey.

She winced as Gage's eyes cut to hers again.

"I haven't asked you," he said evenly, with only a teeny tiny hint of irony, "how this whole pretend relationship thing is going."

Oh boy. "Fine."

"Is it going to stay that way for the rest of the month, no trouble?"

God, she hoped so. "Hey, no trouble is my middle name."

Gage nodded, but his eyes reflected his concern that maybe she was lying through her teeth. She couldn't reassure him because she had no reassurances. None.

Because just behind her façade was a bone deep certainty that she wasn't fine. Not even close. She was falling for a man she had no business falling for, and for a kid that wasn't hers.

Fine didn't begin to cover it.

"Do I need to step in?" Gage asked, holding eye contact, raising a brow. "Kick his ass?"

She laughed, as he'd intended, even knowing that beneath the levity, he'd absolutely do it if she wanted. "No."

He watched her for a long moment. Part of Gage's brilliance was being able to see what people didn't want him to. She had no doubt he knew exactly what was wrong. Just as he knew how important it was to her to handle her problems on her own. Finally he nodded, gave her a surprisingly gentle hug, then moved away.

Sam turned to talk to some of the reporters, moving through, making the rounds, and suddenly Wade was in front of her. He took her hand and pulled her around a corner until it was just them, sandwiched in a hallway between two rolling hampers of towels.

He'd put on the rest of his uniform, thank God. His hair was still wet from his shower, falling silkily over his forehead. His eyes were smiling, though his mouth wasn't. "One week down," he murmured, gently pressing her back to the wall.

"And we haven't killed each other." *Or lost our clothes again.* Good signs, both of them.

Moving slowly but extremely surely, he linked their
fingers at her sides, then slid their joined hands up the wall,
until they were above her head. Then he leaned in so close
there wasn't enough space between them for so much as a
sheet of paper.

"What are you doing?"

His mouth curved. "You were undressing me with your
eyes."

"Was not—"

He kissed her. Well, first he outlined her lower lip with
his tongue, then he covered her mouth with his, and at the
first taste of him, she was gone.

Gone.

She rocked against him and he let go of her hands,
sliding his down her arms to cover her breasts, his thumbs
brushing over her already pebbled nipples. A rough groan
escaped him and he lifted his head. They were nose to
nose, their breath coming as one, gazes locked.

She couldn't tear her eyes off him. His hair was looking a little tousled, his uniform shirt wrinkled now from
her fingers, his eyes flashing heat and good humor as she
tried to smooth it out, pressing it over his broad chest and
shoulders. "Sorry," she murmured.

"For the wrinkles, or that kiss?"

"You kissed me." She sighed. "But if you hadn't, I'd
probably have initiated it."

He smiled against her throat, she could feel it, and heard
it in his voice. "Good to know." He glided his thumb over
her nipple again.

She trembled, which was annoying. She was working!
But when he let his mouth settle against the spot just beneath her ear, she actually tilted her head to the side to
give him better access, which he fully utilized, brushing

his lips against her sensitized flesh once, then again. "You still want me. And God knows I want you.

She slid out from between him and the wall and attempted to recover some dignity. "Have a good game, Wade."

"Nothing to say on the wanting me thing?"

"I'll tell you the same thing I'm going to tell the reporters who ask about us. *No comment*." And with not nearly the dignity she'd hoped for since her nipples were hard and her panties wet, she walked away in tune to his soft, knowing laugh.

At the end of the San Francisco series, the Heat got on their usual chartered jet, and then got delayed on the tarmac for two long hours. It was late, past midnight, and everyone was exhausted, Wade included. Exhausted and restless. And in his case, also oddly . . .

Lonely.

It was a new feeling for him, an unwelcome one, and unable to sit in his seat, he walked the narrow aisle of the plane. His teammates were all in various positions, asleep, reading, or on their PDAs.

Near the back, Tag was sprawled out on two adjacent seats, one leg up, one leg hanging to the floor, his arms flung wide, mouth open, sleeping with the utter abandonment only a kid could pull off. Sam was across from him, and as Wade looked at her, he realized that this was where he'd meant to end up, near her.

As if she felt the same, Sam moved over to make room for him. She didn't speak, and Wade couldn't express his appreciation enough for that. He just wanted to sit, maybe sleep, and he'd wanted to do both those things with her.

His pretend girlfriend.

It didn't escape his notice that he was closer to her, in their pretend relationship, then he'd been to any other woman in a long time.

Or that he'd been having an internal debate with himself about whether they could have something for real.

Half the time he believed it.

The other half, he wasn't so sure. It'd never worked for him before, and if he fucked it up and they ended up in a bad place, then he wouldn't have her in his life at all.

So he didn't go there. Instead, in the dark, surrounded by the low hum of the plane's engine, he just absorbed being close to her in the only way he knew how. After a few minutes, Sam stretched and yawned, shifting, trying to get comfortable. "Here," he murmured, and slid an arm around her shoulders, urging her against him. She looked up at him, and then, as if it were the most natural thing in the world, set her head on his chest.

The simple, easy trust had something catching deep within him. Nothing he wanted to define given that he was fairly certain it would be something he didn't know how to face, so he merely stared down at her, struck by the warmth spreading through his belly as she slowly drifted off, using him as her pillow.

Christ, she was sweet.

"Wade?" she murmured in a low sleepy voice that made him hard.

"Yeah?"

"Cop a feel while I'm asleep and I'll toss you out the window at fifteen thousand feet."

He smiled. "Go to sleep, Sam."

And she did. The plane was comfortably dark and quiet, and it'd been one hell of a long week. Pulling her in a little closer to better support and hold her against him, Wade settled in. He could tell when she let go because she completely relaxed against him, but for him sleep was a long time coming.

Sam coaxed Tag out of bed the next morning with blueberry pancakes. He wasn't thrilled. "I know you're tired," she said when he yawned broadly. "And I know it's early, but I have to—"

"It's okay," he said, bleary-eyed, head dropping to the table next to his plate.

She stared down at him, concerned. Ten-year-olds were supposed to be rough and tumble. She'd looked it up. Ten-year-olds were supposed to be hard to handle and loud and noisy. She wanted him so badly not to be scarred by his parents, by circumstances. But every night she lay in bed and worried about all the ways she might be further screwing him up. "Do you ever complain? Whine? Act like a brat?"

He cracked open an eye. "You want me to act like a brat?"

She smiled and lifted a shoulder. "Maybe once in a while, yeah."

"Okay." He straightened. "I wanna play Xbox in the clubhouse. It really sucks that you don't have one here. I mean who doesn't? You don't even have a GameCube. You've got nothing."

"Sorry, there's no baseball game today. We're not going to the clubhouse. And I don't have kids, so I don't play Xcube or Gamebox."

He snorted.

"Or whatever," she said with a roll of her eyes.

"What if I threw myself down on the floor and yelled?"

"Would you really do that?"

He looked at the floor, then at what he was wearing—Wade's jersey, what a surprise. "I might get the jersey dirty."

"Don't worry. You're going to like what we're doing instead."

Too late. He appeared to be enjoying his temper tantrum. "I don't wanna sit in your office and do schoolwork. Why do I have to do everything with you? At home, I got to stay alone." He paused, then almost as an afterthought, kicked the floor, then repeated his favorite mantra. "I want to go home."

"Okay," she said. "I know I started this, but—"

"I could go home if I really wanted to. I could call Uncle Brett. He'd come get me." He pulled out his cell phone and thumbed through his contacts.

She was no longer sure if they were playing at this temper tantrum or if he was testing her, so she decided to wait him out a minute.

He went still. "Aren't you going to stop me?"

"From calling a member of your family? Never."

Tag stared at her, not old enough to hide his dismay. "But I was going to tell him to come get me. And you don't want me to go. You like me."

"Actually, you silly, cheese-loving, grumpy old man hiding out in the body of a ten year old, I love you, with all my heart."

Tag blinked, and then in his ear Brett said, "Hello?"

Sam reached out and covered the mouthpiece of the phone. "You realize you don't have to talk me into letting you stay, right? That I truly *want* you to stay. If you want to."

"I want to," Tag whispered back, eyes bright. "I really want to stay with you."

"Music to my ears." She closed his phone on her brother, no qualms. Brett would forget they'd called within two minutes. "Now come here," she said softly, slinging an arm around Tag's narrow shoulders and pulling him in.

He was stiff, but didn't shrug her off. "You're not going to kiss me are you?"

She sighed and kept her lips to herself.

Shortly after, they cleaned up breakfast and Sam showered and dressed. She was going to be in professional capacity but a far more casual one than usual, so she went with a pantsuit today. And a Heat baseball cap with Wade's number on it.

It was for appearances, she told herself as she drove her and Tag to the park.

"What are we doing here?" Tag asked.

"It's a surprise.."

Both Pace's and Wade's cars were in the lot. The sight of Wade's gave her stomach a little quiver. Other body parts quivered as well.

On the field, Pace and Wade were coaching two teams of ragtag kids against each other in a game of baseball. Wade stood behind the catcher, his sunglasses catching the sun. He wore battered Levi's and a T-shirt that stretched across his biceps and chest and was loose over his washboard abs. He also wore a smile, the one that did things to her insides.

And her insides didn't need things done to them; they were already fluttering.

From across the field, he met her gaze. She looked right back at him and more fluttering occurred.

"Jeez," Tag said at her side. "Take a picture."

She'd wondered when he was going to act like a ten-year-old. Seemed the real Tag was starting to show himself.

And so were her feelings for Wade.

Wade watched Sam and Tag arrive. That she'd showed up today for the game didn't surprise him. She ran the 4

The Kids charity with the same easy efficiency she seemed to run her life, and though this wasn't one of her events, it was Pace's. Wade was only along because Pace had dragged him out of bed, saying he needed more help than just a check with this one. Sam was here because she'd insinuated herself into their program, for which they were both grateful.

What *did* surprise him was the ball cap on her head.

With his number on it.

It'd been only last night that he'd held her while she'd slept on the plane, and yet he couldn't take his eyes off her. There were no reporters here today, they didn't have to be "on," so probably some space was called for between them.

But he didn't want space.

Sam was running back and forth between her car and the snack bar, setting it up when he cornered her in the lot. "Nice," he said, flicking the cap up to see her eyes.

She lifted a shoulder, but couldn't quite hold back her smile. "It's a girlfriend thing."

"I like it."

"Sorry about drooling on you last night."

"Yeah? You snored, too."

When her horrified gaze flew to his, he laughed softly against her temple.

"I don't snore," she grumbled, smacking him lightly on the chest.

He pressed his face into her hair. "Only a little."

With an eyeroll, she turned away and hoisted a box of candy bars out of her trunk.

"Candy," he said. "The way to every little boy's heart."

"And the big boys?"

He took the box out of her hands and set it on the roof of her car. Then he backed her up against the door, slid a hand to the back of her neck and kissed her. She made a soft sound of acquiescence that sliced straight through him, and when her tongue tentatively touched his, he got hard so fast the blood drained from his brain, leaving him dizzy. "The big boys have a different way to their heart," he said against her lips.

"I can feel that."

"Smart-ass." He stroked a finger from her temple to her jaw. "We should go out for dinner after the game."

"For pretend?"

"For whatever comes to mind."

Her eyes darkened.

"Tell me," he demanded softly. "I want to know what you just thought about."

"Naked. Naked is what comes to mind. And," she said quickly as he skimmed a hand up her back, pressing her closer, "it's a bad idea."

His fingers slipped under the hem of her top to settle on bare skin. Bare, warm skin that he wanted to kiss, nibble, suck . . . "Because . . . ?"

"Because in a few weeks we go back to whatever we were before."

She had him there. Together they walked to the field where Tag was already with Pace and the others. Tag was by far the youngest boy out there, but no one had any problem including him. This would never have happened in an organized league, but these kids were different. At one time or another, they'd all been the misfit and because of it, they were far more accepting.

When the game started, Wade and Pace stood behind the plate coaching their respective teams, tossing out encouraging directions to the kids, most of whom couldn't have caught a ball before this season to save their lives.

By the end of the fourth inning, the game was tied zip

all. They agreed to one last inning, and Wade's team was up at bat. Tag headed out of the dugout, slowing as he got to the plate. He'd struck out twice already and looked a little bit like he was heading to the guillotine. Wade had tried to help him with advice but Tag hadn't wanted any, so Wade kept his mouth shut this time.

Tag let out a breath, bravely took his stance, and his helmet promptly slid over his eyes.

With a sigh, Wade pulled him back out of the batter's box and tightened the helmet. He kept his voice low and soft. "Keep your eyes on the ball—"

"I know," Tag said in a tone that sounded more like, *Well,* duh!

Wade lifted his hands and stepped back. His gaze went to Sam, standing in front of the snack bar watching like a nervous mother hen.

Tag's teammates yelled out some encouragement, and Tag swung at two far outside left balls. Finally, he stepped out of the box, looked at Wade, and sighed.

The only request for help he was going to get. "You're closing your eyes," Wade told him. "It's a family trait." He slid a look to Sam, who smiled. She closed her eyes when she batted, too.

Tag nodded and kept his eyes wide open as he swung on the next one and connected. "Holy crap!" he yelled in ten-year-old glee, tossing his bat, running as the ball sailed up past the pitcher.

Pace was calling out directions to the shortstop, telling him to keep his eyes on the ball, to back up a few feet . . .

The shortstop missed the catch, but scooped it up fairly quickly and probably could have thrown the ball all the way to first, but Tag was grinning and running and tugging up his falling-down jeans as he hauled ass toward the base.

And then something happened that Wade didn't expect. The shortstop held back, looking at the first baseman, who nodded. "Keep going," the kid said to Tag. "Go to second." Then the shortstop threw to second base and the second baseman missed.

Pace clapped his hands to his head in disbelief.

But Wade was grinning. Pace's team was letting Tag take a homer. "Go, Tag, go!"

The kid rounded third and slid into home like a pro. He stood up triumphantly, filthy from head to toe.

Sam was jumping up and down for him. Tag bumped fists with all the members of his team, but Sam was having none of that. She ran around the fence and wrapped her arms around the kid, squeezing and kissing him until he squirmed free.

"Jeez!"

"Sorry, I couldn't help myself," she said, and kissed him one more time.

Tag didn't look like he minded all that much.

Wade knew just how the kid felt. In fact, he snagged Sam by the back of her shirt and pulled her to him for a kiss of his own. "Sorry," he murmured, echoing her own words right back at her. "I couldn't help myself."

That afternoon Wade was working out in the Heat's facility before a mandatory team meeting, pushing himself hard at the bench press in tune to Jane's Addiction on his iPod when Pace sat on the bench next to him.

"Problem," Pace said.

Wade pulled out one of his earphones. "Holly left you for a real man, and she's waiting for me at my place?"

"Funny. No, tonight's fund-raiser."

Which was a full-out carnival to celebrate another year

of the 4 The Kids charity. Professional athletes from a variety of sports were paying out the wazoo for the opportunity to run a booth and be seen doing something charitable, which was a win-win situation for the charity's checkbook. Since Wade had put out a big chunk of money to help fund the carnival, he hadn't committed to running a booth.

"We're short a few athletes," Pace said. "Sam's working the phones right now, scrambling."

"She'll find someone."

"It's the dunking booth that's causing the big problem. She wants a high-profile athlete, but no one wants to do it."

Wade lifted a shoulder. "So get in the dunk booth, man."

"I'm already signed up for something else. And I'm also the MC for the event."

"You like to multitask. Just make sure you don't get dunked with the microphone in your hand. Electrocution isn't pretty."

"Okay, wise guy," Pace said. "Let me just spell it out for you. Sam and I just signed *you* up for the dunking booth." His supposed best friend grinned and clasped him on the shoulder. "Going to be good times."

Wade slid him a look. "If you dunk me, I'll personally put you in the booth for your turn."

Pace stood up and moved out of the reach of Wade's arm. "You'd have to catch me first. And I'm faster than you are."

"Why can't you get Henry to do it? Or Mike?"

"She wants you."

"Why?"

Pace shrugged. "Maybe you're not paying enough attention to her. Maybe you're being a bad boyfriend."

"*Hello*, it's pretend!"

Pace got on the treadmill and he began running steadily, swinging his arms naturally, his shoulder completely healed from the surgery he'd had months ago. "I see you've learned nothing."

"I've learned plenty," Wade told him. "I've learned she likes me best either far, far away, or with my tongue down her throat. We don't do so well with anything in between."

"You haven't *tried* anything in between. You've let the chemical attraction take over. Not that there's anything wrong with that."

"It's not chemical."

"You're right," Pace said, working the touchpad control of the treadmill. "It's not chemical. Given how thrown you are about this whole thing, it's probably love."

Wade nearly swallowed his tongue. He came off the bench, and with a laugh, Pace held up his hands in surrender. "Hey, don't kill the messenger."

"You're wrong."

"Okay, whatever you say, Wade."

"What does *that* mean?"

"I'm pretty sure it means you're an idiot. Look, you drove me crazy last year with all the 'Live your life' shit, and now look at you. You're not doing a fucking thing with yours."

"Not doing a fucking thing—" Wade choked and stared at Pace. "We just started a new season, you dumb ass. We're building a charity that gives street kids a fighting chance."

"Yeah, yeah. You're a great ball player and a great guy, too. You'll get no argument from me there," Pace said quietly, the joking gone. "Without you, I wouldn't be half the pitcher I am." He pointed when Wade opened his mouth. "Shut up. You give big bucks to the kids, more than any of the rest of us. You write checks for your father. You'd write a stranger a check. How many times do we have to talk about this, Wade? You can write all the checks you want, but—"

"Ah, Christ, the *but*. I hate the *but*."

"—*But* when it comes to the actual doing, you're still standing back. You're still keeping yourself distanced."

"That's the stupidest thing I've ever heard. I do stuff all the time. I don't keep myself distanced."

Pace wiped his face with a towel, tossed it aside, and kept running. "Right. You go out plenty—or at least you used to before you got a pretend girlfriend. But that shit doesn't count, that shit isn't even real. Getting your hands dirty is real. Coaching the street kids you're afraid to connect with because you'll see yourself in them is real. Getting behind your dad, supporting him through rehab instead of waiting for him to fail again, that's real. Being a *real* boyfriend to a woman you have feelings for, sticking around when it's not all fun and games, *that's* real."

Wade stared at him, then sank back onto the bench.

Pace watched him warily as he ran on the treadmill. "You going to say anything? Try to hit me? Anything?"

"My legs feel funny. Rubbery."

"Stop working out."

"I think it's what you said, not the weights."

"Which part?" Pace asked. "The love part?"

"No." *Yes*. Spots danced in Wade's vision and he had to put his head between his knees.

"*Love . . .*" Pace said again, a smile in his voice. *Asshole*. The spots danced faster, and now his ears were clanging.

"If I could feel my legs, I'd pound you into next week."

"Even if you could feel your legs, you still couldn't catch me."

Chapter 17

Don't bunt. Aim out of the ballpark.

—David Ogilvy

Sam was late for the team meeting. She was never late. But Tag had asked for a specific cereal for breakfast, and it was so rare for him to care that she'd run out to the store to get it and then she'd forgotten the milk and had to go back out to get it, and then Tag had spilled it down the front of him, and . . .

And she could feel her blood pressure hitting the edge of the healthy range, heading directly into heart failure territory as she ran into the team room, tugging Tag along with her.

She was the last to arrive. She slowed her pace as they entered, wanting to appear cool, calm, and collected. It was her MO, her modus operandi, always.

Never let them see you sweat.

See, she'd learned something from her father after all.

"I'm tired," Tag said.

"Shh." She pointed to a chair away from the large group

of men all now looking at her, a group of men that included an irritated Gage, the entire support team, and every single of one the Heat players along with the one she'd had erotic dreams about all damn night long. "I won't be long," she murmured to Tag, locking gazes with Wade. "Sit."

"Not a dog," Tag muttered, but he sat and pulled out the Game Boy she'd bought/bribed him with yesterday.

"You lose your watch?" Gage asked Sam.

She sighed as she took a seat. "No." Most of the players nodded or smiled at her. Pace's was just sympathetic enough that she shot a second involuntary look at Wade.

He wore workout sweats, and was slouched in his chair, long legs stretched out in front of him. A warm, intimate just-for-her smile crossed his face, completely disarming her.

"Sam, you want to open with a debriefing on tonight's event?" Gage asked.

"Yes." She opened her briefcase and pulled out . . . the box of Frosted Flakes she'd just purchased.

Gage raised a brow. "Hungry?"

Sam slid her gaze to Tag, who bit his lip. "Um," he said, hopping down off his chair and coming up to her. "Sorry, that's mine."

She was well aware of that. Not willing to get into it with him right now in front of the team, she silently handed him the box.

Tag took it and moved back to his chair.

There was about five beats of utter silence—well, as much silence as there could be with a ten-year-old rustling through a box of crunchy cereal—when Wade nodded toward it with his chin. "I'll take some."

Tag offered him the box. Wade patted the seat next to him, and Tag sat.

Gage gave a barely audible sigh. He didn't like delays

or deviations from his plans. And he sure as hell hated having his meetings interrupted.

Wade grinned at him and popped Frosted Flakes in his mouth with one hand, his other on Tag's shoulder, holding him in place. "Sorry, Skip. Carry on."

Gage gestured to Sam, who shot a quick glance at Tag, but the kid was actually sitting still now. Best to move quickly. She opened her file on the carnival. She told everyone their booths—ignoring the friendly jabbing at Wade when she listed the dunk booth—and laid out what she needed everyone to do. Halfway through her spiel, she watched Tag wriggle out of his chair and pull out a stack of baseball cards. Wade's and Tag's heads were bent together, smiling, murmuring in conspiracy. And in that moment, she finally realized who it was that Tag always reminded her of.

Wade.

That evening as the sun gave one last hurrah over the Santa Ynez peaks, glimmering brightly on the Pacific Ocean, Wade and Pace walked through the park-turned-carnival. The other athletes were there, too, each getting ready to work a booth on the grassy field.

The festive strings of lights twinkled in the growing dusk, bright and inviting. The Ferris wheel slowly turned in the salty air, music booming as the place became a hustle of activity.

At the front gates, a crowd lined up, anxious for the grand opening, only twenty minutes away now. Wade, wearing board shorts and a T-shirt in anticipation of the dunking booth, eyed the Ferris wheel with nostalgia. "That's where I'd have picked to work. Easy, fun, and it doesn't require getting wet."

Pace just grinned, and Wade narrowed his eyes at him. "Which booth did you say you were running?"

"I didn't."

"You're an asshole. You got the Ferris wheel?"

"Yep."

Wade shook his head. "You suck."

"Yes, I do. I suck up to our fearless publicist. A method you ought to try once in a while instead of this weird backing off thing you've got going. Since when do you back off on anything?"

Since he'd realized he was in over his head.

"If you wanted, you could be enjoying the last half of your fake relationship while you still have the excuse, and see where it takes you."

"Look," Wade said. "I know you think I'm not trying, but—"

"But you're not."

"Just because it came easy for you with Holly—"

Pace laughed good and hard over that. "Are you on crack? You were there. You saw how it was. We nearly killed each other. And the whole time you were in my ear, telling me to make it work, to give it a shot. Now I'm trying to tell you the same thing, only you're not listening."

When Wade thought about giving a real relationship with Sam a shot, he had two reactions. A surge of adrenaline comparable only to being in the lead in the bottom of the ninth in the playoffs.

And a gut-tightening fear.

He understood the adrenaline part, because when he and Sam were together, the sparks flew hard and fast. He'd been with more than his fair share of women, and he recognized that being with Sam was different.

And a million times better.

What he didn't understand was the fear. It made no

sense to him. He'd been through harrowing experiences, he'd known *real* fear. Sam shouldn't represent anything close to that, and yet every night when he got in his car to drive to her place, something stopped him.

Pace was still looking up at the Ferris wheel. "I used to ride one just like this at the county fair every summer. You?"

"Yeah." Wade looked at the growing crowd, waiting to get in. "You just know there's a whole bunch of teenage boys out there hoping to cop a feel on this thing tonight."

Pace laughed. "I caught my first feel on one just like it."

"When, last year?"

Pace gave him a good-natured shove. "I was fifteen and stupid. I had twenty bucks in my wallet from my father, and Stacy Adams holding my hand." He smiled. "God, she was sweet."

The memory was clearly a warm, happy one. Wade had no such happy memories. At fifteen, he'd been working at McDonald's after school for his runaway fund, and eating free fries after his shifts for his dinner.

It had been a bleak time. He'd not been warm or happy. And rarely safe. Just thinking about it now had him glancing over at the hot dog station. He could go for one or two.

Or five.

These days he had as much money as he could ever want, but back then, having a twenty in his pocket to spend however he'd wanted would have been an unimaginable freedom. It would have boggled his mind to be able to stand in line like he was here tonight and buy himself whatever he wanted, much less know that he could do it all over again the following night if he so chose.

Holly was working at the park's entrance, consulting a

clipboard. She wore jeans and one of Pace's Heat sweat-shirts, hair up, huge diamond glittering on her finger. Wade nodded in her direction. "Looks like you could probably get lucky again tonight if you wanted."

"Counting on it." Pace grinned, then headed toward her. When Holly saw him coming, she set aside her clipboard and walked right into his arms.

Pace pulled her up against him so that her feet were dangling, and her soft laugh echoed across the slightly damp ocean air.

Watching them, something deep within Wade tightened. All his life he'd had one goal—freedom. Freedom from poverty. Freedom to do what he wanted, when he wanted. Freedom to be who he was. Freedom to work hard and play even harder.

He'd gotten that for himself. Maybe at a price.

Okay, definitely at a price.

Because he was alone. And yet, he'd always wanted that, too. Wanted to be responsible only for himself, never anyone else. He'd held himself back. He'd done so with careful purpose, not ever wanting to be responsible for hurting anyone.

And yet . . . and yet, looking at Pace hold Holly in his arms, that look of bliss on his face, made Wade wonder at exactly what he was missing. Shaking his head at himself, he headed to the dunking booth. The tank was huge, and filled with what he suspected was freezing water.

"Maybe no one will dunk you."

He turned to face . . . "Tag."

Tag was staring at the dunking booth. "Can you swim?"

"Worried about me?" He grinned and ruffled the kid's hair. "I can swim just fine, but maybe you want to take my spot in there?"

Tag shook his head. "I just ate three hot dogs. You're not supposed to eat and swim."

"Maybe I should go eat then."

Tag studied the dunking booth seriously. "You could tell Aunt Sam your stomach hurts. She'd get you a 7Up and excuse you."

"That's a good one, but I promised I'd do it, and I couldn't back out on her."

"Yeah." Tag nodded. "She doesn't like when people back out on their word." That said, Tag glanced over his shoulder a little nervously and a lot guiltily.

"What's up?"

"Nothing."

Nothing his ass. "Where is she?"

"She's . . . really busy."

Wade had no doubt that was the truth. She was running this whole show. But if he knew Sam, and he was pretty sure he knew her better than just about anyone else, he'd eat his shorts if she didn't have everything perfectly in control. "There's no way she's letting you run wild out here."

"I'm not wild."

"You know what I mean. She wouldn't leave you alone. You're her top priority."

"No."

Wade turned to face him fully, hands on hips. "Okay, spill it."

"We were at the front gate, in the ticket booth. There's some problem with the food stuff and she told me to wait, that she'd be right back. Three minutes tops, she said."

"And?"

"And she didn't come back."

"Tell me you didn't just walk off."

"I was hungry."

Christ. She'd be frantic by now. Wade pulled out his cell phone. She answered on the third ring with a sharp, curt "I can't talk right now—"

"I have something of yours," he said, eyeing Tag. "About five feet tall with a bit of an attitude—"

"Where are you?" she asked on a rushed breath.

"Dunking booth. I—"

She'd disconnected. Wade looked at Tag. "She's coming." He pulled out his wallet and handed the kid a twenty. "For the next time you're hungry. But you have to ask her before you take off. Always."

Tag pocketed the money. "She sound mad?" he asked in a wary voice.

Before Wade could answer, a figure came running like a bat out of hell directly for them. "Tag," Sam called out, breathless, a look on her face that pretty much squeezed the hell out of Wade's heart.

Her hair was loose and flying around her shoulders as she gulped for more air. He'd seen her in business attire and in heart-stopping cocktail dresses for certain events. He'd seen her naked.

He rarely got to see her casual as she was now, in jeans and a hoodie sweatshirt. He liked the look, a lot. But what stopped his heart were her eyes. She was scared and panicked, and Wade grabbed the back of Tag's shirt just as the kid's automatic flight response kicked in. "Time to face the music, kid."

Chapter 18

The scoreboard is an ass.

—Neville Cardus

Sam skidded to a stop in front of Tag and Wade and put a hand to her chest to catch her breath. "You okay?" she demanded of Tag.

He nodded.

"I think the question is are *you* okay?" Wade asked quietly.

She shook her head. She couldn't talk. The relief at seeing Tag nearly brought her to her knees. She set her hands on his shoulders, searching for invisible injuries. "Are you okay?"

He dragged his toe in the dirt in front of him, watching the motion of his foot intently, appearing to be wishing for a big hole to swallow him up as he nodded.

"I asked you to wait for me," she said, hearing the waver in her voice, knowing her legendary cool was nowhere to be found. "Where did you go?

"Nowhere," Tag told the ground. "You left."

"But I came back and you were gone."

"You said three minutes. It was longer. You didn't come back like you said."

Sam let out a careful breath and tried to pull in another because she hadn't taken in air since she'd realized he'd walked off without her.

Alone.

But even worse, it was her fault. The popcorn machine had blown a fuse and the person in charge of manning the electrical cords wasn't at his station, so she'd ended up being ten minutes instead of the promised three, which she realized now must have felt like an eternity to Tag. Especially since he had a history of people leaving him. "Look at me, Tag. Please?" She waited until he lifted his gaze to hers. "Are you really okay?"

Tag stared into her face, some of his bravado slipping. Finally he nodded.

"You gave me a heart attack," she said fiercely, and yanked him into her arms, rocking him, knowing it was herself that needed the comfort, not him.

Could have lost him . . .

Tag made a muffled sound against her sweatshirt. "Can't. Breathe."

She loosened her grip slightly and he sucked in a dramatic gulp of air. "Next time I'll take you with me, but if I can't, if something happens like this again, I need you to promise me that you will follow my directions and stay if that's what I've asked of you," she said.

"You have a lot of rules."

"Yes," she agreed. "That's what people do who care about each other. We talked about you being happy, Tag. For me to be happy, I need to know where you're at, and that you're safe. Okay?"

"Okay."

She finally let go of him just as Santos Ramirez, the Heat's left fielder, walked by with his three young boys.

"Hey," he said to Sam. "I need one more kid. It takes an even number for the rides." He grinned at Tag. They were old friends from the clubhouse. "Can I borrow him?"

Tag looked at Sam hopefully.

"Do I have your promise about the listening thing?" she asked.

He nodded his head like a bobble doll.

Sam knew it was far too easy, but inside she was still a complete wreck so she pulled out a twenty from her pocket. "For the rides and food—"

Wade wrapped his fingers around her wrist. She knew by the way he took the time to look her over carefully that he could feel her still shaking. "I already have him covered," he said quietly.

"Ah, man," Tag mumbled.

Santos grinned. "You're good," he said to Wade. "I didn't get good until kid number three."

Wade smiled but hadn't taken his eyes off Sam, and she knew he could see how close she was to losing it. He slid a hand up her back, giving her silent comfort as Santos and the kids moved off. "Breathe," he murmured softly.

She couldn't. She'd not taken in a full breath of air since she'd found Tag missing. Hurting or losing someone she cared about was her biggest nightmare. And having it come true had scared her beyond belief. "I'll pay you back for whatever he got out of you," she said, attempting to sound unaffected and failing miserably. "But I ran off looking for him and left my purse at the check-in, and you need to get to your booth."

"Sam—"

"Gotta go," she managed, and literally jogged off. It was rude but she needed a minute.

Or thirty.

She headed to her car, where she'd be alone, to better fight the tears of panic and adrenaline choking her. And maybe then she could do as Wade had suggested, and breathe. But God, anything could have happened to him, anything at all. He could have been kidnapped, attacked, molested . . . anything.

Okay, she wasn't quite ready to breathe yet. The moment she yanked open her car door and plopped into the driver's seat, she put her head down on the steering wheel and burst into tears.

She held a high-powered job working with grown men who acted like children. Watching one ten-year-old should have been a piece of cake in comparison. So why couldn't she do it? Why was it that she could be so successful at work, or at any menial task she put her mind to, and yet when it came down to something like this, something that required heart and soul, something fairly important, she failed?

The answer was simple, and devastating. She failed at relationships. All of them—

The passenger car door opened. She didn't have to look to know that one tall, leanly muscled Wade O'Riley had just slid into the seat next to her. "You're supposed to be at the booth," she murmured, keeping her head down on the steering wheel.

"I was just there. Henry's taking the first hour for me."

"Go away, Wade."

"Can't do that."

"Please."

He just sat there, distinctly *not* going away. *Shock.*

"If you go away right now," she said recklessly. "I'll take you off the dunk booth rotation entirely."

"Tempting. But let's do this instead. I stay, and if I make you feel better, *then* you take me off the rotation."

"Nothing can make me feel better."

She felt his hand on her hair. "It's not your fault," he said very softly.

"No?" She squeezed her eyes tight, feeling another tear escape. The absolute last. "Then whose fault is it?"

"Look, he's a kid. And a boy to boot. By the very definition, he's supposed to drive you crazy. It's his job."

She choked out a laugh, and dammit, it came out sounding an awful lot like a sob. She went utterly still, but it was too late, she'd given herself away.

His hands were gentle but inexorable as he pulled her around to face him, and she could tell by the look on his face that he'd already known she was crying. She was crying, she hadn't combed her hair, and she'd rubbed off all of her makeup.

"You're beautiful, Sam."

She choked out another laugh and tried to turn away but his hands tightened on her. "And you're not yourself," he said quietly.

"No." She sniffed. "I need a tissue."

When he offered her the hem of his vintage Led Zeppelin T-shirt, she had to laugh again. She was laughing while crying, which was a first.

He caught a tear with his thumb. "So you *are* human."

"I am. I'm human. So much so that I'm sitting here in front of you with my nose running."

He smiled. It wasn't his professional smile. It wasn't his on-the-prowl smile. Nope, this one was slow, soft, and devastating for its utter sincerity. "Hello," he said. "My name's Wade. Nice to meet you."

She let out a breath. "Funny."

"Yeah. Thing is, I mean it. This with you tonight, it feels . . . real."

"Don't waste your charm on me, Wade. We were drunk dates once. And then pretend dates. We wouldn't know real if it hit us on the head."

"Truth or dare."

"We've already played that game."

"Truth or dare."

She sighed. "Truth."

"Do you believe I've never lied to you?"

She thought about that, about all the outrageous things he'd said and done over the four years she'd known him, but she'd never doubted a single word that had come out of his mouth. "Yes. I believe you've never lied to me."

"Good. The drunk date in the Atlanta elevator was . . . a surprise," he admitted. "A hot, sexy-as-hell surprise. The pretend dating thing? Even more so." His hand on her jaw, he slowly shook his head. "But something's happening between us here, Sam. And it's not just elevator and bathroom quickies."

She forced herself to meet his eyes, and what she saw in there caught her breath. Heat. The same heat that tended to melt her panties away with alarming frequency and ease. But also warmth. And, gulp. *Affection*. Not to mention a staggering amount of something else.

He cared. Much more than she'd given him credit for being capable of. "Wade—"

He set his finger on her lips. "And I like you this way."

"A mess?"

"Soft, open. Vulnerable." He leaned over the console and slid the fingers of both hands into her hair as he shifted closer. "*Real.*" His lips were only a breath from hers. "It makes you more human than any other time I've seen you, and that's how I know."

"Know what?" She grabbed his wrists but didn't pull him away because he'd begun to massage the kinked, knotted muscles at her neck, and she moaned softly instead.

"I'm falling for you."

She went still as stone, then lifted her eyes to his. "I don't expect you to catch me or anything," he murmured. "But if you could just keep it in mind . . ." And then he kissed her. It was different from all their previous kisses, which had been hard and deep and wet, and instantaneously hotter than flames.

Not this time. This time it was slow and sweet as he kissed first one side of her mouth, then the other before running his tongue along her lower lip until it trembled open. There was no other option, her body always gave itself up to him, caving to his irresistible blend of intuition and assertiveness. Those were the traits that made him a great ballplayer, a strong man inside and out, and an even better lover.

And he was falling for her.

What the hell did that even mean? She'd ask but she realized both her mouth and her hands had made themselves at home on his body, which was all his fault because he had such a good one. She slid her fingers over the tight muscles of his stomach for the sheer joy of touching him, then up his chest, his neck, sinking into his soft, silky hair. "Wade."

"Mmm." He did something incredible with his lips on her throat and her eyes rolled back in her head as she murmured in pleasure, helplessly leaning in for more, but he held back, pulling free to look at her.

"I love your mouth," he breathed, kissing her bottom

lip, and when she made another restless sound and reached for him, he gently took it between his teeth and lightly tugged.

This caused an answering tug in all her good parts, of which there always seemed to be so many when she was with him, and then finally his mouth closed over hers again in a heavenly kiss that made her forget everything, including her own name.

Chapter 19

You can't win them all but you can try.

—Babe Didrikson Zaharias

When Sam opened her eyes after another long, drugging kiss, the windows were completely fogged over. They were in their own world. She met Wade's dark and scorching gaze. "This is bad."

"A good bad," he said, his voice thick with arousal.

"Wade, the last time we did this, I smiled like an idiot for three days."

He smiled now. He had the sleepiest, sexiest bedroom eyes she'd even seen. "No," she said, pointing at him. "Don't look at me like that."

"Why?"

"Because when you do, I tend to lose my clothes in a hurry."

His smile widened, slow and sure, and spoke volumes. He liked when her clothes came off.

Her nipples went even harder. "Fine. I want you. Okay? I admit it. I. Want. You."

"And the problem is?"

That was easy. She had a difficult time recovering afterwards, and he did not. He wanted a physical relationship. She got that. And now he was falling for her. She knew what that meant to her, but what did it mean to him? He'd been rather vague.

He ran a finger down her neck, then lightly back and forth over the base of her throat where her pulse raced, speeding up at his touch. Then his finger took a journey south.

"You know what?" she managed, her brain running on sheer lust, overtaking the thinking cells as he traced the tip of her breast. "I can't remember the problem."

"Atta girl." His mouth was busy on her throat, his hands sliding beneath her shirt, settling on her ribs, making her babble.

"Besides, this is a public event." She gasped when he cupped her breasts. "Which means we have to be boyfriend and girlfriend, right? We're—oh, God"—those fingers, those talented, knowing fingers plucked at her nipples—"entitled."

"I like the sound of that." He hit the automatic locks on the door without taking his mouth off her. She let out a throaty moan, fisted her hands in his shirt, yanked him forward, and kissed him. Kissed him while tugging up his shirt.

No slouch, he unzipped her sweatshirt and slid it off her shoulders, revealing the spaghetti-strapped tank she had beneath. His fingers nudged those straps down as well and then her top was at her waist. Her bra vanished and so did his shirt, and their hands fought for purchase on each other's zippers, all while they kissed; deep, drugging kisses that exploded her brain cells one at a time, an organized war against rational thought. She had no idea how much more time had gone by when she realized she'd lost her jeans and he had his mouth pressed to her belly. "Unbelievable," she panted, leaning back in her seat to give him better access. "We're at it again."

"It was inevitable." He scooted down a little to kiss her hip and bumped his head on the steering wheel. "*Fuck.*"

She burst out laughing, she couldn't help it, but the laughter backed up in her throat when he kissed her inner thigh. And even though she was already panting as if she'd been running a marathon, her breathing quickened even more as his mouth worked its way up her leg.

"You have the softest skin," he murmured against her, his thumbs hooking into her panties, his tongue getting closer to where she desperately needed it. "Lift up, Sam."

She lifted up and then her panties were gone and he was nudging her over the front seat into the back. He followed her, then with a big hand on each of her thighs, urged them open, kneeling between.

Call her slow, but that was when she realized she was completely butt-ass naked and he wasn't. "You're overdressed."

"Sorry." He stripped out of his board shorts so fast her head spun, and then he bent his head and took her nipple into his mouth, teasing it between his lightly clamped teeth, rolling his tongue around it until she cried out, her hands flailing for something sturdy because her world was spinning. She gripped the armrest in one hand and the back of the seat in the other, and when he ran a finger down her belly and between her legs, she arched up to meet his touch. "Hurry."

"Hell, no," he said thickly. "We were in a hurry last time. I didn't get to . . ."

"What?"

"This." And he lifted her to his mouth.

Sweet Jesus.

His tongue shot her into instant overdrive, and when he added a finger into the mix, and then another, she came hard and fast. God, she was such a slut when it came to him.

Her hips were still rocking, her breath still wheezing in her throat, her entire body still wracked in the after-shudders as she sat up and turned her attention to his most impressive erection. He was big and hard and she loved the way his breath caught when she stroked him, so she did it again.

"Jesus." He closed his eyes, his head dropping back. "I hope you're going somewhere with this."

"Yes." And she guided him into her. "How's that?"

His groan of pleasure was her answer as he hooked her legs over his forearms, leaned over her, and began to move.

And oh, God, how he moved. It was as if he took her to another plane, every single time, and she gripped him tight, rocking to meet him, inarticulate, needy, little whimpers escaping her with each breath.

Bending his head, he kissed her as he moved inside her, long and slow and deep, then gradually faster, building the tension, the unbearable need, all of it etched on his face. Just watching him was enough to nudge her over again, and this time he followed her into the abyss.

He collapsed over her for a moment. Then with a groan, he managed to shift his weight, sitting up, pulling her over him, cupping her face until she opened her eyes.

His hair was a little wild on the best of days, but now, from her fingers, it stood practically straight up. He had a mark on his shoulder that looked suspiciously like she'd bitten him, and a gleam in his eyes that said he was a *very* sated man. "You need a bigger backseat," he said, his voice low and sexy.

"I need some self-control."

He grinned. "Control's overrated. But maybe next time we can make it to a bed."

A bed would probably kill her. Her clothes were in the front seat, so with a sigh, she went to climb over, then squeaked in startled shock when he sank his teeth into her butt. Dropping to the front seat, she glared at him. "Hey!"

"Sorry," he said, clearly not sorry at all. "But you have an edible ass." He was all sprawled out, lazily slipping his board shorts and T-shirt back on his body, and he looked like . . . like something she wanted.

Again.

Which was all his fault. Between his soft, "I'm falling for you" and then the wild, almost out-of-body orgasms he'd given her, she knew herself. She couldn't keep it at just "play." Grimly, she told him, "I have to get back."

"I know." He ran a finger over the frown she could feel between her eyes. "I almost had that gone there for a few minutes."

"You did," she admitted. "You have this odd ability to relax me and rev me up all at the same time."

He laughed softly. "Same goes."

"I just have to remember not to get used to it."

"Why?"

"The month'll be over soon enough."

He was quiet a moment, watching his finger play over her throat and shoulder. "We could always keep it going."

She ignored the hopeful leap her heart made. "Okay, who are you and what have you done with Wade O'Riley?"

His lips curved, but to her relief he didn't push as she stared at him, trying to gauge which head that comment had come from, the one on top of his shoulders, or the one in his pants. She decided it was far too dangerous to guess, and grabbed her clothes.

"I've never seen you in jeans," he said as she wrestled back into them.

"I planned on changing before the carnival opened," she said. "But once Tag went missing, I—" *Lost it.*

And he'd helped her put it back together again. He'd

made her feel better—*Ah, hell.* She narrowed her eyes. "I'm not getting in the dunk booth."

"Of course not. You clearly don't feel better at all."

"Okay, stop that."

"Hey, I understand. You're breaking your word."

"That's low," she said on a blown-out sigh. "You know I always keep my word."

He leaned back, hands behind his head as if he'd never been more comfortable, and just smiled.

Dammit! "Fine. But I'm only doing this so you can't hold it over me." She eyed his body and had to fight not to leap over the seat again and eat him up. "And because as it turns out, I could use the cold dip."

His soft laughter followed her out into the night.

Wade stood outside the dunking booth. He was waiting for Sam, who was changing her clothes for the booth. A few women approached him for an autograph, which he gave, but neither tried to write their phone numbers anywhere on his person.

Progress.

He had his picture taken by two other women, who asked where his pretty girlfriend was. He told them she was coming right back, and as they walked away, he realized with surprise that he was smiling.

He liked the idea of being taken. *Go figure.*

Pace and Holly appeared hand in hand, fresh off the Ferris wheel. Holly was glowing, Pace was looking pretty relaxed. Wade recognized the look, since he imagined he was wearing a matching one.

"Where's your girlfriend?" Pace asked. "Oh, excuse me. Your *pretend* girlfriend."

"Shut up."

Holly smiled at Wade. "You're getting close to figuring it out, aren't you?"

"Figuring out what?" Pace asked.

"That it's not pretend," Holly said, still looking into Wade's eyes.

Maybe. Still didn't make it any easier. "Don't you two have booths to work?"

"Aw." Holly let go of Pace to give Wade a hard hug. "You're so cute when you're all turned upside down by a woman."

Pace was grinning over her head at him.

"You're really annoying," Wade told him, and to return the favor, he hugged Holly in tight.

"Hey," Pace said. But when Wade kept ahold of his woman, he just sighed. "You've been getting whatever you want from women for years with one crook of your little finger. Watching you even attempt to get what you want from Sam, when you don't even know what that is . . . well, that's just good entertainment all around. Now, Goddammit, let go of her, she's mine." He grabbed Holly's hand and tugged her to him.

Holly laughed. "We still doing pizza after?" she asked Wade.

Wade sighed. "Yeah." He turned to look at the booth in time to see Sam climbing out onto the platform. He spent a few minutes watching her try to get comfortable up on the bench seat in a borrowed bathing suit top and shorts.

She might be bossy and stubborn as hell, but she was one hell of a good sport.

The line was at least ten people long, which was good. Lots of people meant lots of money, and lots of money meant more resources dumped into the 4 The Kids pockets. That's what this was all about, but he couldn't help but grin as he watched Sam warily eye the little kid at the

front of the line, specifically the lever he had to hit in order to dunk her.

Santos appeared with his boys and Tag at Wade's side.
"What's Aunt Sam doing in there?" Tag asked Wade.

"She's in there because she likes me," Wade said as he
received dark, murderous looks from Sam.

"Are you sure she likes you?" Tag asked doubtfully.

"Yeah." Wade smiled. "She just doesn't know it yet."

"You're weird," Tag said.

The little kid at the front of the line threw his ball and
missed the booth entirely.

From inside the dunk tank, Sam took a visible breath
of relief.

The next kid in line missed as well.

And the third.

"Wow," Tag said. "They all suck."

"Maybe not," Wade said.

"You know she's going to get real mad if she goes in.
She doesn't like it when her hair gets wet after she straight-
ens it."

"No?"

"No. And she's looking at you like you're in big trouble. Are you in trouble?"

"What would being in trouble entail?" Wade asked him.

Tag shrugged. "Maybe no ice cream after dinner."

"Huh. I do love ice cream."

"Yeah," Tag said. "But at least she's nice even when she's
mad. She doesn't ever get scary or anything. Well, except
for tonight when she almost cried. That was scary."

Wade's gut tightened as he took his attention off Sam
and looked down at Tag. "You get scared back home?"

Tag lifted a shoulder. "Sometimes. Like when I get left
alone."

A slow burn churned within him for the way he'd been

treated. Knowing all too damn well exactly how shitty it felt, Wade gently set his hand on Tag, glad the kid was safe here with Sam for now. Tag accepted the touch with only a little squirm—progress.

The next kid missed and Tag made a sound of disgust. "What, can no one throw?" He shoved a hand in his pocket and pulled out a few bucks. "I'm gonna show 'em how it's done."

Wade gently squeezed Tag's shoulder, holding him back. "Wait."

"Why?"

Wade pulled another twenty out of his pocket.

Tag's eyes lit up.

"To *not* dunk her," Wade directed.

"You want me to stand in line and miss?"

"Yep."

Tag eyed the line and all the kids in it, and slid his gaze back to Wade. "You paid all of them?"

Wade smiled.

Tag just stared at him. "You sure she's not your real girlfriend?"

"Just don't hit that lever, kid. I'm a lot tougher than your Aunt Sam."

Tag grinned and pocketed the money. "You *so* like her."

"Yeah." Wade smiled. "Yeah, I do."

At the realization that the big, bad Wade O'Riley was nothing more than a sorry sap, Tag just shook his head. But then he said softly, "I like her, too."

Chapter 20

Baseball isn't a business, it's more like a disease.

—Walter F. O'Malley

The next morning the Heat left early for a trip to Colorado to play the Rockies. Sam brought Tag and his tutor, and on the plane, Tag pulled out his schoolwork. Sam ostensibly did paperwork herself, but in reality she stared out the window and thought about the night before.

The carnival had been an undeniable success business-wise. Personally? She wasn't as sure. She and Tag had managed to turn their misunderstanding into a positive thing, or so she hoped. She felt like he'd let her get closer to him.

Wade had certainly let her get closer as well. So close she still bore the whisker burns on her breasts and between her thighs.

He'd been there for her, from soothing her raw nerves to making her forget the panic with mind-blowing sex. Hell, he'd made her forget her own name.

But she still didn't know what to do with that.

In Colorado, game one, Wade delivered a pinch-hit, two-run, walk-off triple, capping a three-run ninth to give the Heat a series-opening win, three-two.

Afterwards in the hotel, the team ate together at the bar. It was a good crowd, easygoing and laid-back, the mood mellow and relaxed.

Sam did her job, moving between tables, making nice with the few reporters that were around, keeping one eye on Tag, who was once again with Santos's boys. The mood was fun and jubilant. They'd won today's game, the fans were happy, and so were their sponsors, so much so that Wade's face was currently once again all over the country's most popular cereal boxes these days. She caught little pieces of the conversations going on all around her, most of it about Wade.

". . . He's been phenomenal lately . . ."

". . . Amazingly pinpoint with his control, commanding both sides of the plate . . ."

". . . Strategized the perfect game plan, and executed it . . ."

She absorbed it all and felt a warm sense of pride for him, knowing he worked his ass off and had earned it. And yeah, maybe she couldn't take her eyes off him—

"Nice job on the pretending," Gage said, coming up next to Sam. "It's hardly noticeable at all that you're staring at him."

"Just doing my job," she quipped.

"Sam."

She knew that tone, that soft but undeniably authoritative tone, the one that said, "Talk to me." When he used that voice, most people willingly spilled their guts. He had the power that way. And thanks to his Latin father and supermodel mother, he really was almost too gorgeous to look at this close. "Is it still pretending?" he asked, his dark eyes solemn, concerned.

"A little late to ask me that now, isn't it?"

"It's never too late."

She looked at Wade, who was surrounded by the other players, all laughing and having a good time. Wade was smiling but his eyes were . . . locked on Sam. "Actually," she whispered to Gage, her gaze held prisoner. "This time it is."

"A picture," one reporter called out, and gestured for her to move closer to Wade's table. "To show that the mighty Wade O'Riley is still off the market."

Wade stood and took Sam's hand, smiling that warm just-for-her smile. It momentarily caught her off balance, a situation he took full advantage of by sitting back down and pulling her into his lap, cupping her face and kissing her softly.

"Thanks," the reporter said with a laugh after he'd gotten the shot. "You guys are great sports."

Wade pulled back slowly, eyes on Sam. "My pleasure."

Yeah, she thought shakily, feeling his hands on her back, one slipping low enough to cup her ass beneath the table. Her pleasure, too. And wasn't that just the problem.

It wasn't pretend.

And in less than two weeks, it'd be done.

Not letting herself go there, she moved out of the bar and into the hallway to check her messages, only to go still as she felt someone come up behind her and stand close enough to share body heat. Since her nipples hardened, she knew exactly who it was.

"Guess who?" He ran a finger over her shoulder.

She bit back the soft sigh of pleasure. "Oh, Gage."

Wade let out a choked laugh and whipped her around to face him.

She arched a daring brow. They hadn't been alone since

he'd gotten her naked in her backseat at the carnival. It didn't bode well that she felt like dragging him into the closest closet now for a repeat performance. "Nice game today," she said "Actually, fantastic game today, but I'm mad at you, and you know why."

That had him blinking. "Maybe you could remind me."

"You guilted me into getting into that dunking booth, and while I sat up there terrified I was going to get dunked, you were paying people off."

"And that's a problem?"

Her gaze dropped to his mouth. She couldn't help it, it was a damn fine mouth. "You could have told me."

"What, that I was never going to let you get dunked?" He tugged her in hard against him. "Which, by the way, was a luxury you didn't afford me. When I took my turn after you, I got dunked twenty-seven times. I still have water in my ear." He held her, his warm hands stroking up and down her back. "So is that what you're really mad at, or is it the fact that I told you I was falling for you?"

"That," she said shakily, dropping her forehead to his chest. "Most definitely that. People don't just . . . fall."

His hand came up and cupped the nape of her neck. "Sure they do."

"I don't."

"Ah." He said this very gently and brushed his jaw to hers. He smelled like a million bucks, and was warm and strong and so sure. "Maybe it'd help if you loosened up a little bit. Give your heart some rein to fly free." He pressed his mouth to her ear. "Just let go and see where it takes you."

She realized she was leaning into him like he was her own personal support beam. She tipped her head up and stared at him. Just let go? See where it took her? No worrying about the two week expiration date? She understood that was pretty much his life's motto, but she'd never worked like that.

"I can be lots of be fun," he coaxed with a brow wriggle that suggested much of that fun might be had naked.

She had to laugh. He was right. Loosening up and flying free would be fun. Of that, she had no doubt.

But what about after the fun was over?

"I've met some of your family," he said. "They're all pretty intense guys, so I'm guessing fun men aren't exactly familiar to you, but you should give me a try."

"I've gone out with plenty of fun men." She'd done so in a purposeful attempt to find the polar opposite of the doggedly aggressive men she'd grown up with.

"And?"

"And nothing worked out."

"Why?"

"Because their fun always won over substance."

"Common mistake, but you're armed with knowledge now. Give it a try. Kiss me, Sam. I'll show you what I mean. I've got plenty of substance."

Uh-huh. And some of that substance was currently pressing into her belly. With an ache of need drumming through her, she fisted her hands in his shirt, her gaze still locked on his mouth.

With a smile, he bent his head and kissed her. It involved tongue, lots of tongue, and heat slashed through her. She moaned and—

"Ew."

With a gasp, she pushed free and twisted around to face Tag, who stood there watching them.

"Kinda gross," he said, and went into the boy's restroom.

Above her, she sensed Wade smiling. "This isn't funny," she said.

"You're right. It's nice."

"Nice?"

"I get the feeling Tag's view on relationships is pretty fucked up. Having him see two people who have feelings for each other is good for him."

She stared up at him, wondering why the fact that he so obviously cared deeply about Tag reached out and grabbed her by the throat. "Pretend feelings," she whispered.

The crux of her problem.

He was quiet a long moment as he ran his thumb over her jaw. "We're pretending to have a committed relationship, true. But my feelings for you aren't pretend." He leaned in and kissed her again, softly, sweetly. And then he walked away, leaving her standing there shaken to the core, with more questions than answers. But she'd wanted to know this wasn't all play, and it seemed she'd gotten her confirmation.

And yet somehow instead of putting her at ease, she felt a little like she'd just walked off the edge of a cliff into a freefall.

After dinner, Henry, Joe, and Mason ordered up an Xbox for a play-off in their suite. Sam allowed Tag to go with them because one, she knew the guys wouldn't do anything stupid in front of him, and two, she needed a moment to herself. She hadn't had a moment to herself since opening day two and a half weeks ago. Ever since then, when things came up that she needed to think about, she'd had no choice but to shove it into a file in her brain labeled *To Obsess Over Later.*

Except that compartment was now full. Overflowing, in fact. In the glorious silence of her hotel room, she worked for several hours on her laptop, planning the next big charity event—an elaborate, elegant dinner and auction for Santa Barbara's rich and famous. She also worked on some upcoming media appearances and other publicity events for the guys. There were interviews to set up and calls to make, some of which dealt with reporters trying to get the scoop on her brother and her family, or on her and Wade. She deflected the negative into positive wherever she could. That was her job. She was cool, composed. Tough as hell.

No weaknesses.

But she *did* have weaknesses, two of them, and both new to her. Tag, who'd somehow turned her into a fiercely protective Momma bear, and Wade, who lived life like it was a freebie, like he was a cat with eight more lives in the wings, because he knew more than most that life was short and meant to be lived hard and fast.

She got that about him.

She understood that about him.

She just couldn't *be* like him.

Though she'd certainly enjoyed being under him . . .

At the soft knock on her hotel room door, she shook herself and opened it to Wade himself. Tag was suspended by his ankles, draped over Wade's back, laughing, and Sam's heart cracked wide open.

Wade turned so that she could see Tag, and she took in his glossy eyes. He had to be exhausted.

By all rights, Wade should be, too. He'd played a physical game today, but he didn't look tired as he met her gaze. He was wearing jeans and a black sweater over a black shirt and looked lean and predatory as he took her in.

"Got good and bad news," he said, carefully swinging back around and walking into the room without decapitating Tag on the door jamb. "The bad news is that Tag ate all the M&M's and an entire bowl of those mini-chocolate bars before anyone knew what was happening."

Sam slid Tag a look.

"They were busy playing," Tag said in his defense. "And yelling at the TV and each other."

"In good fun," Wade murmured and twisted over the back of the couch, dumping Tag face-first into the cushions, but more importantly, unintentionally giving Sam a nice view of the way the jeans perfectly fit Wade's very fine ass.

"Good fun," Tag repeated, rolling to his back on the couch, grinning up at Sam. "Pace called Wade a dickhead—"

Wade leaned over the couch and covered the kid's mouth with his hand. "Do you remember what I told you?"

"Uh-huh. Not to repeat any of the bad words I heard tonight. Our secret. But I didn't think *dickhead* is a bad word. Everyone says it in the clubhouse and stuff."

Sam looked at Wade in time to catch a guilty grimace as he swiped a hand down his face.

"I won't tell the rest," Tag promised.

Again Sam looked at Wade.

Wade just shook his head.

"The good news?" Sam asked him.

"We already dealt with the sugar high," Wade said. "He's on his way down now."

"Tired," Tag agreed, his eyes drooping at half mast. As he yawned nearly wider than his head, Wade scooped him back up in a fireman's hold, much to Tag's tired amusement. Catching Sam staring, Wade raised his brow in question. "Where do you want him?"

"In here." She'd gotten a suite so Tag would have a room of his own. She opened the door and turned down the bed.

Wade flopped him on the mattress, then pulled off Tag's shoes and sweatshirt, brushing against Sam as he did, smelling warm and sexy.

She needed to get a grip.

Tag was already out like a light. She pulled the covers up to his chin, then stroked a strand of hair off his forehead. She should have made him brush his teeth, especially with all the sugar he'd consumed. Maybe she should wake him up—

Wade took her hand in his and pulled her from the room. He shut the door and gave her an amused look.

"What?" she asked.

"You're getting more comfortable with him."

"Funny thing about ten-year-olds. It's hard to keep your distance."

"Yeah, especially with that one. He's got a way of worming right in." He pressed a hand over his heart. "Here."

She worked at not melting and failed miserably. "Are you just trying to butter me up?"

"No, I'm not crazy about butter. I'll whip-cream you up though. Anytime."

She shook her head even as her knees wobbled at the thought. "Can you be serious?"

"If I have to be." He lifted a shoulder. "I like the kid."

Simple. Easily admitted. No angst over the admission. Well, wasn't he just free with his emotions lately? "It's easy to like him," she said. "It's not so easy to be responsible for him."

"It's not supposed to be easy, but you're doing great. You're falling for him. No, don't be embarrassed," he said, tugging her around when she tried to walk away, holding on to her, dipping his knees a little, to look into her face. "It's cute."

"*Cute?*"

"Sexy, too."

She had to laugh. "How is me caring for Tag sexy?"

"Hell, I don't know, Sam. Everything you do is sexy to me."

She felt her body react to his words and crossed her arms. "Okay, you know what? You need to stop talking. And—" she said quickly, when he took a step into her, the intent in his heated gaze quite clear. "No sex either."

"How about just fooling around? We could just feel each other up." He ran a hand down her arm and then settled it on her hip, his fingers slipping beneath her shirt to graze bare skin. "That's not technically sex, right? I could still call for that whipped cream."

Tempting as that thought might be, she shook her head. "You're leaving."

"Yeah." He smiled. He'd known that. He'd been messing with her. "Have dinner with me when we get home." He took his hand on a tour upward, over her ribs, gently gliding over her breast.

"W-what?"

"Dinner." His thumb teased her nipple into a tight bead. "It comes after lunch. We have a game tomorrow night, so how about the day after, back in Santa Barbara? After our Houston game."

"Wade."

"Sam."

His other hand joined his first under her shirt, and she shivered in pleasure. "J-just dinner?"

"For now. We'll wing the rest."

"You're good at that, but I'm not."

Something came and went in his eyes, so fast that she thought maybe she'd imagined it—regret? "Stop thinking so much," he said softly. "Let one area of your life just happen. Dinner," he repeated. "Dinner, because I like food and I like you. And you like me, too. It's what two people in like do, they go out to dinner."

"Fine. But no elevators, Wade. No bathrooms. And no backseats."

"Tag's right. You sure have a lot of rules." But with a small smile, he leaned in and kissed her, a soft, surprisingly gentle kiss that lingered long after she'd locked the door behind him, making her ache just a little as she wondered how nice it would be if there was no rules at all.

Thanks in part to his own ninth-inning catch at the plate, Wade assisted the Heat to a satisfying win the next day. After the game, he sat with some of the guys at the hotel bar in front of a flat screen enjoying a few beers. They were flipping between basketball and wrestling when a group of well-dressed women showed up and started flirting.

And then began the silent pair-off as his teammates settled into a different kind of game for the evening. Wade used to be the king of that game but tonight, as he had for months now, he held back because his idea of fun was eight floors up, working on her laptop and hanging out with her nephew.

Still, one of the women playfully asked him to autograph the napkin her drink had been set on, and then she took the pen from him and settled a hand on his. Turning it over, she wrote her number on his palm. He had no idea why so many women did this, if they thought it was unique or what, but she was looking at him, soft and willing, waiting for a sign that he might actually use her number when a familiar female voice spoke from over his shoulder.

"Sorry. He's already got the only number he needs tonight."

Wade looked up into Sam's steely gaze just as someone in the bar took a picture, making them all grimace at the unexpected flash.

The woman with the pen smiled with some chagrin and moved away to join her friends.

Wade smiled up at Sam. "Sit with me."

"I have a meeting with Gage and then I'm going back to Tag. You do know that picture will show up all over the Internet tomorrow, right?"

"Yes. My protective girlfriend, saving me from myself."

She shook her head and walked off. Wade sipped his drink, watching her go, thinking how radically things had changed for him, that for the first time in his life he was the one being walked away from.

The next morning the picture of Sam standing over Wade indeed appeared everywhere, the reports claiming she'd been possessive, protective, and gorgeous with it.

The guys loved it.

Wade did as well.

But Sam appeared to hate it, and ignored anyone who teased her about it, including Wade.

Back at home, the Heat played Houston. Wade loved a home crowd, and today's was particularly, satisfyingly rambunctious. The Heat trailed by one for the first five innings, then erupted for seven runs in the bottom of the sixth to take a twelve-eight lead. Wade took a hard kick to the thigh in a home slide by the Astros center fielder but with no other mishaps, they held the Astros scoreless in the eighth and ninth innings, and took the win.

Afterwards, Wade limped into the clubhouse thinking he'd slap on a little Icy Hot and be good to go for his date with his crazy, jealous, gorgeous girlfriend tonight. After a shower, he sat on the bench in front of his opened locker, hurting but happy. The guys were messing around on either side of him, still high on adrenaline, planning some fun for the night ahead.

"You coming with?" Joe asked.

"Got a date," Wade said.

"Catch up with us when you're done."

There'd been many nights when he'd done just that, gone out with a woman, had his fun, then joined up with the guys. But tonight, he had a feeling the only person getting kicked to the curb would be him.

He pulled on his clothes and found Pace watching him. "If you wanted to see something," Wade said. "You should have watched while I was still in the shower."

Pace sat next to him. "I didn't want to tell you before the game. Your father called me."

"Son of a bitch."

"Have you thought about actually talking to him?"

"I send him what he needs."

"Yeah. A check isn't going to solve this one. He wants out of the center you got him into."

"So? No one's holding him there." Wade tied his shoes and stood up. "He can do whatever the hell he wants. He always did."

"I think what he wants is you."

"He had a health scare. Doctor told him to quit drinking. He's got it in his head that he can't quit drinking without me."

"So give him you."

"Hell, Pace, he's had me all along. But I no longer even attempt to compete with the booze."

"Maybe if you just talk to him instead of—"

"Not interested." Wade could talk until he was blue in the face, it never changed anything. Grabbing his keys and his things, he headed out of the facilities and made his way to Sam's condo. Downtown was crowded, the streets packed as usual. He had to park a few blocks down and was recognized several times as he walked the street toward Sam's building. He stopped to sign a few autographs and climbed the stairs to her condo.

Tag answered the door. "Hi."

"Hi. You stay out of trouble today?"

"I did . . ." He winced. "Not."

"What did you do?"

"Sort of scared the babysitter off."

Wade tucked the kid's head under his arm like a sack of potatoes, mussed his hair with his knuckles, and with Tag letting out a belly laugh and trying to swat his hand away, stepped into the entry.

Samantha turned from the window. She was still in her work clothes, a wraparound shirt dress the color of the day's sky. Her usual elegant and sophisticated business style.

But she didn't look her usual cool, calm, and collected in the face of any storm. She had a stress line dividing her forehead, shadows beneath her eyes, and on the windowsill, her fists were clenched.

She was a woman on the edge.

For most of his life, he'd run like hell from this very thing, from worrying about someone else, from caring. But when it came to her, no matter how often he'd tried telling himself it was just the pretense, the great sex, it didn't fly.

Because even he didn't believe that was all there was when it came to her.

Chapter 21

Baseball fans are junkies, and their heroin is the statistic.

—Robert S. Wieder

"**I'm** sorry," Sam told Wade. "But I have to cancel dinner."

Wade's stomach tightened. He'd been thinking about tonight all day, looking forward to it far more than he'd even admitted to himself. "Why?"

"Because the babysitter—"

"Yeah. I heard." He gave Tag another head noogie.

Tag let out a belly laugh, and Wade smiled at the sound as he looked at Sam. "You don't have to cancel because of the kid here. We'll just bring him."

"Wade, he had the babysitter believing he had three physical disorders, two behavioral disorders, one psychosomatic disorder . . . and a bladder control problem."

Wade arched a brow and let go of the kid's head. "That took talent," he said into Tag's eyes with a smile. He looked back at Sam. "I say we make him watch us while we eat burgers and play games on the wharf."

Sam sighed. "Wade—"

Wade looked at Tag. "Why don't you give us a minute."

Tag, no dummy, ran down the hall and slammed a door. "I can't hear a thing!" he yelled through it. "I swear."

"It's not going to work," Sam said quietly to Wade. "He's acting out. Yesterday he didn't want me to leave him here with his tutor when I had a meeting. He left the water running into the tub and just about flooded the entire condo so I'd have to stay." She shook her head and spread her hands. "Stick a fork in me, I'm done."

"You're quitting him?"

She stared at him in shock. "What? No, of course not! I'm quitting *you*. Obviously Tag has separation anxiety."

"I think it's more than that," he said quietly, knowing firsthand what abandonment issues felt like.

She nodded and lowered her voice to a thread of a whisper. "I realize that. There's going to be an adjustment period, and clearly he's testing me. I get that. I'm trying to prove myself to him, trying to show him that I won't up and leave him, ever, but I can't screw this up, Wade. I won't do that to him."

He felt his heart catch hard, and all he could manage was a nod. She got it. She got Tag.

And she'd get you, a small voice said, but he told the small voice to shut the hell up.

Sam drew a deep breath. "The bottom line is that I just can't do this thing with him correctly, and also whatever the hell it is we're doing at the same time."

Okay, now this he didn't get. "Why not?"

"Why not?" She gaped at him as if he were an idiot. And maybe he was, because he didn't see the problem.

"Because," she said in a low whisper. "It's taking all I have to handle him the right way."

Risking his neck, he stepped closer to her, running a

finger over her jaw. "I'm pretty sure there is no *right* way, Sam. All you can do is your best. And for the record, you're doing a great job at that." He settled a hand on her hip. "He doesn't mean to be a pain in the ass, he's just hurting and scared."

"I know that, don't you think I know that?" She looked destroyed over her inability to solve this with her usual strength of will. "It's just that he's good at pushing my buttons."

"Well, maybe if there weren't so darn many of them." He laughed when she growled, and then he pulled her resisting body in for a hug. "Dinner," he said softly, running his hand up her back. "You need to eat, he needs to eat, it'll serve a purpose."

He took it as a good sign when she snuggled into him instead of shoving him away, pressing her face to his throat and wrapping her arms around his waist. "Is this just an attempt to get back into my pants?"

"Baby, rest assured, *everything* I do is an attempt to get back into your pants."

She surprised him by letting out a low laugh, and pulled back to look into his eyes. "I can't do this, Wade. I can't fight him and you at the same time."

"So quit fighting." He ran his fingers over the tense muscles of her neck. "We've talked about this. Loosen up a little and go with the flow."

"And if I screw up?"

"With Tag?"

Something flickered in her eyes, making him realize she'd meant him. Them. "Yes," she said, trying to recover. "With Tag."

He pulled her back into him, body to body. "He has a mother who couldn't give a shit, a selfish bastard of a father, and a nonexistent grandpa. By housing and feeding him, you're already ahead of the game." He entangled her fingers in his. "And as for what you really meant, with us . . ." He held her when she would have turned away embarrassed, bringing her hand to his mouth to brush his lips over her knuckles. "Not much you can screw up, Princess."

"Right. Because we're just . . . winging it."

Okay, not what he meant. "Sam—"

"No, you know what? I don't want to go there right now. Not now, maybe not ever." She dropped her hand to his chest. "Yes to dinner," she said, muffled. "Because I'm too tired and defeated to even call for take-out." She hesitated, then surprised him by lifting her face and pulling his down for a soft, warm kiss, one that she initiated. "And thank you."

He felt emotion spread through his chest. "For what?"

"For keeping it together, even when I can't . . ."

Wade nodded, but in truth, he didn't have it together at all, not when it came to her. Not even close.

He drove them to the wharf, where they ordered burgers and watched the early evening surfers. When the food came, Tag stared down at his burger but didn't touch it.

Wade nudged him. "What's the matter? Not cooked the way you want it?"

"I thought I had to watch the two of you eat."

Sam stared at him for a beat, then met Wade's gaze, hers filled with guilt as she set her burger down. "Oh, Tag. We were kidding."

Tag put his hands over his eyes. "But I really was bad. On purpose." He ducked his head even farther. "Probably so bad you would never even *think* about letting me play in the arcade . . ."

Christ, the kid was good, Wade thought with admiration. Shaking his head, he pushed the plate back in front of Tag. "Knock it off. Consider manipulating a no-go around here, along with scaring babysitters and trying to drive your aunt out of her mind."

"Wade," Sam said softly. "He's—"

"Got your number," he said bluntly, watching the realization that Tag had been playing her come into her eyes. He turned to Tag. "Eat your burger, kiddo, and think about this—you can be a little punk all you want, but Sam's not going anywhere, not without you. She sticks."

Tag lifted his gaze and settled a heartbreaking look on Sam.

"It's true," she whispered, her eyes unusually bright. "You're stuck with me."

"You're not mad?" Tag asked her.

"Not at this moment, no. Can't say that that won't change, but one thing that for sure won't change is your address for the rest of the next three months."

"Yeah, because you *have* to keep me," he said a little bitterly. "No one else wanted me."

Sam put her hand over his. "Maybe I didn't *know* I wanted you, but I do. And your father wants you and loves you, he's just got to take care of himself right now before he can take care of you again."

Tag nodded and stared at his burger.

"It's true," Sam told him. "I want you with me, I love having you with me. Because of you, I've expanded my food horizons to include cheese on everything. I watch *SpongeBob SquarePants*. And I'm getting good on the Xcube."

"Xbox," Tag corrected with a snort but he did let loose a reluctant smile as well.

"And my refrigerator is always full of good stuff," she went on, smiling, too. "And best of all? Because you're always at work with me, no one can yell at me. Plus, you're fairly entertaining."

"I am?"

"Yeah, and you're also pretty darn cute when you're not scowling. Now eat your burger."

Tag grinned and ate his burger. Sam looked at Wade with a soft smile. He had no idea what it meant, but he liked it. A lot.

After dinner, they walked along the beach, with Tag managing to get wet up to his waist because he couldn't resist the lure of the ocean. Nor could he resist kicking up a wave at Wade, splashing him down the front.

Wade merely stripped off his shoes and shirt and went in after the kid. When they were both good and drenched, they returned to the shore to face a clearly bemused Sam.

"You're both . . . wet," she said, trying to pretend she wasn't staring at Wade's chest and failing.

"That's water for you," Wade said.

"She doesn't like to get wet," Tag reminded him. "Her hair frizzes up like a squirrel's tail."

"Tag," Sam said.

"Oh. Right." He winced. "That was a secret."

"I like squirrels," Wade said to Sam with a smile.

"Don't even think about it," Sam warned him.

Oh, he was thinking. He looked at Tag, who nodded, and the two of them engulfed her in their arms, pressing their wet bodies close to her squirming one, not letting go until she was as drenched as them.

"Nice," Wade said, and tousled her frizzing hair.

Tag ran ahead, toward the car, and Wade grabbed Sam's hand, following more slowly. She was using her free hand to try to flatten her hair.

It wasn't happening.

He let his gaze dip down her body. Her blue dress was soaked, clinging to her hips, belly, and breasts.

She was cold.

She looked down to see what he was looking at. "Great." She hugged herself. "Feeling a little embarrassed here."

"Yeah, that's not what I'm feeling."

She rolled her eyes and tried to get the material away from her body. It broke free with a little suction sound that went straight through Wade, then replastered itself to her like a second skin. She gave up. Not him. Christ, she was hot, and he stepped toward her.

"Oh, no," she said quickly, with a short laugh as she backed up, holding out a hand to ward him off. "No touching."

"Give me ten seconds to change your mind."

He expected her to laugh. Instead she nodded, a heat coming into her eyes. "You could do it in zero point four," she said softly. "But you won't. Not here, not now."

"Why not?"

"Because Tag's here . . . and because you're a good guy."

He stared into her eyes. "Don't tell anyone."

"You secret's safe."

He drove them home, and walked her and Tag to their door. Tag ran inside, leaving them alone. Sam leaned back against the door jamb. "Thanks for tonight."

"Yeah. The burgers were good. I love that place."

"I meant for helping me with Tag."

"He's a great kid."

Her head was back against the wood, tilted up to look into his eyes. "He is." She licked her lower lip, an unconscious gesture.

She wanted him to kiss her.

Leaning past her, he took a peek inside. Tag wasn't visible. Good. He put a hand on either side of Sam's head and crowded in a little bit, being careful not to touch her. "'Night," he whispered.

She stared up at him, her eyes dilated, her lips open just a little.

She was waiting. Waiting for the good night kiss. And she was so hopeful, so damn sexy with it, he nearly groaned.

"Night," she said a little breathlessly, her eyes drifting closed, her mouth gravitating to his, only a breath away now. It took everything he had to remain utterly still. Even more to push off the door and back away.

Her eyes flew open. "What are you doing?"

"Not touching you."

She stared at him for a beat, then clearly remembered her own words and sighed. "You think this is amusing."

"I'm feeling a lot of things, not a one of them amused." He looked at her in that wet dress and this time he did groan. "Okay, got to go."

"Wade?"

When he turned back, she was in the middle of the doorway, nipples still pressing against the wet fabric of her dress, begging for attention. "Yeah?"

"You want me to throw myself at you, right? Which, admittedly, I keep doing." She shook her head. "I'm onto you."

"I *wish* you were onto me. Or better yet, all over me. I'm not picky."

She actually took a step toward him, the interest in her eyes making him insta-hard, but Tag appeared behind her with a bag of Cheez Doodles and a DVD in hand. "Wanna watch with me?" he asked.

Sam, her back to him, closed her eyes for a second, then let out a breath. "Yeah. We want to watch with you."

Wade ruffled Tag's hair and grabbed Sam's hand. Which is how his date ended up being PG instead of his usual NC-17, or better yet, X.

Chapter 22

The season starts too early and finishes too late and there are too many games in between.

—Bill Veeck

The Heat played Washington at home in a five-day series, and went into the fifth game tied up two to two. Sam and Tag sat in the stands next to Holly, and at the first media break, Sam loaded up on snacks, handing Holly a full tray.

"You okay?" Holly asked.

"Of course. Why?"

Holly passed Tag the tray. "Go for it, dude."

"Sweet!" Tag said, and dug in. When he was occupied, Holly said quietly to Sam, "You look stressed."

Sam slunk down in her seat. It was a sunny, gorgeous, warm day. The air was scented with fresh cut grass and sea salt. The stands were filled with hometown fans. Sitting up here like this was as comfortable as being at home. "I'm out of control," she whispered.

"Work?"

"Among other things."

Holly smiled. "You know what's good for stress?" She leaned in close and lowered her voice. "Sex with your big, bad, sexy pretend boyfriend." She put air quotes around *pretend*.

"Ha. Thanks for the tip."

"Anytime." Holly turned forward to watch Pace pitch and Sam spent the next inning watching her big, bad, sexy "boyfriend" work his magic on the field.

Tag was sitting on her other side, eating more than five truck drivers, but totally into the game. Whenever Wade came up to bat, Tag held his breath along with Sam. He jumped up and cheered and yelled along with Sam. He swore at the umpire along with Sam. And when, at the bottom of the third inning, Wade hit a homer the two of them jumped up and down, and then turned to each other and hugged. Sam felt his scrawny arms go around her and her heart swelled until it was too big for her chest. "I love watching games with you."

With a grunt, he sank back to his seat and stuffed the last of his third hot dog into his mouth.

Sam looked at Holly, who laughed and shook her head.

"And you're having fun with me, too," Sam said to Tag, suddenly needing to hear it, needing to know he wasn't still pining away for home too badly, feeling as lost as she had for most of her childhood.

"Uh-huh," he said, mouth full, still focused on the game. "Even though you make me use soap every night."

At the bottom of the fourth inning, Tag groaned.

"Tag?" Sam's brow knit. He was green. "You okay?"

He opened his mouth and threw up.

She got him to the clubhouse where he threw up some more.

And some more.

Sam panicked. She'd never had so much as a hamster. For all she knew, he was dying of some horrible disease. Whipping out her phone while Tag hunched miserably, bow-ing to the porcelain god, she called medical and brought them in from the dugout.

By this time, Tag had started to feel better, but he gamely answered the medic's questions.

"What did you eat?" the medic asked after checking his vitals.

"Four hot dogs, popcorn, and a soda."

The medic gestured with his chin to Tag's pockets. "And?"

Tag slid uneasy eyes to Sam but didn't answer.

"What?" she asked. "What aren't you telling me?"

Tag remained mute, and after exchanging a look with the medic, Sam hunkered down on her knees, level with Tag, who was still sitting on the floor next to the toilet. "Okay, let's do this," she said. "You tell me whatever it is that you're not telling me, and I won't get mad."

"Promise?"

Oh, boy. "Promise."

Tag pulled out a can of tobacco.

Sam gasped. "I told you that you couldn't have any of that."

"I took it from Santos."

"Define took."

He hesitated. "You promised not to get mad."

She drew a deep breath and looked at the medic. "Is he going to be okay?"

"You'll need to hydrate him." The medic gave Tag a long look. "And he'll need to lay off the chew until he's legal."

She gave Tag ginger ale to settle his stomach, and when he swore he was all better, they went back to the game.

Holly smiled at their return. "So maybe only two hot dogs next time?" she asked Tag.

"Yeah," Tag said with a sigh.

At the top of the fifth inning, the Nationals third baseman popped a foul. Wade tossed off his mask, keeping his face up as he ran back and back . . .

He caught the ball and hit the fence at the same time, right at a fencing joint, which was a steel pole. At the impact, he crumpled to the ground.

By some miracle, the ball didn't pop out of his glove but stayed tight in the mitt, and the Nationals player was out.

The crowd went crazy.

But Wade didn't move.

Pace ran off the mound toward him. Gage always moved with easy, economical grace, no unnecessary movements, but even he jogged out of the dugout at the sight of Wade so utterly still. Sam was already on her feet, trying to get a better view.

"Is he okay?" Tag asked.

With Pace and the coaches hunkered over him, she couldn't see.

"He's not moving." Tag tugged on her arm. "Do you see him moving?"

Sam's gut was too tight to answer. Wade had tossed off his headgear to catch the ball, so when he'd hit the pole and then the ground at full force, he'd had no head protection at all.

Around her, the crowd had grown eerily quiet, anxiety and worry humming across the field. Holly quietly slipped her hand in Sam's.

Just wriggle a damn toe, she thought, shielding her eyes from the piercing sun to watch what was happening down on the field. *Just a single toe and then I'll be able to take a breath—*

"Maybe his brains are leaking out," Tag said, looking serious and solemn and a little frightened. "Do you think his brains are leaking out?"

Sam drew a sharp breath but slipped her arm around him. "No, I do not."

"Okay." He was quiet for a single heartbeat. "Look, the same guy who helped me is helping him. It's probably just broken bones. Maybe he can get one of those wheel-chairs with the motor in it."

"I'm also hoping no broken bones." *Move*, she silently begged Wade. *Get up . . .*

Nothing.

And then finally she saw a foot kick out, and she nearly dropped to her seat in overwhelming relief. The people huddled around Wade moved back to give him some room. He sat up, nodded in response to whatever Gage was say-ing, and got slowly to his feet. To the relieved cheers of the crowd, he walked unaided, but he immediately left the dugout with three staff members.

Leaving Tag with Holly, Sam raced down to the club-house to see him, but security was blocking the medical room, letting no one through, not even her. The place was completely closed off until the end of the game.

Her thoughts were racing in tune to her heart. What if he wasn't okay? *Focus, Sam, focus . . .* She needed to tell the press something—*Jesus, screw the press*, she thought. Why should she worry about the press when her heart was lying on the other side of that door? She whipped out her cell phone and called Gage, who told her to sit tight, he'd let her know Wade's status ASAP.

Wade didn't return to the game.

Gage didn't call her. Her cell phone was going crazy with media outlets wanting the scoop. The Heat lost seven to six, and afterwards, Sam rushed Tag back to the club-house, hoping for at least a glimpse of Wade.

She didn't get it.

Instead, she finally got her call from Gage, saying that she could report that Wade had been taken in for X-rays and more information would be forthcoming soon. After doing that, she stood in front of Wade's locker and eyed his things. His street clothes were there, and the crumpled, dirty jersey that had been taken off him. She picked it up, clutched it to her chest, and felt her eyes burn.

Pace came up behind her and set a hand on her arm. "You hear anything?"

She blinked the tears back and took a deep breath. "Official word is he's getting X-rays."

Pace just looked at her.

"Unofficially? I've heard nothing." She glanced down at her phone to make sure.

Pace reached into Wade's locker and lifted Wade's phone. "He didn't grab his stuff." He put the phone back down and scrubbed a hand over his face, which was lined with worry.

Her phone rang and she quickly answered. "Okay, possible slight concussion," Gage said. "Bruised but not cracked ribs."

She let out a low breath, disconnected, and repeated Gage's words for Pace, who squeezed her shoulder and moved off to shower and change.

Sam laid Wade's jersey on the bench, smoothed it out, running a finger over his number, imagining colliding with that fence at full speed and hitting the ground as hard as he had. A lump clogged her throat. When Wade's cell phone vibrated, she jumped, then automatically leaned in to read the ID.

Dad.

That's all the readout said, and she bit her lower lip, staring at it. What if his father watched every game? What if he'd been on the edge of his seat, missing his son, aching to be there in person, and he'd seen Wade get hurt? He was probably waiting tensely for news.

None of your business, Sam, she told herself. *None. By your own doing, you and Wade aren't a real thing. You're just winging it.*

And having the occasional mutual orgasm.

That was it. *You do not answer his phone. He wouldn't want you to.*

But the phone kept humming and vibrating, and with a low exhale of breath, she grabbed it. "Hello?"

There was a pause, then the low, throaty laugh of a man who sounded as if he'd been smoking for two hundred years. "Well, well. Who's the pretty lady answering my son's phone?"

"Samantha McNead," she said. "Publicist for the Heat." *And your son's occasional booty call partner.*

"I don't suppose Wade would be around?"

"No, I'm sorry. He's . . ." She didn't want to alarm him, especially on the off chance he hadn't seen the game. "Temporarily unavailable."

Wade's father laughed again, heartily. "Darlin', that boy has been *temporarily unavailable* all his damn life. Can you get him a message for me? One that he'll actually listen to?"

She sincerely doubted there was a soul on earth who could make Wade O'Riley listen if he didn't want to. "I can get him a message," she said carefully.

"Tell him I'm at the bus station. I made the trip, the least he can do is pick me up."

"You're in Santa Barbara?"

"That I am. Tell him to hurry, darlin'. It's damn hot out here today."

Sam looked across the clubhouse at Tag, who was sitting in a huge leather recliner, playing his Game Boy, quietly waiting for her. That he was quietly waiting for her at all had a whole lot to do with Wade, and the patience and understanding he'd shown Tag.

She owed Wade for that.

She took a deep breath. "Wade had a game today," she said into the phone. "He's . . . a little busy at the moment."

"Yeah." His father sighed. "He usually is."

She pictured an older man, all alone, tired and hungry from his long trip, and her gut twisted. "No, he . . . there was a problem. He—"

"I know. He's got things to do, places to go, people to meet. It's okay. I'll just . . . wait."

"I'll make sure you get a ride," she said. "Just stay right where you are." She didn't want to leave the facilities now, not without seeing Wade if at all possible, but she knew that wasn't going to happen for a while anyway. She looked around for someone that she could task with going to the bus station, but she couldn't put that on anyone without invading Wade's privacy even further. So in the end, she grabbed Tag and her things, and then she was driving through town toward the bus station.

Darlin', that boy's been temporarily unavailable all his damn life.

Gage called her again just as she arrived at the bus station. "He's on the DL. Day-to-day status. Probably only going to be off a few days, but with the slight concussion and those banged-up ribs, we want to be careful."

"Is *slight* the official word, or the real word?" she asked.

"Both." Gage was as tough as they came, but his voice softened. "He's really going to be fine, Sam. You know how it works. The disabled list just gives him a few days recovery, that's all. I'll call you when he's released from the ER."

The relief left her weak-kneed. "Does he need a ride?" she asked, even while knowing Wade wouldn't need for anything. He was a big-ticket player, and the Heat took care of their own exceptionally well.

"I've got him," Gage confirmed.

Sam parked at the bus station, and with Tag in hand, she crossed the street, eyeing the benches lined with people. The far right bench had only one man on it, and he stood as she stepped onto the curb. Tall, lanky, and lean, with a weathered face and a mop of gray wavy hair falling over his temple, he looked like a California surfer plus half a century. Contradicting his years, he wore a loud Hawaiian shirt over a set of cargo shorts and mirrored Ray-Bans, which he lifted to the top of his head, leveling a set of green eyes on her, and she knew.

John O'Riley.

"Hello," she said, holding out her hand. "Samantha McNead."

"Aren't you the prettiest publicist I've ever seen." He reached out to shake her hand but his hand was already occupied. He glanced at the brown sack in his fingers as if he'd forgotten the alcohol was there, then shrugged apologetically. "Liquid courage."

Sam wondered how he'd pulled off traveling with an open container, but then her gaze shot up the street and she saw the liquor store.

John took a sip and staggered unsteadily on his feet. "Sorry. My feet aren't what they used to be."

Tag appeared fascinated. "Are you drunk?"

"Nope. Never." John tipped his nose down at him. "Are you Wade's?"

"No!" Sam grabbed Tag's hand. "He's my nephew, Tag."

"Well, hello-ooo, Tag." John tossed his "liquid courage" into a trash bin. "And good-bye, Jack Daniel's. I'll miss you." He sighed dramatically. "That was my last drink. I'm ready for my ride to Wade now, though knowing him, he's probably ordered you to try to dump me somewhere along the way."

Sam didn't have the heart to tell him that she hadn't told Wade about the visit at all, or that she was stepping over all sorts of boundaries. She didn't know how to explain it to herself, much less him. "Do you have a suitcase?"

"Bus people lost it. Bastards," he said amicably.

"Bastards," Tag repeated gleefully, rolling his lips inward when Sam gave him a look.

"Maybe we could make a quick stop, darlin'?" John asked Sam. "I need a few things."

She had a hundred things to do. A thousand. The first and foremost being checking in on Wade. She needed to report to the news outlets, check on the schedule . . . But she'd started this, she had to finish it. She couldn't ditch him now. "Okay," she said. "A quick stop."

"So how did Wade talk you into doing this for him?" John asked as they walked to the car. He tripped over the curb and nearly fell.

Sam quickly locked her arm in his. "I'm just doing him a favor."

"Ah." John nodded and patted her hand. For a quick beat, his easy smile faded, revealing the anxiety beneath. "Nice of you."

"Everything's going to be okay, Mr. O'Riley."

"John. Call me John." He looked into her eyes, his mouth curved. "And I bet you make a good publicist, don't you?"

She decided not to comment on that. In her car, John

fastened his seat belt and slid his sunglasses back on. "It's bright in California."

Sam checked Tag in the rearview mirror, making sure he had his seat belt on, then pulled out of the lot. "So what brings you to Santa Barbara?"

"My mule-headed son." John looked out the window at the ocean on his right. "I need something from him, and though he doesn't know it, he needs something from me, too."

She didn't want to argue with the man, but the truth was, Wade didn't need much from anyone. "You mentioned a quick stop?"

"I need clothes. And cigarettes."

"Tobacco makes you sick," Tag said from the backseat in an *I learned this the hard way* tone.

John slid him a look. "You're a quick one, aren't you?"

"The quickest."

Sam's phone chirped. It was Gage again. "He's been released and is sore as hell, but everything's okay."

She released a pent-up breath. "Is he home?"

"He will be, soon enough."

Sam pulled into Walmart and looked at John. "Is this okay?"

"Sure."

Sam rushed out of her door and ran around to help him before he stumbled again, but he seemed surer on his feet now. "It's the damn shoes," he murmured. "The laces get me every time."

He was wearing slip-on athletic shoes. No laces. Sam locked arms with him. He leaned on her and grinned. "You're sweet. Are you Wade's?"

"That's . . . complicated."

He sighed mightily. "It always is."

"Tag," Sam said. "Grab my purse?"

Tag handed it over and they all went inside Walmart, stopping at the McDonald's first to get John a large coffee to help the sobering up process along.

Then John settled into one of those motorized scooters and took off with a wave toward menswear. Tag hopped into another motorized scooter and would have followed except that Sam blocked his path.

"Aw, man," Tag said.

She occupied him by taking him to the electronics aisle, where she called Wade's house to no avail as Tag picked out a light saber that made the most god-awful, obnoxious sounds on earth.

"Stand back, Earthling," Tag demanded and playfully jousted Samantha in the gut.

"Ow."

"You're supposed to fall to the floor in agony and die a slow, painful death," he said with some disappointment.

"Maybe later," Sam said. "Let's go find John."

With a sigh, he hit a button and the neon green "laser" telescoped in on itself, collapsing.

"Cleanup on aisle eight," said an annoyed voice over the loud speaker.

With a very bad feeling, Sam craned her neck and took in the sign over aisle eight. *Wine and Beverages*.

Crap. "Come on," she said, bum-rushing Tag over there, where she found three employees mopping the floor and a case of Jack Daniel's shattered at their feet.

"What happened?" she asked them.

One of the employees wielding a mop shook his head. "No one saw anything."

Sam dragged Tag up and down the aisles, looking for John. They found him at the checkout. He smiled broadly at them as he unloaded his things onto the conveyor belt. Socks, underwear, another pair of cargo shorts, another brightly colored Hawaiian shirt, and a basketball.

And two bottles of Jack.

"I thought you quit," she said.

"I did. These are in case it doesn't stick."

Sam nearly rolled her eyes, thinking of course it wasn't going to stick if he had his crutch readily available, but she bit her tongue. She couldn't comprehend an addiction of this caliber . . . and it wasn't really her place to get involved. A thought that almost made her laugh out loud. She was already way more involved than she should be.

Back in her car, she tried Wade's house again, still no answer. She called Pace, and confessed what she'd done just in case someone had to locate her body.

"Problem?" John asked when she'd hung up.

"No. No problem." Pace had assured her he'd have done the same thing. Didn't make her feel any better about blindsiding Wade with his father, even though it'd been entirely accidental.

"Darlin'."

She met John's gaze, his eyes surprisingly sober now. "He has no idea I'm here, does he?" he asked.

She grimaced. "Not exactly."

"Then what, exactly?"

"There was a game today."

"There's always a game."

"Yeah, but today Wade body-slammed into a fence," Tag said. "He caught the ball though. It was pretty sweet."

John looked at Tag, then back to Sam. "Is he hurt?"

"Slight concussion and bruised ribs," Sam said.

"Take me to him."

She understood the sentiment. She just wasn't sure Wade was going to appreciate it.

Chapter 23

Sports do not build character. They reveal it.

—Heywood Hale Broun

Once Wade was released from the hospital, Gage drove him back to the Heat's facilities. Wade moved slowly and carefully into the clubhouse, greeted by his agent and trainers. He heard Gage give a quick statement to the press, and wondered why Sam hadn't done it. He told himself it didn't matter that she hadn't waited to see if he was okay.

Didn't matter at all.

She had Tag to worry about, and . . . and hell, he'd been alone for most of his life, he didn't need anyone to hold his hand just because he hurt like a mother. At his locker, he picked up his things including his phone and noticed the twelve missed calls.

"Hey."

Wade very carefully turned around, wincing at the movement in both his ribs and head, and found Pace sitting in one of the leather chairs, sprawled out comfortably. But after four years of being together, Wade knew that the lazy pose was deceptive. "Hey yourself."

"Word is you're going to live."

"Apparently so."

Pace pushed to his feet and came closer, looking him over carefully.

"I'm not circling the drain," Wade said. "At least not yet."

"Well, that's a relief. Come on, I'll take you home."

"Gage has a car out front for me."

"I have a car, too." Pace grabbed Wade's duffel bag and slung it over his shoulder, adding it to his own bag. He opened the front doors of the facility for Wade and waited for him to go out first.

"You know something I don't?" Wade asked him, bemused.

Pace tossed their two bags in the back of his car. "You scared the shit out of me."

"Aw, that's sweet."

Pace didn't look amused. "I don't want to pitch to anyone but you, Wade."

"Is this going to end in a marriage proposal, cuz I'm not sure Holly—"

"God, you are such a dick."

"Don't be mad. I love you, too."

"Laugh all you want," Pace said. "But I need you to remember exactly how much you love me when you feel the need to kill someone later tonight. I want you to also remember that if you're in jail, I can't pitch to you."

Wade's smirk faded. "What the hell are you talking about?"

Pace didn't answer as he drove them out of the parking lot and hit the highway. Night had fallen. The moon was sitting on the horizon, a few inches above the Pacific Ocean, casting a blue glow over the rugged mountain bluffs.

"You going to tell me what's going on?" Wade asked.

"You access any of your messages yet?"

"No."

"Your father's in town."

Wade shook his head. "No, he's not. He's still in Oregon."

"He bailed." Pace pulled up to Wade's house. "And here's the biggie—he's here. As in inside."

Wade stared at the car in his driveway.

Sam's.

The sight of her car gave him a rush, but his brain was feeling a little sluggish from the hit it'd taken earlier. Pain from that, mixed in with the news from Pace, suddenly blossomed into a full-fledged migraine. He opened Pace's passenger door and started to get out but Pace snagged the back of his shirt. "Remember what I said. Remember I'll only pitch to you, and that if you do anything stupid, I can't do that. Plus you don't want to go to jail. You'd hate being Bubba's bitch."

"Bubba?"

"Probably he's three-hundred-fifty pounds and would expect you to squeal. I mean you're not really my type, but he might think you're pretty."

Wade just looked at him. "You need help," he finally said.

Pace turned off the car and started to walk Wade to the door. Wade blocked his way. "Go home to Holly, Pace."

"You shouldn't be alone."

"I'm getting the feeling I'm not going to be alone. Go home," he repeated. "I'll deal with whatever's waiting for me."

Pace stopped and sighed. "Call me if you need me."

"Yeah." Bells were going off in Wade's head. Hard to

tell if it was his concussion, or just a general sense that his life was about to go straight into the toilet.

He was betting the latter.

Sam was sitting on Wade's couch holding her breath when his front door opened.

He walked in wearing a T-shirt and washed-out Levi's. Hands on hips, he looked at the group in his living room. His gaze touched first on Sam and Tag, softening on both of them before locking in on his father.

The softness vanished and the air crackled with tension as he turned and tossed his bag aside with slightly more violence than necessary.

"Hello, son." This from John. "How are you?"

Wade just looked at him.

"I guess you're surprised to see me, huh? Samantha was kind enough to give me a ride."

Wade sent Sam a look that made her squirm before turning to Tag. "Hey, man," he said.

"Hey. Your head okay?"

"I'll live."

Tag waited a beat. "You going to start drooling or anything? Cuz that's what happens sometimes with head injuries."

"This is more of a brain problem," Wade said, and looked right at Sam. "It's on overload and might explode."

She winced.

And John sighed. "Always was dramatic," he said to Sam.

Tag looked back and forth between father and son. "So . . . you guys in a fight or something?"

"No," John said.

"Yes," Wade said at the same time.

Tag was playing with the basketball that John had gotten from Walmart, trying to twirl it on his fingers as John had taught him. The guy might be a drunk but he was incredibly athletic. Not a surprise really, considering Wade's abilities.

Wade watched Tag fumble with the ball a moment, then slid a look at his father. "Your doing, I assume."

John nodded. "It's just not quite as impressive to twirl a baseball, sorry."

Wade just shook his head. "Tag?"

"Yeah?"

"I got a bunch of new equipment delivered. Bats, gloves, athletic shoes. Want to look through it?"

Tag dropped the basketball. "Yeah!"

"Second room on the left at the top of the stairs."

"You rock!" Faster than lightning, Tag was gone.

Sam watched Wade walk into his open kitchen. He pulled open the refrigerator door and grabbed a beer. He wasn't moving with his usual, smooth easy stride. She knew he had to ache like hell, and when he put a hand to his ribs, she ached right along with him. She stood up, thinking he needed to be in bed, preferably with an ice pack for his ribs, since he hadn't been given pain killers because of his slight concussion. "Are you really okay?" she murmured.

"Fan-fucking-tastic."

"Wade—"

"Really?" John asked from the couch as Tag came back down the stairs carrying a new bat and glove. "No hello, Dad, great to see you? Not even a fuck you?"

Tag's eyes got big at the forbidden F-word, and he opened his mouth to repeat it but Wade pointed at him, then twisted off the top of his beer and tossed it over his shoulder into the sink. "Watch your language in front of the kid," he said to his father.

Sam moved closer to Wade and put her hand over his on the beer. "Wade, I think alcohol's a bad idea."

"Why, because I'm forty percent more likely to be an alcoholic since my father's one? Well, guess what, Princess? My mother was a drunk, too, so I believe that gives me an *eighty*-percent chance." He gestured with his beer. "Bottoms up."

Sam's heart constricted at the pain in his voice, the one that matched the pain in his eyes, and she realized there was a whole hell of a lot more going on between father and son here than she could understand. "I only meant it's a bad idea because of your concussion," she said quietly.

Obviously not caring, he tipped the bottle up to his lips, then lowered it before taking a sip with a softly uttered, "Goddammit." He set the bottle on the counter with more force than necessary and drew a deep breath.

"Actually," John said. "Your mother always was more of a social drinker than an alcoholic."

Wade narrowed his eyes but didn't speak. He didn't have to, his eyes spoke volumes.

John patted his hands down his body as if looking for something. Like a flask.

No one spoke.

"Maybe I'd better go," Sam said.

Wade turned to her for the first time, his eyes dark and dilated. "I'd like to talk to you first."

She just bet he did. "Oh. Well, it's late, and—"

He wrapped his fingers around her arm, his grip inexorable. "Now."

"Yeah." She nodded. "Okay."

He pulled her out into the hall and pressed her back

against the wall. His mouth was tight, his body even more so as he held her arms. "How?" he asked in a low, controlled voice. "Why?"

"He called your cell phone."

"Yeah? So? He always calls my cell phone."

Their gazes locked for a long moment while she considered how to reply.

"You answered it," he said.

"It said *Dad* on the ID, and you'd just been hurt," she said in her defense.

He blew out a breath. "I'm doubting he knew that."

She didn't tell him that was the truth. "I saw his name and I thought . . . I don't know. I guess I thought family is family, and—"

"Hell, Sam. You should know better than anyone that blood ties don't necessarily make a family."

She stared up at him, knowing he was right, so damn right. "He said he needed a ride," she whispered. "And I pictured a helpless old man—"

"That man is the *opposite* of helpless."

"Well, I'm beginning to see that now." She winced. "And he thinks he's staying with you."

He leaned into her, and over her shoulder thunked his head to the wall, which had to hurt.

"I realize he arrived without your knowledge or permission," she said softly. "And I'm sorry if you're upset that I gave him a ride from the bus station, but he would have found one here with or without me."

"Don't be so sure. There are plenty of bars between the bus depot and here."

She'd seen Wade in tense situations before. After a bad loss. Before a big game. Having a disagreement with Gage. When Pace had needed surgery in the middle of last season.

But never once had she seen him be anything but cool and calm and unflappable about all of it.

He wasn't close to any of those things now, and it was an entirely new side to him. "You're furious with me because I invaded your privacy. I'm sorry, Wade."

Still leaning on her, his head against the wall, he craned his neck and met her gaze, his brimming with hostility, and even worse, a vulnerability she knew he hated. It was that, more than anything else, that put her heart in her throat. "I screwed up, and I *am* sorry. But you can't just ignore him."

"Why not? He spent the first eighteen years of my life ignoring me."

"Was it always just you and him?"

"No, it was him and his booze. I wasn't really much of a factor. I've asked him for years to quit, he was never interested. Now he gets a health scare and is staring his mortality in the face, and suddenly he's all about quitting. He has it in his head that he needs me in order to do it. He needs a relationship before it's too late."

Sympathy filled her, but the look on his face dared her to show a single ounce of pity or he'd toss her out the same way he intended to toss out his father. The way he'd challenged her *not* to toss out Tag. "He did mention the senior center was for the elderly," she said. "Which apparently he doesn't consider himself. I'm not sure I understand a lot about addiction, but I do know that just asking someone to quit is rarely enough motivation. It doesn't mean he doesn't want to. Or that he doesn't love you."

He stared at her for a long beat, but whether he was soaking that all in or planning her death, she didn't know. "He's timeless, you know," he finally said. "Probably even immortal due to the fact that he's spent so many years carefully and purposely pickling himself, preserving his parts for the next millennium." He sighed and scrubbed a hand over his jaw, which had two days of stubble on it. But it didn't escape her notice that he was still leaning on her, holding her against the wall, as if he were too tired to hold himself up on his own.

"Maybe if you help him out," she murmured. "He'll do this. Really quit."

He let out a harsh laugh. "I've heard it a thousand times, Princess."

He looked exhausted, his eyes lined with pain, so she was well aware that she was risking her neck by wrapping her arms around him. "You have nothing to feel ashamed of, Wade."

"I'm not ashamed. I'm pissed off. Did you search him for alcohol?"

At the flicker of guilt she couldn't hold back, he ground his back teeth together. "What?"

"We stopped at the store."

"Jesus. Don't tell me you bought him some."

"By accident!"

Once again he *thunked* his head on the wall just over her shoulder.

She slid a hand up between his forehead and the wall. "You're going to hurt yourself even more."

"Not possible."

"Look, I threw the alcohol out, okay? I'm sorry but your dad can be a little slippery."

He let out a short laugh, his tone saying it wasn't actually funny, and left his forehead against her hand, rubbing his head back and forth against her palm.

"Wade." She ran her other hand up his back, aching for him again. *Still.* She let her fingers brush over his temple as she gently tipped his head up to look at him. "I'm so sorry."

He caught her wrist so that she couldn't keep touching him, in spite of the fact that he still had her pinned to the wall with his entire lower body. "Don't."

She had no idea what the gruffly uttered word meant. *Don't talk? Don't care?* Far too late for that. His body's heat radiated through her. She stirred a little, curling into him, careful with his ribs, wanting only to soothe, to offer him some gentleness. "Let me check him into a hotel somewhere nearby, and I'll come back to take care of you."

His eyes were dark. "What did you have in mind?"

"You in bed."

"I like it so far. Keep going."

"You in bed, *asleep*," she corrected.

He sighed.

She stared up into his face, deeply tanned from the long hours out in the sun, though not enough to hide those shadows beneath his eyes or the pain tightening his mouth. His eyes were dilated, but she suspected that was still temper, and yet when she snuggled into him, she could feel his body stirring with a different sort of tension altogether.

He was hard. "You have a concussion," she marveled. "Bruised ribs. You have to hurt like hell, not to mention you're mad at me. How can you even think about sex?"

"God-given talent." He slid a hand down her back and cupped her ass.

And now it was *her* body stirring. Hell, who was she kidding? Her body was addicted to his. She'd reacted to him the minute he'd walked in the door. "Wade."

His mouth brushed her neck. And then her jaw . . . He made his slow, purposeful way to her mouth and as she made a low sound of helpless arousal, he wrapped his arms tight around her and kissed her with a lot of tongue and temper and desperation.

"We have to deal with your dad," she murmured.

With another rough breath, he let her go and turned away, temper winning. "Don't worry about the hotel. Just get Tag out of here before my dad teaches him any more bad tricks. The rest is my problem, not yours."

Sam hated doing as Wade asked, but short of forcing herself on him, she had little choice. So she took Tag home, tucked him into bed, and then herself. Lying there staring at the ceiling, she thought about Wade's father, and then hers, who'd never so much as checked on her and Tag. She chewed on that for a while, his utter lack of support with the Jeremy thing, the complete non-help he'd given her with Tag, and she knew they had to talk. She was finally over being a part of the McNead empire. There in the dark, she nodded at her decision. It was a good one. And for the first time since Wade had hit the post, she relaxed.

First thing the next morning, she was back at Wade's, knocking with determination on his door.

No one answered.

She looked back at her car. Tag was bouncing on the front seat eating an Egg McMuffin. Breakfast of champions. She reassured herself that she wasn't a bad pseudo-parent, that this was only the second day this week that she'd fed him fast food.

Okay, third.

But she was going to work on that. Really, she was.

Unfortunately she had a crazy schedule today. She had a Heat team meeting to get to in one hour, then she'd take Tag to the tutor's and herself back to work, where she had

to oversee an ET photo shoot, finish organizing the upcoming charity dinner, and arrange for several etiquette
workshops for the bull pen players per Gage's order. She
had a conference call scheduled with her father as well, at
her own request. He wasn't going to like their conversation, as she was going to tell him she didn't plan on re-
newing her contract for next season.

This McNead was going off on her own, thank you
very much.

She knocked on Wade's door again.

Still no answer. She pulled out her cell phone and called
Wade's. After two rings, the shade on the window next to
the front door opened.

Wade stood on the other side of the glass. He wore gray
sweatpants low on his hips, a wrap around his ribs, and
nothing else. His hair was wet from a recent shower and
messily falling over his forehead. His eyes were shadowed,
and so was the jaw he hadn't shaved.

He had his cell phone in his hand at his side, attitude
blaring from every pore of his mouth-watering body.

She met his gaze and waited expectantly with her phone
to her ear.

With a slow shake of his head, like maybe she was an
unfathomable pain in his ass, he opened his phone and put
it to his ear.

"Hi," she said.

He just lifted a brow.

She wished she could do that, convey so much with
one look. It sure would save a lot of time, something she
was extremely short of at the moment. "I brought you and
your dad breakfast." She hoisted the bag to show him. "Not
your beloved fries because it's too early, but I hear that
their Egg McMuffins clog arteries just as effectively."

He didn't smile. "How do you know my dad's still here?"

Ah, he speaks. "Because you wouldn't have kicked him out. Even though I'm sure you gave it more than a passing thought," she added politely.

He sighed and shoved his fingers in his hair. "I'm not opening this door to you. One houseguest is my limit at this time."

Ouch. But she'd figured he'd still be mad at her for interfering, even if she'd done so with only his best interests in mind. Telling herself she'd worry about the consequences later, she took another glance at Tag—still behaving—and opened the front door herself.

"I should have locked that," he said, slipping his phone into his sweatpants pocket.

She handed him a coffee.

"Bribery won't work."

She was betting otherwise. "Drink up."

He blew out a breath and did as she asked. She waited, and he drank some more, and they shared breathing space for a few minutes.

"Okay," he finally admitted. "So I needed caffeine."

She arched an agreeing brow and handed over the food.

He set the coffee down on the window ledge and opened the bag. Grabbing an Egg McMuffin, he sank his teeth into it.

She waited.

After another moment, he nodded.

"Feeling human again then?" she asked, keeping her smile to herself.

"I've got a start on it anyway."

"Good." Going up on her tiptoes, she brushed her lips over his. His eyes revealed their surprise. She rarely made the first move, instead letting him be the aggressor, sexual or otherwise. The realization startled her, and made her want to touch him more. She took a peek at Tag. His head was down. He was playing his Game Boy. "How are you feeling?" she murmured to Wade, setting a hand to his chest.

He looked down at her hand. "What did you have in mind?"

"Not the same thing you do."

He let out a breath. "I'm good enough to play today."

"You're on the DL."

"I'm good." His eyes darkened and he wrapped his fingers around her wrist. "Keep touching me like that and I'll show you how good."

"Your dad—"

"Sleeping off a hangover, no doubt."

"Nope. I gave that stuff up, remember?" John stepped in the foyer. He was dressed in yet another eye-popping Hawaiian shirt and cargo shorts, a newspaper tucked beneath his arm, looking chipper but a little edgy. The lack of alcohol was definitely getting to him. "Hello, kids."

Sam smiled and handed him a coffee.

"Thanks, darlin'." John eyed his son. "I meant what I said, Wade. I'm here to quit."

"And I meant what I said," Wade told him. "I catch you with an ounce of alcohol, even cough syrup, and this little *Brady Bunch* experiment is over."

John nodded. "I'll be in the other room. Don't want to cramp anyone's style."

"You're cramping my life," Wade said.

John's mouth curved. "At least you admit I'm in your life."

He was gone before Wade would comment on that but Sam heard the low, inaudible growl deep in his throat and gently pushed on his chest to hold him in place. "I see it's going well."

"Don't worry," Wade said, looking down at her. "I'm not going to kill him. Yet."

"Wade."

He closed his eyes. "Is this where you lecture me on being nice?"

"This isn't my job. I'm not going to lecture you on anything. I just wanted to say—"

"I don't want to talk about it."

"But—"

"Ever."

She studied his dark eyes, the muscle ticking in his jaw. "That's ridiculous."

"Really?" he asked. "Because I seem to remember a situation in reverse, only a few weeks back, when Tag got delivered to you. You didn't want to talk about it. And you sure as hell didn't want help from me either."

True enough. "But I wasn't being stubborn and obstinate."

He laughed and pressed his fingers to his eyes.

"Okay, maybe I was a little."

"Yeah. Thanks for breakfast."

"But good-bye," she guessed. "Right?"

"Unless you're packing some TLC."

"Is that code for sex?"

He gave her a look that singed her eyebrows.

"Yeah," she said shakily. "It is."

He set down the bag and pressed her back against the foyer wall and kissed her. It wasn't soft and gentle. It was all heat and tongue and aggravation.

And all of her bones melted.

"Ah, jeez," came Tag's voice. *"Again?"*

Sam nearly leapt out of her skin as she jerked back from Wade. Tag had gotten out of the car and stood there slurping from his orange juice, studying them critically.

Into the silence, Pace drove up the driveway. He got out of his classic Mustang with a bag of McDonald's and eyed Tag's Mickey D's. "I'm too late."

"Pace!" Tag said with great pleasure, and took in Pace's warm-up sweats. "You going to practice?"

"Yep. Soon as I check on Wade here."

"They're *kissing.*"

"Are they?" Pace asked mildly, his eyes reflecting his amusement.

"Yeah. Can I ride in your car?"

"I'll take you to practice with me, sure. If it's okay with your Aunt Sam."

Tag whirled on Sam. "Yeah?"

A cab pulled up and honked.

Everyone looked at each other. *What now?*

"That's for me." John nudged his way past the four in the doorway, smiled at Tag, and headed down the walk.

"Where are you going?" Wade asked him.

"Progress that you even asked. I'm off to my first AA meeting."

"You've been to AA a hundred times. A thousand."

"Maybe a thousand and one is the charm."

Wade frowned as his father waved over his shoulder and got into the cab, which drove off. He looked at Sam, his gaze inscrutable though she was pretty sure it still had retribution in it. *Oh, boy.* "Time to go, Tag," she said.

"I want to go watch Pace practice. Please?"

Pace tossed Tag his keys. "Wait for me in the car. Just don't take it for a spin without me."

"Next time?"

"When you're sixteen, we'll talk. Go." Pace looked at Sam and Wade. "You two going to play nice?"

"I always play nice," Sam said.

Wade let out a barely there snort.

Pace grinned. "Just don't do anything I wouldn't do." He nudged Sam. "Don't worry about the kid. You know where we'll be."

And then it was just her.

And Wade.

Who stood there bare-chested in just those sweatpants, that edible body tense and unhappy. "I feel like this is my fault," she said.

He softened with a low sigh. "It's not. Okay, it is . . . but it's not."

"You're hurting."

"Yeah. Want to kiss it better?" He ran a finger over her collarbone, then along the edges of the deep V-neck of her dress.

Her breath caught.

He closed his eyes as his finger slid beneath the material. A muscle jumped in his jaw, then he opened his eyes again and stepped back. "You should probably go to your meeting."

That had been her plan but now she wanted to stay and have him keep touching her. "Not for forty-five minutes."

"Sam," he said warningly. "I'm pissed off and really want to stay that way."

"Pissed off isn't productive to healing."

Again, he ran a finger over her neckline. "What are you wearing beneath the dress?"

Empathy and lust warred within her, along with a genuine, bone-deep affection that shouldn't have surprised her but did. She already knew she liked him, more than she'd meant to, more than she'd ever wanted to. Her dress was just another wrap dress, professional and relatively modest, and not at all overtly sexy in any way. Except that when Wade looked at her like that, with frustration and heat, with those green eyes at half mast, she felt sexy as hell. "Maybe you should find out yourself."

As agile-minded as he was able-bodied, he reached around her to hit the lock on his front door. "Best idea I've heard all morning."

Chapter 24

The best way to catch a knuckleball is to wait until the ball stops rolling and then pick it up.

—Bob Uecker

Wade pulled Sam in, his eyes quietly and powerfully intense, all the more so because she knew what it meant. He wore that look when he was on the baseball diamond and going for the win.

And he wore it when he was making love to her.

And did he make love. He was good at it, so damn good.

"I dreamed you started your own PR firm and left us," he murmured, pressing his mouth to her jaw.

She choked out a startled laugh even as she tilted her head to give him better access. "I'm thinking about it."

He lifted his head and stared at her, then nodded solemnly. "Yeah, you should. You'd be great."

"So in this dream," she said. "I was gone. Did you miss me?"

His hand splayed over her hip, playing with the tie on her dress. "More than I can say."

"Aw."

"Fucking pathetic." He pulled the tie until it gave.

"You're still hurting," she murmured, pressing a hand between her breasts, holding the dress together. "Probably you shouldn't be doing anything . . . strenuous."

He took her hands in his, spreading them out at her sides so that her dress loosened and unraveled, then slipped to her elbows, aided by his hands. He pushed her backwards until she bumped up against something.

The table behind the sofa in the living room.

On it sat a bowl with keys, a stack of mail, and Wade's wallet. Clearly the dumping grounds for his pockets when he walked into the door at night. With one sweep of his hand, the entire contents were knocked to the floor.

She gasped. "But your ribs—"

"I'll tell you when I need help."

"Your head—"

"Is fucked up," he granted. "But mostly just on the inside." He urged her up on the table, then stepped in between her legs, bringing himself up snug to her body.

With her dress hanging off her elbows, she could feel the soft cotton of his sweatpants on her inner thighs, the contrasting heat of his bare, hard abs against her softer body.

Then he kissed her. And Lord, the man could kiss. He slid his tongue to hers and kissed her until she was nothing but a puddle of pulsing need. She tried to go for his sweats but found her arms caught in her dress. "Wade."

He dipped his head to take in the sight of her sitting there, arms held at her sides, legs spread wide around his hips, wearing only a plain white cotton bra and matching bikini panties with a single tiny pink rose in the middle of the elastic edging. He ran a finger over that rose, then straight down between her legs, and heat shot through her body like lightning, centering on that fingertip.

"Pretty," he said, and unhooked her bra. He pushed it

and her dress off her arms, sending both to the floor. Dipping his head, he kissed her neck, making his way over her collarbone to her breast.

Her nipple.

Her belly . . .

He dropped to his knees, running his hands up from her feet to her inner thighs.

She gripped the table on either side of her for all she was worth. "*Wade*—"

His fingers hooked in the sides of her panties, then kissed her hip, his mouth lingering. "I'm going to put my mouth on you, Sam. I'm going to lick you until you come."

There was something about being naked and literally spread out for him, something about him being so fully in charge of the situation. She shouldn't like it. She really shouldn't. She was sure of it.

A single tug and her panties were gone, which left her in nothing but her heels. Nothing between her and his hot gaze, which had a front-row view of *exactly* how much she liked what he was doing. She held her breath as he let out a low, rough breath of his own, one filled with heat and hunger.

And then he leaned in and put his mouth on her.

She'd had lovers, some of them even very good. But still it tended to take her awhile to climax. It was because she had a hard time turning her mind off and completely letting go. And if it took too long, she'd been known to give up, even worse, been given up on.

She never had that problem with Wade. After the elevator episode, where she'd gone off for him in under five minutes, she'd attributed it to the alcohol, to the hotness factor that was Wade himself.

She hadn't yet worked up a reason for the wedding bathroom incident.

Or the backseat of her car.

Or today. Because after only about two minutes of having his mouth on her, that clever, oh-so-talented, greedy mouth, her toes were already curling.

"Good?" he murmured against her skin, then did something amazing with his tongue.

She cried out and arched up, unable to stop herself. "Better than my showerhead."

Letting out a soft huff of laughter, he slid his hands beneath her ass to pull her a little closer. "Nice to know."

"Don't stop. Please don't stop."

He didn't. Not even when she cried out his name and shattered.

Wade shifted his mouth to Sam's inner thigh as her shudders finally slowed. He loved her like this, all hot and bothered and breathing like crazy. "You okay?" he murmured against her soft, delicious skin, kissing her because he couldn't seem to stop.

Her fingers loosened their death-grip on his hair. "No. I'm blind."

He tilted up his head and felt a smile curve his mouth. "Your eyes are closed."

"Oh. Right." She opened them slowly, leveling the dreamy, dazed orbs on his, which cracked his heart wide open.

It was a shocking feeling, a new feeling, and he found himself just staring up at her, a bit stunned. He went to stand and felt a stab in his ribs, and shocked at the pain, sat back on his heels instead.

Sam hopped off the table and in just her heels, crouched at his side, her hand on his abs. "Your head or your ribs?"

"I'm fine."

"You're gray."

He let out a careful breath. "It's nothing. Christ, you should see how gorgeous you look right now in only those heels."

"You are such a guy." She helped him to his feet. "Come to the couch. Sit a sec."

He allowed her to draw him around to the couch, and then held on to her hand when she would have moved off.

"I was going to get you Advil from my purse." Her questioning eyes ran down his body, snagging on the tented front of his sweats.

"Advil isn't going to help my condition," he said.

"What will?"

"Looking at you."

She let him tug her closer so that one knee hit the couch next to his thigh. Surprising him, she used her own momentum to lift the other leg over and straddled him.

His eyes met hers as his hands went to her hips. "I'm already feeling a little bit better," he said.

"I think I can improve on that." She tugged his sweats down enough to wrap her hand around him and stroked. "How's this?"

He rocked helplessly up into her fingers, and pain speared through his ribs. He went very still and carefully didn't breathe. He didn't dare.

"Wade? Dammit—" She tried to lift herself off of him but he dug his fingers into her hips.

"No, don't," he grated out. "I just—I can't move like I want to," he admitted hoarsely.

"Then let me." She lifted up, guiding him to her, slowly, holding his gaze as she sank down on him. "Okay?" she whispered, eyes locked on his.

He could barely speak as she held him inside her body. "Yeah." He stared up at her, taking in her hair, long ago rioted from his fingers. She was still flushed, and she had a red mark on her jaw where he'd gotten her with his stubble. *She looked like she'd been claimed*, he thought.

As his.

And then she began to move, and as was usual when he was with her like this, he couldn't think at all.

"So," she murmured some time later. "Still mad at me?"

Cradling the warm, sated, naked woman in his arms, Wade stirred. His face was plastered against her sweet-smelling neck, her hair drifting in his eyes, a strand of it sticking to his unshaven jaw. He'd just had an orgasm that had rocked his world. In truth, he couldn't have summoned mad to save his life. "Let's go to my bed."

"I have a meeting," she said.

"Be late."

"Gage hates late."

"Not if there's a good reason."

She smiled. "According to Gage, the only acceptable reason to be late is death."

"Or sex."

She laughed, the woman he'd only meant to play with, the woman who instead had become the only steady hold on reality that he had. "I'm pretty sure the only sex Gage would consider as an excuse would be his." She rose off him and began to gather her clothes.

Watching a woman dress was usually fascinating for Wade, and one of his favorite pastimes. Well, actually, watching a woman *undress* was his favorite pastime.

But dressing was fun, too.

But now, all he could feel was the dull thump of his heart as he watched her pull on her panties and turn around, looking for her bra.

He scooped it off the coffee table and handed it to her, not letting go when she tugged. "It's not the meeting," he said.

"Of course it's the meeting." She yanked hard and he let go of the bra.

"It's the bed," he said. "I said *bed* and you got all flustered."

She covered her gorgeous breasts with her bra and hooked herself in without answering.

"Yeah," he said grimly, some of his after-sex glow fading. "The thought of my bed scares you."

"Don't be ridiculous."

"What then? Tell me."

She grabbed her dress off the floor. "Why would a bed scare me?"

"I don't know, we've never done it in a bed. Maybe a bed represents something other than sex. Maybe a bed says we mean more to each other than just a quickie on a couch."

"Or in a backseat," she said.

"Yeah, or an elevator." He held her gaze. "Or a bathroom."

"Wade." She covered her eyes and breathed in deeply. "Do we have to do this now?"

Quiet, a little unnerved at the urge he had to try harder to coax her into staying, he watched her nip and tuck herself together, then twist her hair up.

And voila.

In less than three seconds she went from sweet, warm, tousled Sam to all-business Sam.

Frightening how good she was at that.

She moved past him to the door, and he barely caught her hand.

She looked down at their entwined fingers instead of meeting his gaze, and suddenly he was forced to face an unsettling fact.

For the first time in his life, he wasn't trying to figure a way to get rid of a woman he'd just slept with. He wasn't running for the door. He wasn't working up an excuse or a pretty lie about why he had to go. Because he didn't want to get rid of her. He wanted more.

He honestly hadn't seen that one coming.

"I have to go," she whispered.

"Yeah." He waited until she met his gaze, her own unusually bright. "I see that." Still a little bowled over by his own thoughts, he dropped his hand from hers, watching as she stepped to the door.

"It's not what you think," she said, her back to him.

He'd never pushed for more with a woman, ever. It made him feel a little bit like he was standing balls-out-naked. *Oh, wait.* He *was* balls-out-naked. "What do I think, Sam?"

"That I don't want to be with you. I do." She paused, then turned to face him. "I do. But I know your terms, Wade. Light and fun and easy. Only sometimes something inside me forgets, and I have to back off to regroup."

At her words, his chest ached. "Sam."

"I just need to regroup," she repeated softly. "That's all. I'll see you later."

And with that, she was gone.

Sam ran into the meeting with one minute to spare. Gage looked up, then frowned. "You're almost late and you're . . . smiling. What's up?"

She'd noticed the smile in the rearview mirror on the way over here. Even with the seriousness of the conversation she'd had with Wade after the whole couch-sex thing, she couldn't get rid of it. Damn multiple orgasms. "Nothing."

He looked her over very carefully, then let out a low breath. "I could use a *nothing* smile like that."

Sam survived the meeting, and then the phone call with her father as she informed him of her intention not to re-sign her contract when the season was over, that she'd instead be starting up her own PR firm. She'd sounded cool and collected as she told him that she hoped he would hire her an as independent contractor to continue to run the Heat's PR needs, but that she'd have other clients as well, and would no longer be a McNead employee.

He'd argued. He was unhappy with her decision, and claimed that she was letting the family down, but she thought the truth of it was that he didn't want her out from beneath his thumb.

But for her it was as good as done. Maybe she couldn't choose her family, but she sure as hell could choose her own path.

And when she hung up, she was still smiling. Seems sex really did a body good.

She was still smiling that night over macaroni and cheese with Tag. But when she got up the next morning, the smile was finally gone. She lay in bed and thought about getting herself over to Wade's for another twelve-hour smile, but she couldn't come up with an excuse so she called him. "How are you?"

"Define okay," he said, his sleepy morning voice rough and sexy enough to make her nipples hard.

"Not a murder suspect would be good."

He blew out a breath. "Then I'm okay. At least for now. But don't worry, I've seen a lot of movies. I think I can get away with it without getting arrested."

"What's he doing?"

"Breathing."

"Is he drinking?"

"Oddly, no. At least not that I've caught him at. But he's eating me out of house and home, and he won't stop talking."

"Are you feeling better?" she asked. "Your head? Your ribs?"

"I can't feel anything but my blood pressure rising. Can your blood actually boil? I think mine's boiling."

"You need to watch a movie," she suggested. "Or eat some brownies. Relax."

"I've got a better way to relax."

She actually felt herself go damp. "Sex isn't the answer."

"Sam, sex is *always* the answer. Come over."

"By the time I got there, we'd only have five minutes."

"Five minutes is all I need."

"Maybe I need more." Like six. She could probably do it in six if they skipped the preliminaries and got right to it.

He sighed. "You're right. Maybe you'll come over tonight."

"I've got Tag and you have your dad."

"I'll hire us both babysitters, and we can sneak off. Maybe to the beach. Since a bed scares you, let's do it on the cliffs," he said, his voice husky, like he was already picturing it.

And now so was she . . . "Wade."

"See this," he said, "this is why life is better when it's all fun and games."

She laughed and disconnected, then woke up Tag for breakfast.

"Outta milk," he grumbled sleepily. "What are you going to put in your coffee?"

"You're worried about my coffee, or your Frosted Flakes?"

"That, too." He smiled sweetly.

Her heart tugged. She knew he wasn't missing his dad as much these days, if he'd ever really done so. Most likely what Tag had missed was being at the only home he'd known, and Sam wanted to think that she'd given him a more than decent replacement. Given the lack of recent complaining on his part, she figured she was at least on the right track. Problem was, she'd gotten herself good and attached to him, and knew that at the end of the three months, when Jeremy came for him, it was going to hurt like hell.

Apparently that was the story of her life. Fall in love for a predetermined amount of time, then get her heart stomped on. "How about we go out for breakfast?"

Tag sat straight up. "Really?"

"Not fast food this time, but really."

Tag leapt out of his chair and headed for the door.

"Bring your backpack, your tutor's meeting us at my office today."

"'Kay. Can we get pancakes with strawberries and whipped cream?" He batted his already gorgeous eyelashes at her, reminding her that someday in the not so far future, he was going to be charming girls with little to no effort. "I know how you love pancakes," he said, making her laugh.

She should have said no, but just as it was with Wade, it was also happening with Tag—she was losing her famed self-control. "If we hurry."

Chapter 25

No matter how good you are, you're going to lose one-third of your games. No matter how bad you are you're going to win one-third of your games. It's the other third that makes the difference.

—Tommy Lasorda

Wade pulled on a pair of running shorts and a T-shirt, and tried his usual morning run. He got a quarter of the way through his five-mile route before caving in to the rib pain, which sucked. He sank to the curb and called Pace. "Come get me."

"Can't. I'm in the middle of an ET shoot, and I'm looking damn fine, too, I should add."

Wade disconnected and called Sam. "Come get me?"

There was a beat of disbelieving silence. "I can't drop everything and have sex with you!" she whispered, clearly trying to sound appalled, but really sounding very interested instead. "I'm inspecting the hotel's ballroom for the auction." She paused. "How about later?"

He had to laugh, and didn't bother to explain. *Hell, no.* Not if she was going to give him a booty call out of the deal. "Later." He limped home and found his father passed out cold on the damn couch. "Ah, just like old times."

"Except I'm not hungover." John sat up, and Wade had

to admit, he wasn't drunk. He was bright-eyed and strung out, but not drunk.

And he was trembling ever so slightly. His entire body was in alcohol withdrawal. "You okay?"

"No, but I'll get there. Let's do something father/son-like. Bowling. Surfing. Anything."

Wade raised a brow.

"I'm serious."

"How about we just try to coexist."

"I need more." John paced. "I really need more to pull this whole quitting thing off." He looked down at his hands, which even when he fisted shook badly. "Need to," he repeated.

"You need a drink," Wade said flatly.

"More than I need air."

Wade let out a breath. "Go to rehab, dad. I'll take you. I'll pay."

"Don't you get it? I need more than your money, Wade."

Christ, and now Wade could hear Pace's voice in his head saying, *Writing a check won't solve everything.* "Look, you said you were tired of the trailer park and needed a house, so I bought you one. You got tired of the house and decided you needed freedom, so you sold it and lived on a campground with five other homeless guys until you got kicked out of there for disorderly conduct. Then you said you needed to be with others like you, so I found you a nice senior center—"

"They weren't like me, they were old."

"The median age was five years younger than you."

"I got bored."

"Ah. And now we get to it. You got bored and thought you'd try me on for a change."

"You say that like you were my last choice."

Wade let out a laugh. "Dad, I've always been your last choice."

John was quiet a long moment, and when he spoke, his voice was filled with regret. "I'm sorry for that, you know. I'm sorry for a lot of things. I've screwed up, but it was the alcohol, Wade. I've been lost in the alcohol."

"There are always choices. You made yours."

"Yes, and I'm making another one now." John's voice dropped to a near whisper, as if he were almost afraid to hear Wade's reaction. "I choose you."

Wade leaned back against the wall and closed his eyes. "Because you got sick, and scared."

"Better late than never, right? And don't you ever get scared? Scared of ending up alone like me?"

"Alone, maybe. Like you? No. I don't drink like you."

"But you push people away like me. Listen to me, Wade. My time is limited, and I'm not getting any younger. I don't want you to feel bad if something happens to me and we haven't made peace."

Wade opened his eyes, his gut clenching. "Did you learn something new from the doctor?"

"No."

The clenching eased slightly.

"People make mistakes," John said softly.

"Yeah." Wade ran his hand over his aching ribs. "Like miscalculating the distance between the plate and a fucking fence."

"You doing okay?"

Wade just looked at him.

"I know. I have no right to ask."

"Have you ever even seen a game, Dad?"

John was quiet for so long that Wade turned away, frustrated and disgusted at the both of them.

"What if I said I've seen every game," John finally said. "Including yesterday's?"

Wade turned back. "I'd say you're so full of shit your eyes are brown."

"Okay, I've *wanted* to see your games, but you never invited me."

Jesus.

"I've screwed up, okay? I am readily admitting that. But I want to fix it, I want to change."

"Then change."

"I'm working on it. Jesus, Wade, you don't give an inch, do you? It would help if I knew exactly what you're so mad at."

Wade just rolled his eyes.

"Hell, son, I've been drunk for thirty years. Help a guy out, throw me a bone."

"Okay. Let's start with kindergarten, which is the year I understood that no one else's dad passed out in their front yard every night, too drunk to get inside."

John winced. "Okay, my bad on that one."

"When I turned seven and reminded you it was my birthday, you gave me a flask of whiskey and then stole it back from me in the middle of the night. The next morning you told me the Easter Bunny did it."

"Christ." John closed his eyes. "Are you sure?"

"Yeah. I'm sure. And then there's how you got fired from every single job you ever even halfway held, including the school's janitor position, because you whipped out your dick to urinate in the principal's trash can while his secretary was in the room. That was a fun one to live down, by the way, so thanks for that."

John grimaced and scrubbed a hand down his face. "That one I remember. She called me a loser."

"You *were* a loser!"

There was a profound, sudden, thundering silence, and then John sank to the couch, looking sucker-punched. Wade felt like he'd just kicked a puppy, but even sick with it, he couldn't find it in himself to apologize.

"I kept you fed and clothed, you could give me that much," John whispered.

"I kept myself fed from working at McDonald's. And I kept you fed, too. I brought home food that I stole from work."

John swore beneath his breath and sighed, leaning his head back on the couch, eyes closed. "It's no excuse, but can't you see I wasn't thinking about anyone but myself? It was wrong of me, and I can't go back and change it, but I'm trying to change now." John opened his eyes. "I'm sorry that I didn't realize how much anger and resentment you were holding on to. But I guess I should have, since I'm holding on to stuff, too."

"Like what? What did I ever do to you?"

"Well, you never liked me much." John tried a smile to signal he was only kidding, clearly trying to lighten the mood, but Wade didn't feel light. For once in his life, he couldn't find the light and easy. Shoving his fingers into his hair to try to ease the pounding in his head, he turned in a slow circle away from his dad, coming to a dead stop at the sight of Sam standing in his opened doorway.

He'd wanted to see her. He'd wanted to kiss her, touch her . . . definitely lose himself in her, but she'd been standing there listening, soaking in things he hadn't wanted anyone to hear—

"I'm sorry," she whispered. "I've got to get back, but I came to . . ." She lifted a bag. "Lunch from the hotel."

"Ah, what a darlin'," John said kindly.

"Not hungry," Wade said.

"But you're always hungry." She winced, probably because she was remembering what she just heard about his childhood, about him stealing food.

Which was perfect. Just perfect. Now she felt sorry for him. "Thanks," he said. "Maybe another time." Gently as he could, he nudged her backwards over the threshold. Then shut the door in her face.

"No wonder I'm not a grandfather yet," John said, then shook his head. "You have some serious issues."

Wade rested his head on the door. His dad was right. He did have some serious fucking issues.

"That rudeness must come from your mother's side because I'd never have shut the door on that pretty face. Good to know I didn't screw you up all by myself."

Wade felt the muscles in his jaw clench, and he hauled open the front door in time to see Sam power-walking to her car. "Sam."

She looked up, gaze shuttered as he made his way to her. He tried not to wince but her eyes narrowed in on his ribs, though she remained silent.

"Where's Tag?" he asked.

"With his tutor. I have to get back to the hotel. I ran out on my meeting."

Since she didn't move, he took advantage, taking her hand so she couldn't escape. He looked back to make sure his dad was still in the house, and then pulled Sam a little farther away, out of earshot. They stood on the edge of the grassy bluff and looked at the ocean.

"If you're still looking for those five minutes," she said. "I've decided not to share them with you."

"Can't blame you." He closed his eyes and absorbed the sun, trying to find peace. It didn't come to him like it usually did. "I'm sorry I acted like an ass," he said quietly. "But you should know, it probably won't be the last time.

My dad brings it out in me, and I think he's staying. He seems to believe he can't quit drinking without me. And though I'd love to quit him, I don't seem to be able to just walk away this time."

"You want to believe he's really quitting."

He looked into her slay-me eyes. "Yeah."

She let out a breath. "Seems neither of us can cut our dads out of our lives entirely, even though neither of them has been much of a parent." She surprised him by taking his hand in hers. "I'd like to believe that makes us good people."

He nodded. "I'd like to believe that, too."

Her mouth curved slightly as she stepped close and slowly set her head on his shoulder with a sigh. "I suppose I can forgive you for being an ass."

He let out his own sigh and wrapped his arms around her. "Thank you."

The waves were low and mellow today, the sun the same. Looking down at Sam's head on his chest gave him the sense of peace he'd been looking for.

"Too bad we can't pick our families," she said, watching the water.

"Too bad."

She cocked her head and looked at him, really looked, as if she could see right through him. Aware that she now knew far more about his childhood than he was comfortable with, he had to resist the urge to squirm. "What?"

"I feel for the boy you were," she murmured. "So much. But mostly I'm glad you made it, and very proud of the man you've become, Wade. You should be, too."

He let out a breath and stroked a strand of hair off her face. "You have this way of getting straight to the heart of the matter, don't you?"

"I don't care that you have bad days. I don't care that you have a very busy life with lots going on. I care about the fact that all I can think about is how you said you were falling for me, or how in spite of myself, I'm doing the same. I only care that suddenly I feel like I'm hanging out here all alone because you've changed your mind."

He met her gaze. "I haven't."

"No?"

"No," he said firmly. "It's just that I thought we were moving along nice and slow, seeing where it takes us."

"Such as maybe some more elevators, bathrooms, and couches."

He let out a little smile. "Well, actually, I'm really hoping for that bed. I'm getting a little old for that back of the car shit."

"It's been a little crazy," she allowed, not committing.

Which was usually his MO, the not committing. "Yeah," he said, wondering where this was going. "Just a little crazy."

"And not quite the easy and light and fun you expected."

Unease settled in his gut like a lead ball. "True."

"Problem is, you didn't see the fatal flaw in your plan," she said, watching him carefully. "That nothing is easy and light and fun all the time."

"Also true," he admitted.

"As is the fact that you've never tried to manage a relationship during a season, correct?"

"Not so much as a pet snake."

"And yet here you are with a woman looking at you," she said. "One with an impressionable kid in her care, taking a serious bite out of the light and easy. Not to mention a father who needs your attention."

Yeah, he thought a little bitterly. *Let's not forget him.*

Sam turned to face him, staring deep into his eyes. "Maybe it's a good thing you only have a week left on your sentence, and then your biggest problem is over."

The words tugged low in his gut. "Is that what you want? For it to be over?"

"This was never about me, Wade." She took his hand and walked with him down to the beach. They kicked off their shoes and sat on the big rocks, hidden from the rest of the world. "Since you're unnerved and I'm not that far behind you," she murmured, leaning back, tipping her face up to the sun, "maybe for now we should just stick with what we're good at."

"Which is?"

She smiled. "It's more of a show than tell thing."

"Yeah?" Just her sultry smile made him feel better. It made him hard, too. "Show me then."

She shrugged out of her jacket, leaving her in just that little tank top he loved. Her breasts strained against the material, her nipples hard. "You have my full attention," he murmured.

She very carefully peeled his T-shirt off over his head. "Good to know."

"Even though I was a jerk?"

"The fight's over, Wade." Her finger ran down his chest, his abs. "Now we're making up." Her mouth curved warmly. "Keep up."

She undid him. Completely undid him.

And clearly knowing it, she just smiled. "I'm quite sure this will put us back on that light and fun and easy track."

"Tell me more about this making up."

"It involves me having my merry way with you."

He pulled her in against him, the circuits in his brain blowing. "I'd like that. I'd really like that."

She smiled and straddled him, a move that had her skirt

hiking up, revealing a pink silk thong that made him groan. He stroked a hand up her thigh, letting his thumb brush across the center of the silk.

She was wet. "God, Sam, is this for me?"

"Well, there was this really cute guy back at the hotel—" She started to crack herself up but it backed up in her throat when he slid a finger beneath the wet silk and inside her.

"Wade," she gasped, wriggling her hips for more, which he gladly gave. She leaned over him and nipped his bottom lip, sucking it into her mouth as she rocked into his touch. "How am I doing on the making-up thing?" she asked breathlessly.

With his free hand, he tugged the thin straps of her tank down, baring her breasts. He kissed first one, then the other, stopping to suck a nipple into his mouth. "Good. God, so good."

Her eyes were fixed on the bulge in his shorts, which she liberated. "Inside me. Now."

He wanted that, too. Leaning back against the rock, he lifted her up so that she could sink onto him, inch by inch. When her muscles clenched around him, his eyes drifted shut. He was breathing like he was running his five miles, but then she began to ride him, grinding her hips against his, increasing her pace with the steady pounding of his heart, and he stopped breathing entirely. "God, Sam." He groaned, his fingers digging into her hips to slow her down, probably nearly bruising her in his attempt to keep himself from coming too soon.

Curving her body over his, she put her mouth to his shoulder, kissing him, softly breathing his name over and over, panting for him, and when he reached between them to stroke his thumb over her in just the right rhythm, she burst, her explosion triggering his.

They leaned against the rocks together, out of breath. He brushed her damp hair out of her face and pressed his mouth to her temple, then lifted her face so he could see into her eyes.

She smiled.

And just like that, everything truly was okay in his world.

Chapter 26

Well, boys, it's a round ball and a round bat and you got to hit the ball square.

—Joe Schultz

The Heat played San Francisco at home for two more nights, which Wade was forced to sit out.

They lost both games.

The following day, they flew to Florida, where he was finally cleared to play. They lost that first game, and frustrated, Wade turned down Joe's and Mike's offer to go out and shake it off, which was code for trolling the bars. Instead, he went up to his hotel room and called Sam. "Hey."

"You okay?" she asked.

"No," he said. "Maybe you should come cheer me up."

"You think wild monkey sex can cheer you up from a loss like that?"

"Who said anything about wild monkey sex? I was thinking of playing cards or something."

"Uh-huh," she said, and he could hear the smile in her voice.

"But hey, if you want wild monkey sex, I suppose I could oblige you."

She laughed softly. "You're such a giver, Wade."

"That I am."

"I have to get Tag fed and in bed. Then his tutor is going to stay with him. I have a quick meeting with Gage and a local reporter in the bar."

"I'll meet you down there."

He showered and changed and hit the bar. Some of the guys were still there. He pulled up a chair to where Kyle, Henry, and Mason were sharing a pitcher and a few laughs.

Mason nodded at a group of women walking into the place, working their way closer. "Think they're Marlin fans and just feel sorry for us?"

"I wouldn't mind that," Kyle said, smiling at one of the women, a pretty blonde. "Sometimes pity's hot."

"When?" Henry asked. "When is pity ever hot?"

"When it looks like that," Mason said, winking at the blonde, who winked back.

Sam walked into the bar with Gage and they ended up on the other side of the room at a table with some suits, one of which was her father.

Wade watched as Mr. McNead barely greeted Sam or Gage. They'd lost today and the man hated to lose. In fact, steam was practically coming out of his head, and after a few minutes, the suits left and Sam's father proceeded to chew off Gage's ear for a good five minutes. Gage, never one to back down, coolly said his piece in return. Then McNead started in on Sam.

Meanwhile the women at the bar had made their way to the table with Wade and the others, and the introductions were made. There were four players and six women, two of whom sat one on either side of Wade. They were pretty and smiley and touchy-feeling, a situation that only a few months ago might have made his night.

Instead, he couldn't take his eyes off Sam. He was hoping she was going to work her way over here and kick some ass. He loved it when she did that, when she claimed him as hers.

After a few more minutes, Gage got up, squeezed Sam's shoulder in silent commiseration, and left. Sam and her father continued what looked to be a heated conversation, and though Wade couldn't hear their words, he could sense the anger vibrating off her.

Wade pushed away his drink. His own father was doing God knew what back in Santa Barbara. He'd stayed to attend his AA meetings, saying he wasn't ready to travel and face all the hotel bars.

"He's not usually so deaf," Mason said to the woman on Wade's left, nudging Wade with his foot as he answered a question that had been clearly meant for Wade. "He loves dancing."

"Then let's go," one of the pretty blondes said, and everyone rose but Wade.

"I'm sorry, but you should go on without me."

Kyle reached down and laid a palm on his forehead. "You sick?"

"Management's waiting to talk to me," he said, standing.

"Are you in trouble for today?" the blonde asked, eyes wide. "For losing?" She pressed herself close and kissed his jaw. "Dancing will make you feel better."

"Sorry," he said, gently disentangling himself. "I'm . . . taken."

She sighed. "Still?"

"Yes."

"I'll be with the others if you change your mind," she said.

"Thanks." He headed across the bar, toward the woman he was "taken" by, for the next few days anyway, and suddenly wished he'd argued for two months instead of one.

Hell, maybe he should look up Tia and get her to stalk him some more, and get himself "taken" by Sam for the rest of the season . . . .

Sam was sitting with her father when Wade came to their table. Her father was still brooding over Sam's decision to open her own PR firm, but she'd already been approached by several potential clients, and nothing was going to change her mind now. She knew she'd been good enough at her job that he would still want her to handle the Heat's publicity, and she looked forward to doing so as an independent contractor, not a Heat employee. They'd just finished discussing it when Wade had been kissed by the woman.

Her father had looked amused.

Sam didn't feel amused, so she doubted she looked it. For how aggressive Wade could be on the diamond field, when it came to women, he tended to be laid-back and easygoing, letting them come to him.

And come to him they did; big, little, curvy, skinny, they came in all shapes and sizes and ages, most falling all over themselves for a piece of him.

He'd been good at doling out pieces. He'd had girlfriends, casual relationships that he'd played at. But Sam had never, not once, seen him hand over the whole of his heart and soul.

And in spite of the fact that he clearly felt something for her, maybe something more than the usual, in the end, she knew she'd be no exception. Not a pleasant realization, especially since she could honestly say she'd most definitely given him a piece of her heart and soul.

Which hadn't been in her plan.

"Is the month up already?" her father asked Wade.

"No," he said, looking at Sam.

"Tomorrow," she said, and saw his surprise.

"Tomorrow?" Wade frowned. "I thought we had a few more days."

"Time flies." Her father gestured to a chair for Wade. "Wanted to thank you, O'Riley. I appreciate you handling the month with as much grace as you did, pretending to have a relationship with Samantha here. I know it wasn't what you wanted, and it probably wasn't easy." He smiled at Sam. "She's good, but never easy."

Sam stood up and grabbed her purse. Wade stood as well, and set a hand at the small of her back in silent but clear support. "Ready?" he asked her.

Beyond ready. "Yes."

Wade nodded, then looked at her father. "You don't have to thank me. Sam did all the work, and that she did so was because of me in the first place."

"Any problems that she couldn't fix?"

Sam opened her mouth in protest but Wade shook his head. "She pulled the job off like no one else could have."

Satisfied, her father nodded, and Sam somehow managed to hold her tongue. She held it as they walked through the lobby, but it was difficult. She could fight her own battles, dammit, and more than that, she hadn't liked the feeling that all she and Wade had accomplished was hiding behind the *pretend* clause.

"Don't take this the wrong way," Wade murmured as they waited for an elevator. "But he's really a very scary man. How'd you turn out so normal?"

She had to force herself not to hug him on the spot. "You think I'm normal?"

He smiled, and slid the hand he'd never taken off of her up her back in a soothing gesture, as if he knew just how on the edge she was. "Relatively speaking. You okay, Princess? You're practically vibrating."

She sighed. "I've just had a really bad hour. You just had a bad game. And tonight is our last night of being boyfriend and girlfriend—" She broke off, unhappy that had slipped out. It felt needy, and she hated needy. "I don't know about you, but I could use some . . . I don't know. Alcohol. Cookies. Sensitivity. Something."

"Our last night," he repeated softly.

Her breath caught. "Yeah."

The elevator opened and he nudged her in ahead of him. As the doors closed, he backed her up against the wall and pressed into her, looking into her eyes for a long enough beat that her heart skipped. "One thing," he whispered.

"What?"

"You're beautiful." And then he kissed her, long and deep. When he slid a hard thigh between hers and moved against her, she completely lost herself and didn't come up for air until the doors dinged and slid open.

He pulled back, ran his thumb over her lower lip, his eyes all hot and sleepy and sexy as hell. "I have something I want to show you in my room," he said.

"I bet."

He grinned, and looking like sin on a stick, took her hand. And instead of putting voice to her insecurities, or wishing for things that weren't meant to be, she called and checked on Tag, then went with Wade to his room and let him show her whatever he wanted.

Twice.

And then once more in the shower for good measure.

The next day, the Heat arrived back in Santa Barbara. Wade entered his house for the first time in a week to a crowd of old men sitting on his couch in various stages of paunchy, wrinkled baldness, all wearing their pants up to their armpits, swirling their dentures in their mouths, passing his Xbox around. "What the hell?"

The room erupted into cheers and requests for autographs, except no one could seem to get up; they were all fighting their walkers and canes.

John came close as Wade watched in disbelief. "Found myself a geriatric AA group."

"Of course you did," Wade said. "They're playing video games."

"Yeah, but they're not drinking."

"Aren't they a little old for you?" Wade slid his father a glance, then took a double take at the very loud, red Hawaiian shirt, plastered with green parrots, which almost but not quite distracted him from the edgy expression on his father's face. He was still missing his booze like he'd miss a limb. "Dad. You realize it's hard to take you seriously with that shirt, right?"

John looked down at himself. "I like this."

Wade shook his head. "Are you scamming them?"

"We really have to work on your impression of me."

Wade sighed. "You're scamming them."

"Hey, they just wanted to see where the great catcher Wade O'Riley lived."

"So you what, charged entrance fees?"

John smiled. "I thought I'd earn my keep."

"Jesus." Wade walked to the wall where the TV was mounted and hit the power button. The TV went black, and a bunch of groans rose in the air. Wade pulled out his wallet, and the room fell silent. "I'm paying you back whatever you paid to get in here, and then I'm sorry, but you have to go."

It took him an hour to clear the place out, and when they were all gone, John shook his head. "You're a party pooper."

Wade let out a rough laugh. "Yeah, well, congratulations. You've managed to do what the Heat management hasn't, you've turned me into a burnout before age thirty-five."

John grinned. "See, admit it, I'm good for you. So . . . how did the series go?" He followed Wade into the kitchen. "Where were you again?"

"Forget it." Wade opened the refrigerator, and stared in shock. He'd been cleaned out.

"Ah, come on," his dad said behind him. "I've been lonely. Talk to me."

Wade rounded on him, unable to hold his silence. "Do you know how many words you spoke to me when I was a kid?"

John's eyes flickered. "Uh, not many, I imagine."

"Less than you've spoken to me since you've gotten here. So you'll have to excuse me, but I'm about at my limit." With that, he took himself off to his room.

His bedroom was large, done up in low, muted, warm earth tones. Dark wood dresser and armoire, huge king-sized bed. Minimal furniture, thousand-count chocolate brown sheets, and thick bedding. He didn't have a TV in here; he'd never needed one in his bedroom before because when he was around, which wasn't much, he watched in the living room, usually with the guys.

But now he was stuck in here with his father holding the rest of his house hostage, and he had nothing but a big bed to look at.

And no woman in it.

A knock came on the door. "I'm hungry."

Wade sighed. "So call for food."

"No credit card."

"My wallet's on the counter."

There was blessed silence for two minutes.

Then John was back on the other side of the door. "Chinese?"

"No, thanks."

"I thought your wallet would be filled with condoms."

Wade didn't bother to answer.

"In fact, I sort of pictured your house filled with women. I thought I'd have to fight them off with a stick. Don't you ever have this place filled with women?"

"Almost never."

"Really?" John sounded disappointed.

"I don't have the life you seem to think I do, Dad."

"Well, damn." John was silent for another beat. "Pizza?"

"No."

"What, have you gone all metrosexual on me? Watching your diet?"

Wade flopped to his bed spread eagle and stared at the ceiling. He was a free man again. There were a ton of places he could go tonight and none he wanted to go to.

Except maybe one.

"You getting fat in the middle?" John asked through the door. "A double chin? Is that it?"

Wade closed his eyes. "A meat lover's special," he said. "Extra large."

After two days off, the Heat flew to New York for a three-day series. Sam brought Tag, the both of them hoping he'd get to see his uncles, but they didn't come. Jeremy still hadn't called Tag, who was doing shockingly well in spite of the odds.

Sam was not.

She'd been swamped with work and hadn't had a moment to breathe much less miss Wade.

Or so she told herself.

But she had no idea where they stood. And she hated not knowing.

In the guest clubhouse before the game, she kept herself busy with reporters, with Tag, with . . . "John?" She looked at Wade's father in surprise as he grabbed a bottle of water.

"Hey, darlin'."

"You came to a game," she said, happy to see him, hoping it meant good things for his and Wade's relationship.

"Well, Wade's gone all the time." He ruffled Tag's hair fondly. "Coming along is the only way I can irritate him."

"Have you tried not irritating him?" Sam asked dryly.

John smiled. "I'm working my way up to that."

In the stands, it was Ladies Day, so the place filled up. Tag inhaled his typical mountain of food, and Sam and Holly assisted.

"So," Holly said. "Your month is up."

Sam sipped her soda as if they were discussing the weather. But discussing the weather had never given her a stomachache before. "Yep."

"That's it then?"

Her heart executed a somersault but she didn't answer because she didn't have one.

On the field, Wade pulled his mask down and went into a crouch to catch for Pace. His hair was a couple of weeks past needing a cut, curling from beneath his headgear over his ears, down to his collar in back.

Pace threw, and the ball snapped into Wade's glove with a *thwack* that Sam could hear from the stands. Rising, Wade nodded as he called something to Pace. His eyes were shadowed by his cap, and though his mouth was slightly curved, she sensed a tension in him. The muscles in his arm flexed as he made his throw, the movement of his body tightening his jersey across the muscles of his back.

Though Sam believed in a woman going after what she wanted, she also believed in self-preservation. Wade didn't know what he wanted. Well, he wanted her body. She knew that. Just the thought brought hers to life. But she wanted him to want more.

She wondered how he was dealing with his father, if he was doing okay. If he was fully recovered . . .

He turned back to the plate, and looked right at her as he did. She couldn't see his expression, or even his eyes, but heat slashed through her anyway.

"Whew," Holly said. "I recognize *that* look."

Yes. So did Sam. So did Sam's body.

Tag was being very quiet, minding himself, which was so odd, she stopped watching Wade and looked at him.

He had her binoculars out and was using them. Not on the guys on the field warming up, but in the stands.

"What are you looking at?" she asked.

"There's a bunch of girls in bathing suits painting on each other."

She and Holly and exchanged a glance, and then Sam took the binoculars. Yep, he was right, the bathing beauties were painting on each other, writing their favorite players' names across their bodies.

"There's a girl with *Wade* across her butt," he said. "Can I have the binoculars back now?"

"No." Sam lifted the binoculars up to her face, and look at that, they focused right in on Wade. *Bad binoculars.*

"What are you looking at?" Tag wanted to know. "The players?"

"Yes." *Well, one player . . .*

"And how is that different?" he wanted to know.

"I'm old."

Tag sighed, and beside her, Holly laughed softly.

Chapter 27

Baseball is an island of activity amidst a sea of statistics.

—Author Unknown

Pace pitched a no-hitter, and Wade had a two-run double in the eighth. It added up to a nice win for the Heat, ending their losing streak.

That night in the hotel, Tag went to Santos's room. His kids and wife had traveled for this series, and Tag was off playing with the boys. Restless, Sam looked at her empty suite. Funny how last season she happily spent every night alone in her hotel room, and now she had one single night to herself and she was feeling lonely.

Tag had more than grown on her. She loved him. She wanted to keep him. And that wasn't all. Wade had grown on her as well. And truth was, she loved him, too. And would like to keep him . . .

And yet she was alone.

Even worse, soon Tag would leave.

And Wade was already out of her life.

Dammit. She grabbed her key card and went downstairs in search of something chocolate. To her surprise, she found Wade in battered jeans and a T-shirt in the lobby. He was surrounded by a group of women seeking autographs and probably his body as well, but she told herself it was no longer her problem.

He'd served his sentence, he was free.

She started to walk on, but something made her turn and take another look at him.

He was smiling and talking easily. But . . . but she knew him now, maybe better than just about anyone. His smile wasn't anywhere close to his eyes and he was even more uncharacteristically tense than he'd been during the game.

Don't do it, Sam.

But she did. She fought her way to his side and stared down all the woman, who slowly scattered.

"Thanks," he said gratefully pulling her in for a hug as if it were the most natural thing in the world, as if maybe he'd missed her.

"Consider it a freebie." She hugged him back, pathetically pressing her nose into his chest, inhaling the warm, male scent of him. Her hands ran up his back, feeling the bunched muscles. "What's the matter?" she asked.

"I came down here to find my dad. He's missing. Have you seen him?"

"Not since right after the game in the clubhouse. And speaking of which, it was nice of you to fly him out here and get him that box seat. He was raving about it after the game."

"Good, but now he's gone." He turned toward the hotel bar.

"And you think—"

"I'd bet my last buck he's somewhere near a bartender."

She looked into his face, tight with strain, and took his hand, entwining her fingers in his. "There're three lounges and four bars. We'll split up."

He looked down at her hand, then into her eyes, his own warm as he stroked a finger over her jaw. "Thanks."

Not trusting her voice, Sam nodded. She let him check the entire ground floor. Nothing. She walked through the garden, eyeing each bench, and then walked through the pool area, just as Wade came out on the other side to do the same.

They saw John at the same time, on a pool lounge chair in a loud Hawaiian shirt and cargo shorts, a pretty woman on either side of him, all three sipping drinks, a bunch of empty glasses scattered around them.

Clearly, they'd been there awhile.

"We're like this," John was saying, holding up his free hand, his first two fingers twisted together. "Father and son. Tight as can be."

"Can you get us Wade's phone number?" one of the women asked.

"Sure," John said, and seeing movement out of the corner of his eye, turned his head and met Sam's gaze.

And then Wade stepped into view as well.

"Son," John called. "Good to see you. Great game to-day." He waved wildly. "Come join us."

At the sight of Wade, the two girls leapt up and squealed with delight. Sam watched Wade wrestle a rare temper with his usual charm. The charm won, but it cost him. He wasn't smiling as he signed autographs, or in this case, body parts. When they were gone, Wade looked at John coolly. "Where to now, Dad? Off to give some more women my phone number? To drink until you fall in the pool and drown? To act like an idiot half your age?"

"Would that bother you, son? Having me act like you?"

Wade stared at him, stunned. "What?"

"You don't think I know anything about you, but I've read enough to know your ladies-man rep. The apple doesn't fall far from the tree, Wade, which means you're acting like a hypocrite. So tell me. Are you pissed because I'm acting like an idiot? Or because you recognize that idiot and see yourself?"

Wade turned and shot a look at Sam, clearly not happy to have her listening to this. But she knew who he was, then and now, and yet before she could tell him so, he walked off.

"Sorry," John said to Sam. "That wasn't very kind of me."

"He's changed," she said quietly. "He's not the happy-go-lucky party boy you're thinking of, not anymore. He's changed, grown up . . ." She met his gaze. "And if you want him in your life, you're going to have to do the same."

He gestured to the empty glasses. "Virgin daiquiris. No alcohol."

Sam looked into his clear eyes. "Why didn't you just tell him that?"

"And ruin the fun he was having hating me?" He sighed. "I want him to believe in me on his own."

"That might take a while. You're going to have to be patient. And probably nicer."

"I understand why you'd defend him. He's so in love with you he can't see straight."

Her heart squeezed. "You're wrong. He likes me. He . . ." *Wants me*. "It's not what you think."

John smiled knowingly, and a little sadly, "So you're just as stubborn as he is."

The Heat flew directly to Chicago. Wade walked into his hotel room, wishing he was alone, but unfortunately, he was followed by his father.

"How many times am I going to have to say I'm sorry for last night?" John asked.

"Zero." Wade ran a hand down his face. Sam had told him what she and his father had talked about last night, and the fact that John hadn't been drinking. "You should have told me yourself."

"I wanted you to see it. But I guess it was too soon. I shouldn't have baited you." John sat on Wade's bed and picked up the remote, flicking through the channels.

Wade sighed. "What are you doing?"

"Looking for a diversion from the Jack Daniel's I smuggled from the flight attendant. I thought maybe a porno channel would do it."

"No porn. Jesus, just what I need is for it to get out that I charged porn to my room."

"Maybe it'll get you another month with Sam."

Wade looked at his dad. "How do you know I'd want that?"

"I've pickled my liver, not my brain."

Wade shook his head and held out his hand.

"What?"

"The Jack."

John raised a brow.

"Give me the fucking Jack Daniel's, Dad."

John pulled it from his bag. Wade snatched it and despite wanting to down it himself, dumped it down the bathroom sink.

"I *have quit*, Wade. I just . . . sometimes it's hard. I need you."

"What makes you think I have any help to give? Christ, Dad, you'd be so much better off in rehab."

"I don't want to be babied, or pitied. And dammit, I don't want to die alone."

"You're not going to die, you're too stubborn."

John smiled grimly. "True enough. Look, it's just that I figured you were the only one in the world who'd be fresh out of pity for me. You're just what I need."

Wade sighed. "You're right about the lack of pity."

"So we going to do this?"

Wade looked at him for a long moment, knowing in spite of himself there was no other choice he could really live with. "If it'll get me my remote back."

At the gate before the Cub's game, they were handing out stick-on tattoos of the player's numbers. Tag grabbed a handful of Wade's and plastered them all over himself. For fun, he also put one on Sam's shoulder, and she had no idea what it said about her that she liked being branded with Wade's number.

They were in the stands when Sam's cell vibrated, and she answered without looking at the ID. "McNead."

"I'm out."

Jeremy. Her stomach dropped. Her gaze slid to Tag as her throat tightened at the thought of giving him up. "After only one month?"

"Yeah. It . . . wasn't for me."

Oh, God. She couldn't let him take Tag back to his world. Wouldn't. She stood up, gestured to Holly to watch Tag, and moved out of earshot. "What do you mean, it wasn't for you? You have a kid to think about, you *have* to get better."

"Yeah. Listen, Sam, I'm sort of on my way to Amsterdam to meet up with Lynn."

She blinked. "Lynn as in the woman who destroyed you about ten years ago? Lynn as in Tag's mom?"

"She called me out of the blue, wants to work things out—"

"Wait a minute. Exactly how long have you been out of rehab?"

"Few days."

"*Days*?" And he hadn't called Tag. *Bastard*.

"Okay, a week. You—"

"I thought you two were long over."

"Me, too."

"You can't go back to her," Sam said. "She's not good to Tag. She—"

"I know. She's . . . too young to be a mom."

Sam was thinking Lynn was too mean and selfish to be a mom, but it didn't matter. No way was she letting Tag go back to Jeremy with Lynn in the picture. In fact, if Jeremy asked her to bring Tag to Amsterdam, where they'd expose him to God knew what, Sam was going to have to kill him, strangle him with her bare hands. "You know what, Jeremy? You don't really have a lot of choices here. You have a child. You need to live your life for him, not you. Do you even have any idea at all what this is doing to Tag? What it will do to him?"

"I was thinking that maybe you could hold on to him for a while longer."

"Yes," Sam said so quickly her head spun. "Yes, I'll hold on to him. Frankly, I'll hold on to him forever, you son of a bitch. In fact, my lawyer will be calling yours to see if we can't work that very thing out."

"Jesus, Sam." He paused, then spoke very quietly. "But thank you."

She held her tongue with great effort, because it would only hurt Tag to alienate him. "Do you want to talk to him?"

"Who?"

Sam opened her mouth but then simply shut her phone. "*Whoops*, bad connection," she said, and went back to her seat and hugged Tag hard.

He only made one fake strangling noise, then let her continue to hold him for a minute, even setting his head on her shoulder before he squirmed. She released him and messed up his already messy hair. "Tag?"

"Yeah?"

"How would you feel about staying here with me even after your dad is done in rehab?"

He slid only his eyes toward her. "My mom still in Europe, huh?"

"Yes, but that's not why I'm asking."

"Why are you asking?"

"Because I like having you around. A lot."

He was silent, and she shifted to catch his line of vision. "I was hoping you feel the same," she said.

He looked at her, then nodded.

"So it's okay with you? If you continue to stay with me?"

"Can I stop using soap?" he asked.

"No."

"Can I have Frosted Flakes each morning for breakfast?"

"No, but I'll keep ice cream in the freezer for dessert."

"And Cheez Doodles."

"Always."

"Cool." And he smiled.

Her heart swelled in her chest until her ribs nearly burst. "I love you, Tag," she whispered, and kissed his cheek.

"Jeez!"

She laughed. "We have to run to the clubhouse at the first media break. I'm giving a quick clip to some foreign reporters today."

"Can I wait here?"

Progress. He was asking. "No," she said gently. "I want to watch your intake. The last time I didn't, you liberated Santos's tobacco, ate too much, and puked up everything but the kitchen sink."

"Aw." But he dropped it. And on the walk to the club-house at the media break, he tugged on her hand. "Sam?"

"Yeah?"

"It's more than okay. Being with you." He grimaced when she grinned and hugged him again.

The game went late. At eleven that night they were tied and heading into extra innings. Sam sent Tag to the hotel room with Gage's assistant, and he was crashed out cold in his room when she staggered in two hours later at one in the morning after a tight win.

Two seconds later, there was a soft knock at her suite door. She opened it to Wade. "Congratulations on the win," she said. "Nice homer in the fourth. And eighth." She smiled. "And tenth."

"Thanks."

She leaned against the doorjamb and looked him over. He wore jeans and a slightly oversized button-down, un-tucked, looking like his usual million bucks. But unlike always, his expression was actually open, and just a little vulnerable, which she found devastatingly charming. "You hurting?"

He shook his head.

"You upset with your dad?"

"Yeah, but that's more a way of life."

"Then what?"

He put his hands on her hips and nudged her into the room so he could shut the door. Pulling her in close, his voice dropped to a soft murmur against her ear. "Maybe I just want to be with you."

Her heart caught. "No reason?"

"Lots of reasons. Many, many reasons." His hands swept up her body and made it quiver. "Where's Tag?"

"Asleep in his room." And damn, but she wrapped herself around him like she hadn't seen him in months. "I was about to shower."

"Yeah?" He guided her into the bathroom, reaching behind him to lock the door. "Don't let me stop you."

She flipped on the hot water. He stripped. Apparently he was joining her. When he was gloriously naked, he divested her of her clothing as well, stopping to stare in surprise at his number tattooed on her shoulder.

"I know," she said, embarrassed. "It's so middle school, but—"

He dropped his head and kissed it, backing the words up in her throat as he continued with the kisses to her breast. "I like it. You're branded as mine."

At the mine, her belly quivered. "Tag's just in the next room," she whispered.

"The kid sleeps like the dead, I've seen him." He ran his tongue over her nipple, and at her throaty gasp, looked up. "But to be safe, you'll have to try to keep the 'harder, Wade, harder' down to a minimum."

"I don't—"

He grinned against her breast and she closed her eyes. She did, God she did. There was no doubt he brought out her wild side.

He made his way to her other breast and ran a finger along her bikini line. "My name or number right here would be nice . . ." He slid a hand between her legs. She sucked in a breath as he dropped to his knees.

"Shh," he reminded her softly, then pressed her back against the sink and put his mouth on her. He drove her straight off the edge—and even had to reach up and cover her mouth with his hand at the end when she cried out and shuddered.

Rocked off her axis, she slid bonelessly toward the floor, but he caught her in his arms and stepped into the shower with her, then pressed her against the wall and slid into her with one flex of his hips.

Then it was his turn to let out the low, husky gasp, and hers to cover his mouth.

And this time, when Sam came back to herself, she burrowed into the man who held her, feeling something new, something catch deep inside of her. She'd tried it his way. She'd given the light and easy thing her very best shot, but she'd passed light and easy a long time ago. She'd fallen completely, head-over-heels in love with Wade.

And probably, it was going to kill her.

The Heat took the Cubs series three-two, which made the fans and management and the sponsors happy. That should have been enough for Wade. At one time it'd most definitely have been enough.

And then the hurricane named Samantha had hit, and things had changed.

On the late night flight home, the plane was quiet and dark as Wade slipped into a seat next to Sam, who was working on her BlackBerry. Tag was passed out cold across from her, sleeping in his favorite position—arms and legs akimbo. Wade smiled as he pressed his leg into Sam's. "Hey."

"Hey."

She didn't seem nearly as sated and relaxed as she had in the shower the night before last, and he took another look at her, seeing the strain in her eyes. "You okay?"

"Yes."

"What are you working on?"

"Last-minute details for the charity dinner in two nights."

He nodded. The event was a big one and required one of his least favorite things—a tux. But as he'd be Sam's date, and she would no doubt wear something that would make his tongue stick to the roof of his mouth, it'd be worth it.

She didn't say anything else. She always said something . . . He nudged her again. "You sure you're okay?"

"Mmm-hmmm."

She hadn't take her gaze off her BlackBerry, so he dipped his head to make eye contact.

She swiveled her head toward him—a distracted question mark in her eyes.

Huh. He took in her slight frown, and the way her brow was furrowed. "You have a headache?"

"No." Her voice was soft. Not unfriendly, but . . . not warm either.

"Okay." He kept looking at her, trying to understand what was going on, because something *was* going on. "I'm getting the feeling I'm missing a memo."

She set her BlackBerry down and looked at him, really looked, as if she were searching for something important inside his head. "And what would that memo say?" she finally asked.

"It would tell me how I'd fucked up, with instructions on how to fix it."

She sighed and went back to her phone.

"Are we having a fight?" he asked.

"Are you mad at something?" she asked.

"No."

"Then no. We're not having a fight."

He watched her work for a moment, at a complete loss. The last time she'd been upset had been the other night at the bar with her father. Wade had been able to take her mind off that pretty easily by getting her naked. Served to reason it might work again, so he slid his arm around her, cuddling her in against him to kiss her neck. God, she smelled good. "Ever join the mile-high club?" he whispered.

She slid him another look, this one inscrutable. "Are you suggesting we hit the bathroom and have sex?"

The tone froze his eyebrows. "Um . . . yes?"

"Let me ask you something, Wade. The month's over, right?"

"Right."

"So what exactly are we doing now?"

"Uh . . ." He figured whatever he said had better be really, really good and convincing. "Seeing where things go?"

"With a purely physical relationship."

He knew a trap when he saw one. "No." He shook his head. This one he knew. "We have more."

"Really? Like what? I'm just trying to define this. For me."

"Well . . . we laugh." He flashed her a grin, but she didn't return it. "And we talk."

She just looked at him. *Great.* Now *she held her tongue.* "*Usually* we talk," he amended, and pulled back a little, stroking a strand of her hair behind an ear. "What's the matter, Sam? Just tell me."

She closed her eyes and shook her head. "I wanted to be able to do this, the light and fluffy nonsubstance thing." She opened her eyes again, and they were filled with frustration and a sadness that wrenched at him. "I really thought I could jump in and jump out again at will.

But as it turns out, it's hard to turn it on and off." She pressed her lips together. "I'm having a really hard time with the off part, Wade."

He stroked a finger over her jaw, thrown by the pain in her voice, by the way his own throat felt too damn tight. "So leave it on."

"For now, you mean. Open-ended."

"Yeah."

She let out a laugh that tore at his heart. She nodded, but then shook her head in the negative. "I wanted to," she whispered. "Because I want you. But I'm not getting any vibes from you that justify the risk. I'm sorry, Wade." She looked away, and then when she met his gaze again, her thoughts were successfully hidden from him. "I can't."

He hated the panic tightening his gut. "So . . . where does that leave us, Sam?"

"With no us."

Chapter 28

More than any other American sport, baseball creates the magnetic, addictive illusion that it can almost be understood.

—Thomas Boswell

The next day, the Heat took Seattle at home by the skin of their teeth, and Wade took a cleat to the shin. It happened in the last inning, and he spent a long time in the shower afterwards trying to get the ache out. But his shin wasn't the only thing that hurt. His chest hurt, his gut hurt.

Everything fucking hurt.

By the time he dressed, the clubhouse had pretty much cleared out. Pace had gone home with Holly. Most of the guys, happy to be back in Santa Barbara, had plans with family. Sam had avoided him pre-game, and was doing the same now, so Wade grabbed his keys and left.

He went home, but the empty house mocked him. Even his father had somewhere to be, leaving Wade truly the only one with nobody. He got back into his car. He drove, having no idea what his destination was.

He ended up at Sam's building. He wasn't sure why, but hell, now that he was here, it'd be rude not to go in and see her. Tag opened the door to his knock, and with a look of disappointment, peered behind Wade.

"You got someone better coming over?" Wade asked him.

"Pizza," Tag said.

Wade nudged the kid aside and walked into the condo, staring in surprise at his father, who was sitting at the dining room table. "What are you doing here?"

"Keeping the kid and his tutor company."

Wade took a long look at his dad, who seemed more than a little strung out. "You okay?"

"Trying to be." John was indeed fighting his addiction, but Wade wasn't sure he was winning.

"Anyone know where Sam went?"

"*No se.*" Tag grinned. "That's Spanish for I don't know. Your dad taught it to me. Want to know what else he taught me?"

"Uh . . ." John was frantically trying to get Tag's attention, making the motion of a knife slicing across his neck. "Ixnay on the haring-shay, please."

"*Comer mierda,*" Tag said proudly.

Eat shit? Wade narrowed his gaze at his father, who had found something fascinating to study on the ceiling.

"He paid me to say it to the cab driver who brought him here," Tag said.

"Christ, Dad."

"Sorry, but the guy was a real prick."

"Prick," Tag repeated.

Wade pulled out his wallet and handed Tag a ten.

Tag pocketed the money and when it was out of sight, he asked "What was that for?"

"To *not* repeat anything my father says."

"Sweet."

"Got any for me?" his father asked, palm out.

"No. You've bled me dry." He pointed at Tag. "Behave yourself."

"Okay. So are you going to go out, too? Like Aunt Sam?"

Wade's world stuttered to a halt. "What?"

John fake coughed and said, "You snooze, you lose," at the same time.

"Dad, a moment?" Wade jerked his head toward the kitchen.

"Can't. Sorry. Very busy."

"Now."

John sighed and rose to his feet, meeting Wade in front of the stove. "This isn't my fault. This time it's *your* bone-headedness, son, all on your own. I'm completely innocent."

"Where is she?"

"Don't know."

Wade gave up on him and went to Tag. "Do you know how to reach your aunt?"

"Uh-huh. I always know, on accounta' we're family," he said, clearly repeating back Sam's words verbatim.

"Okay, good. So . . . ?"

Tag slid him a sly look. "So now it's okay to tell a secret?"

Shit, the kid was good. "*Is* it a secret?"

Tag just looked at him.

"Sorry, man, but no more cash tonight."

Tag sighed. "I can call her and she'll come back. She told me to call her if I needed anything, that she'd be here in a jiffy."

Which was no help for Wade. "Same goes for me, kiddo. You need me, you call. Anytime, okay?"

"''Kay."

With one last long look at his father, Wade headed out. Stopping in front of his car, he reached into his pocket for his keys and glanced at the window of the Italian restaurant across the street.

Sam was sitting inside at a table near the window. She was with a man, talking animatedly, and laughing. Then the man reached over and kissed her right on the lips, and Wade abruptly shoved his keys back in his pocket and strode inside.

Sam looked up as he got to their table, still laughing at something the man with her had just said, her eyes widening in surprise. "Wade."

"That was quick," Wade said, surprised that his voice sounded normal since he felt like his guts had just been ripped out.

The man sitting across from Sam, the one who was going to lose his face to Wade's fist if he kissed her again, smiled and leaned back in his chair, studying Wade thoughtfully. "I think you were wrong about him, babe."

While Wade chewed on the endearment *babe*, Sam looked Wade over.

"No," she finally said cryptically. "I wasn't wrong."

The man squeezed her fingers and brought them to his lips. Wade nearly leaned across the table to break his wrist, but Sam shook her head. "Ernie, stop it."

"Aw," Ernie said on a smile. "You're no fun."

And since he didn't *stop it*, or drop Sam's fingers, Wade softly said, "Drop her hand or lose it."

Ernie laughed silkily as he let go of Sam and slid her a look. "How about now? Still going to try to tell me he's happy it's over?"

"Ernie . . ." she warned.

"Fine." He stood and held out a hand to Wade. "Ernie Rodriquez. Nice triple homer in Chicago."

"Thanks." Wade felt Sam watching him with a look he couldn't begin to comprehend, and he met her gaze.

"Ernie and I were putting finishing touches on the charity dinner," she said. "Ernie's catering."

"My first over-three-hundred-person event." Ernie grinned. "Looking forward to seeing you in a tux, big guy." He patted Wade's arm, lingering at the biceps, letting out a hum of pleasure before walking into the kitchen.

Wade stared after him until Sam cleared her throat. He looked down at her.

"You look confused," she said.

"A little."

"Poor baby." She stood, gathering files and pictures and her BlackBerry, shoving them into her briefcase. "Let me give you the short version. First you dumped me, then you see me out with another man and come charging in here to . . . Well, I don't know what exactly, but you end up getting hit on by the very man you wanted to protect me from. I can see why you'd be confused, seeing as you've acted like a complete ass."

"Wait a minute." He shook his head. "I didn't dump you. You dumped me."

She made a sound that managed to perfectly convey what she thought of his intelligence level, and walked out of the restaurant.

He followed.

"Fine," she said. "I dumped you. A minute before you could dump me. It was self-preservation."

"What the hell does that mean?"

"I don't have time to explain it to you. I've got to go." She gave him her professional smile, the one that was chilly enough that he suddenly needed a coat. And then left him standing on the sidewalk wondering what the fuck had just happened as he was ogled by Ernie from the restaurant window.

Not surprisingly, the next day Wade played like shit. He had no explanation for why he struck out twice, missed an easy fly, and overthrew to third, causing two runs, which was the exact number they lost by.

No explanation at all. Everything was fine. *Fucking fine.*

The guys didn't say much to him as they left the field, though their bafflement was clear. Wade was usually the rock, the motivator, the go-to guy. He didn't have off days, he didn't let anything get to him.

"You sick?" Henry asked him.

Wouldn't that be a handy excuse? He shook his head.

"You sure? You're flushed. Maybe you're coming down with something."

Joe nodded. "Tea, man. Try chamomile."

"Or Earl Grey," Henry said. "You need to be on tomorrow."

Wade nodded. He'd be on.

Or dead.

He wasn't sure which. But the ball of anxiety, frustration, and temper sitting on his chest had to go away or explode. That simple. He was self-destructing. He'd self-destructed with Sam by letting her believe it was only great sex, by not letting her know what she meant to him. He'd self-destructed with his dad by holding back when the guy was trying, finally giving all he had. It should have been easy to hurt John O'Riley. Instead, it left Wade feeling sick inside, because it was one thing to hold on to his self-righteous anger when his dad was being a drunk.

It was another entirely when his dad was being a remorseful ex-drunk.

Pace slung an easy arm around Wade's shoulders, slowing him down, separating him from the rest of the team. "What was that?"

"No idea."

"You need to talk?"

"If you suggest a tea, I'm going to hurt you."

Pace studied him for a beat. "You letting John fuck with your head?"

"No."

"Sam?"

Wade closed his eyes. "It's me. *I'm* fucking with my head. I screwed up. I'm an ass."

"Hey, knowing it is half the battle."

Wade tried to shrug him off, but Pace was like a pit bull when he wanted to be. "*Fuck*, Pace. Now what?"

"Just giving you a minute to collect yourself." Pace was looking at the entrance to the locker room, where Gage stood waiting, dark eyes fixed on Wade. "Gage's going to bust your ass."

"I'm fine." Wade walked up to Gage to get it over with.

The youngest, smartest, sharpest, shrewdest team manager in the MLB looked Wade over carefully. "Talk to me," he said.

Wade shrugged. "Bad night."

"That's all you've got?"

Well, he sure as hell had nothing else.

Gage blew out a breath. "Does the bad night have anything to do with the fact that Sam dumped your sorry ass?"

"How did you know that?"

"Fuck, Wade. I told you this was a bad idea. You don't even *want* a woman in your life. Right?"

"Right."

"So get over it. Get over it by tomorrow's game or I'll kick your ass until you're over it. And if anyone asks, I already kicked your ass."

Wade showered, changed, and slinked out into the shower room, hoping like hell to just be alone.

He got his wish. It was quiet, and though a few of the guys were moving around, no one was talking. And Sam was nowhere to be seen, which shouldn't have mattered, but did. She was almost always around after a game.

Not today. She and Tag were gone.

Torn between relief that he didn't have to face her, and a bone-deep regret that made his chest ache, he drove home.

And was shocked to find Sam sitting on his porch step waiting for him. He sat in his car staring at her through the windshield. *Don't fuck up*, he told himself, then had to laugh because that's all he'd ever done when it came to her. With a sigh, he shoved out of the car and took the walk to the gallows. He sat down next to her and let out a breath, prepared for her to let him have it, and she didn't hold back.

"You're either an idiot or a moron," she said.

He dropped his head into his hands. "Is there another choice?"

"That weekend we went to Mark's wedding, when we were in our *pretend* relationship . . ." She paused until he looked at her. "Up until that point, I had a pretty hard-core crush on you, Wade. I think it was your green eyes. They're the color of moss on a rainy day."

Surprised, he blinked. "You had a crush on me?"

She smiled a little sadly. "I know. I always acted like I couldn't care less, but that was just self-preservation after

Atlanta." She shrugged. "I always felt off balance around you."

He understood that. Sometimes he had trouble finding his balance around her as well, though she usually located it for him just fine.

"The truth is," she said. "Pretending to be with you was harder than I could have imagined, because I kept forgetting to pretend."

He understood that, too. "Sam—"

"I watched you with Tag, saw how you put yourself out there with him, no hesitation. I watched you with your father, how even when you were so angry, you couldn't turn him out. And I realized my feelings for you had . . . deepened."

Despite feeling the urge to hide, he couldn't look away to save his life. "You weren't alone in that," he managed. "I told you I was falling for you."

"Yes. In a light and easy way. But as it turns out, I fell harder. As hard as you can, actually."

His brain froze, like it did when he drank a slushee too fast or inhaled ice cream. And like a complete idiot, he just stared at her. "Sam—"

She stood up. "I get that I was rough on you. Unfairly so. I expected too much and I'm sorry for that. I just want you to know, I can be a grown-up about this. It won't be awkward at work or anything."

Awkward? She was worried about awkward? She had no idea that absolutely nothing was the same when she wasn't in his life. Awkward didn't even begin to cover it. How about devastating and empty and . . .

Hell. His mind was spinning and it couldn't seem to touch down. "Sam." *Shit.* He'd already said that. "I—"

"I'm trying to make this easy. Because that's how you

like things. Easy women, easy job, easy everything. I can give that to you. Good-bye, Wade." With one last look into his eyes, she walked away.

And though he hated himself for it, he let her. Because she was right. He liked things easy. He *needed* things easy.

Except nothing about any of this felt easy . . . .

Chapter 29

Baseball? It's just a game—as simple as a ball and a bat. Yet as complex as the American spirit it symbolizes. It's a sport, business—and sometimes even religion.

—Ernie Harwell

Wade spent several hours slouched on the couch with his remote all alone, which given his last two weeks, should have been heaven. Not only was the silence perfect, but everything was fucking perfect. No demands on his rare time to himself, nobody talking to him, nothing on his plate except whatever he chose. He could call the guys. Hit a bar. Find a willing woman.

Except none of that appealed. He felt restless and frustrated.

And then he realized what the problem was.

He didn't want to be alone.

Alone felt easy but all of a sudden he didn't want easy either.

He called Sam to tell her but she didn't answer. He called his father. No answer there, either. And then he called the one person he knew could help him. "Tag."

"Yo," Tag said into the phone.

"You know where your Aunt Sam is?"

"Again? How come you keep losing her?"

"Because I've been stupid. But trust me, I'm getting smarter. Where is she?"

"Not supposed to tell."

Wade sighed. "How about my dad?

"Same thing."

Well, that was unexpected. "Okay, I realize you probably want me to pay you for the info but from now on, I'm only paying you when you earn it. With work."

"Ah. That's no fun."

"Trying to be responsible here."

"Really? That's what your dad's doing. Trying to be responsible. It's what he said. Sam drove him."

"Sam drove him where?"

"Promises."

Wade rubbed his temples. "I know. You promised not to tell, but he's my dad, Tag. It's okay to tell me."

"No, he's at a place called Promises. Sam took him."

Wade made the hour drive south over Highway 1 to Promises, an upscale rehab center in Malibu. But by the time he got there, Sam had already left, and he wasn't allowed to see or talk to his father, who'd been admitted.

The drive back felt twice as long. The sports news was all over his crappy game, saying he looked tired coming off all the road trips, not fresh, not sharp.

And that he'd been dumped.

Well, they had that right. And yeah, he *had* lost his edge, he felt it in his gut. It wasn't a flu, nothing so easy to get over, though he did feel sick to the depths of his soul.

Back at his place, he plopped down by his pool as the moon rose, staring moodily at the shimmering water.

Somehow he'd managed to rise up from the gutter that had been his childhood. For a long time now he'd had it all, whatever he'd wanted at his fingertips. Four shining years in college. Four years playing for Colorado, then nearly four of the best years of his life in Santa Barbara.

Until he'd gotten one little stalker and the press had taken notice of his hard partying ways and had turned on him.

He'd felt restless. Unsettled. Unsure.

And then had come the weekend with Sam at the wedding. That had changed him. She had changed him. Suddenly the things he'd thought he'd wanted—mostly the freedom to do as he pleased—had changed.

It had taken him some time to realize it.

Too much time.

Because now that he finally had it all figured out, the things he'd somehow managed almost by accident to surround himself with, things like the love of a good woman, the love of a kid, the love of a parent, things he now knew he wanted, *needed*, he'd blown them all apart.

But he wasn't ready to admit defeat. Not on the season, not on his dad, and not on his life.

And especially not on Sam.

The next day Sam worked her ass off for ten straight hours to get the charity dinner and auction set up. Finally, half an hour before the start, she ran up to one of the hotel rooms to change. Her dress for the evening was a black spaghetti-strapped cocktail dress, clingy in the front, dipping low in the back. She looked in the mirror, knowing she'd picked out the dress for Wade and that it wouldn't matter.

With five minutes to spare, she raced back downstairs. She purposely stopped to look at the beautiful view of the ocean against the cliff, the moon rising high as she took a deep, calming breath. Security was tight tonight. With tickets costing a grand a pop, they were expecting Santa Barbara's rich and famous.

Ahead of her, Henry and Joe were checking in, their dates on their arms. Sam was used to seeing the guys in their uniforms, in sweats, in jeans, or even the suits they wore for traveling. Hell, she was even used to seeing half of them nude, given how much she was in the clubhouse during the season, but she'd never get used to the sight of them, big and bad and gorgeous, in tuxes.

Their dates looked beautiful and excited about the evening ahead. Sam wished she could say the same, but as she was dateless, she could summon little excitement. She handed over her ticket to the hotel greeter at the doors, waiting while the woman consulted her clipboard as instructed by Sam herself and frowned. "Says here you're a party of two," the woman said. "Where's your date?"

Ah. Well, wasn't that perfect? She was going to have to say it aloud. Her heart pinged once, hard, and she opened her mouth to say she was flying solo tonight, and that the way she was feeling, she'd be flying solo until the cows came home, when a warm hand settled on the small of her back. She didn't have to look to see whose hand, or whose hard chest, was brushing her spine, because both brought a heat that pooled low in her belly.

"Her date's right here," Wade said.

The woman took in the sight of Wade in a tux and her mouth fell open.

Sam couldn't blame her. She was nearly drooling herself. And shaking a little bit. "W-Wade." Her tongue tripped all over itself because she honestly hadn't figured on him doing this. She was embarrassed that he thought he had to, and also suddenly incredibly nervous that she was going to do something stupid, like throw herself at him. "I didn't expect—"

"Excuse us a minute," Wade said to the woman, and took Sam's hand, pulling her away from the doors, off to the side.

She looked up into his face, which was tight with strain, and she immediately clutched his arms. "What is it? Your dad? Is he okay?"

"He's fine. They still won't let me talk to him, but they swear he's great. And I got a text from him today."

Her eyes searched his, waiting.

"He wanted me to know that sometimes the apple *does* fall far from the tree." He let out a small smile. "That I rolled all the way down the hill and then showed him the way."

She felt her throat tighten, and she slowly smiled. "That's sweet."

"I texted him back, told him to get the thirty days under his belt, then come back to my house to finish his rehab."

It took her a moment to be able to speak. "You're a good man, Wade O'Riley. A really good man." Her heart was having a rough time. It'd skipped a few beats and couldn't seem to get back on track. And she was still trembling, shaking from the strain to keep it light, to keep smiling.

"Sam." His voice was low, husky. "Look at me."

God. Okay. She slowly met his gaze. She'd promised him no awkwardness, but she was dying at the sight of him, tall and gorgeous and far too close. She gestured to the photographers who were taking so many pictures of them the flashes were making her dizzy. "They're having a field day with this, the whole are-we-or-aren't-we thing. Making for good press, I guess."

"I don't care about the press." He pulled her closer. "What I care about is what you said to me on my front steps, about how you feel."

"Yeah." She cringed at the memory. "Listen, I'm really bad at telling people how I feel. Please don't make me explain it again."

"We're *both* really bad at telling people how we feel," he said softly. "In fact, I never told you at all. That makes me worse at it than you."

Again she tried to pull free. "I really need to get in there—"

"I know. This first. You've been there for me, Sam, and tonight I'm here for you."

"Okay. Thanks." She smiled and nodded, but though she could pretend with the best of them, she thought this one last night might do her in. She walked into the ballroom, and though her throat and eyes were burning, she did her best to handle it. She grabbed a flute of champagne from a passing waiter. Though she was tempted to guzzle it, she sipped slowly as she took in the ballroom. It was full and getting fuller, the dance floor beginning to fill up as well.

"Sam."

God. What now?

Wade took the glass from her fingers and set it on a table, then held out a hand.

Her first thought was no. No slow dancing. No possible way could she handle the forced intimacy. But that thought was fleeting because she understood something that she'd possibly always known—she couldn't tell him no. And in any case, he didn't give her a choice. He pulled her into his arms and then she was up against that body that knew hers inside and out. In spite of herself, she melted into him. He was warm and smelled like heaven, and she set her head on his shoulder, her hand on his chest.

He murmured something soft and wordless in her ear and stroked a hand up her back. Beneath his jacket she could feel the steady beat of his heart, in sharp contrast to hers, which was racing. Worse, she was still shaking like crazy; she couldn't seem to stop.

"It's okay, Sam," he said very softly in her ear, running that big, warm, callused hand up and down her back with terrifying gentleness. "It's going to be okay."

How? How was it ever going to be okay? An involuntary shiver wracked her, one he chased away with his hand. "Sam," he murmured, regret heavy in his husky voice.

"Please." She tensed against him. "I don't want to do this. I lied. I can't do this. I can't fake this with you, not even for the team."

Wade tipped up her chin and looked directly into her eyes. "I know. I can't either. When I'm with you, I can't fake anything, I've *never* faked anything. That's what tripped me up at first, I think."

She just stared up at him, not sure if he was speaking the same language as she was. "Tripped you up?"

"You didn't like me for the usual reasons," he said. "The fame, the fortune, the fun. In fact, I'm not even sure why you liked me at all. All I know is that when I'm with you, I feel more like myself than when I'm not."

"Wade O'Riley!" A woman reporter shoved a microphone in their faces. "Nice tux. Dolce&Gabbana?"

"Uh . . ." He looked down at himself as if he couldn't remember. "Armani. If you could give us a minute—"

"And your date. Samantha McNead, right?" the reporter asked smoothly. "Gorgeous dress. Can I get a shot of you two kissing?"

Sam felt herself tense. The last time someone had asked this of them had been at Mark's wedding—the first day of their "relationship."

Wade pulled her into his warmth and pressed his mouth to her ear, his voice soft. "The real thing this time, Sam. No pretending. Because when I'm with you, I don't have to pretend at all, and neither do you. It's just us. And there is an us."

"It's not just us now," she said. "I have Tag—"

"I know. I love that kid. And I have my dad in my life, too. No, it's not just us, but that makes it even better."

She stared up at him, some of the tension leaving her body. He was right, he'd always been right. And she needed to see this through, fear or not. She loved him too much not to. The rest of her tension left when he dipped his head and kissed her, a kiss that went on for so long the reporter gave up on them. Finally Wade pulled back a fraction to whisper, "Truth or dare."

"Wade—"

"Truth or dare."

"Dare," she said, not ready for a truth.

"Kiss me again."

She did, with all the pent-up adrenaline and fear and love she felt for him. He touched her face, gentling her, and when she pulled back, she knew she had tears in her eyes.

"Now ask me," he murmured, pressing his forehead to hers.

"Wade—"

"Ask me."

"Truth or dare?" Her voice was low and thick, she could barely speak.

"Truth."

She stared into his eyes. "Do you love me?"

"Yes, I love you. More than you can possibly imagine."

Chapter 1

Kate Evans would've sold her soul for a stress-free morning, but either her soul wasn't worth much or whoever was in charge of granting wishes was taking a nap. With her phone vibrating from incoming texts—which she was doing her best to ignore—she shoved her car into park and ran across the lot and into the convenience store. "Duct tape?" she called out to Meg, the clerk behind the counter.

Meg had pink and purple tie-dyed hair, had enough piercings to ensure certain drowning if she ever went swimming, and was in the middle of a heated debate on the latest *The Voice* knockout rounds with another customer. But she stabbed a finger in the direction of aisle three.

Kate snatched a roll of duct tape, some twine, and then, because she was also weak, a rack of chocolate mini donuts for later. Halfway to the checkout, a bin of fruit tugged at her good sense so she grabbed an apple. Dumping everything on the counter, she fumbled through her pockets for cash.

Meg rang her up and bagged her order. "You're not going to murder someone, are you?"

Kate choked out a laugh. "What?"

"Well . . ." Meg took in Kate's appearance. "Librarian outfit. Duct tape. Twine. I know you're the math whiz around here, but it all adds up to a *Criminal Minds* episode to me."

Kate was wearing a cardigan, skirt, leggings, and—because she'd been in a hurry and they'd been by the front door—snow boots. She supposed with her glasses and hair piled up on her head she might resemble the second-grade teacher that she was, and okay, maybe the snow boots in May were a little suspect. "You watch too much TV," Kate said. "It's going to fry your brain."

"You know what fries your brain? Not enough sex." Meg pointed to her phone. "Got that little tidbit right off the Internet on my last break."

"Well, then it must be true," Kate said.

Meg laughed. "That's all I'm saying."

Kate laughed along with her, grabbed her change and her bag, and hurried to the door. She was late. As the grease that ran her family's wheel, she needed to get to her dad's house to help get her little brother, Tommy, ready for school and then to coax the Evil Teen into even going to school. The duct tape run wasn't to facilitate that, or to kill anyone, but to make a camel, of all things, for an after-school drama project Tommy had forgotten to mention was due today.

Kate stepped outside and got slapped around by the wind. The month of May had burst onto the scene like a PMSing Mother Nature, leaving the beautiful, rugged Bitterroot Mountains, which loomied high overhead, dusted with last week's surprise snow.

Spring in Sunshine, Idaho, was MIA.

Watching her step on the wet, slippery asphalt, she pulled out her once again vibrating phone just to make sure no one was dying. It was a text from her dad and read: Hurry, it's awake.

It being her sister. The other texts were from Ashley herself. She was upset because she couldn't find her cheerleading top, and also, did Kate know that Tommy was talking to his invisible friend in the bathroom again?

Kate sighed and closed her eyes for a brief second, which was all it took for her snow boots to slip. She went down like a sack of cement, her phone flying one way, her bag the other as she hit the ground butt first with teeth-jarring impact.

"Dammit!" She took a second for inventory—no massive injuries. That this was in thanks to not having lost those five pounds of winter brownie blues didn't make her feel any better. The cold seeped through her tights and the sidewalk abraded the bare skin of her palms. Rolling to her hands and knees, she reached for her keys just as a set of denim-clad legs came into her field of vision.

The owner of the legs crouched down, easily balancing on the balls of his feet. A hand appeared, her keys centered in the big palm. Tilting her head up, she froze.

Her polite stranger wore a baseball cap low over his eyes, shadowing most of his face and dark hair, but she'd know those gunmetal gray eyes anywhere. And then there was the rest of him. Six foot two and built for trouble in army camo cargoes, a black sweatshirt, and his usual badass attitude, the one that tended to have men backing off and women checking for drool; there was no mistaking Griffin Reid, the first guy she'd ever fallen for. Of course she'd been ten at the time . . .

"That was a pretty spectacular fall," he said, blocking her from standing up. "Make sure you're okay."

Keep your cool, she told herself. *Don't speak, just nod.* But her mouth didn't get the memo. "No worries, a man's forty-seven percent more likely to die from a fall than a woman." The minute the words escaped, she bit her tongue, but of course it was too late. When she got nervous, she spouted inane science facts.

And Griffin Reid made her very nervous.

"I'm going to ask you again," he said, moving his tall, linebacker body nary an inch as he pinned her in place with nothing more than his steady gaze. "Are you okay?"

Actually, no, she wasn't. Not even close. Her pride was cracked, and quite possibly her butt as well, but that wasn't what had her kneeling there on the ground in stunned shock. "You're . . . home."

He smiled grimly. "I was ordered back by threat of bodily harm if I was late to the wedding."

He was kidding. No one ordered the tough, stoic bad-ass Griffin to do anything, except maybe Uncle Sam since he was some secret army demolitions expert who'd been in Afghanistan for three straight tours. But his sister, Holly, was getting married this weekend. And if there was anyone more bossy or determined than Griffin, it was his baby sister. Only Holly could get her reticent brother halfway around the world for her vows.

Kate had told herself that as Holly's best friend and maid of honor, she would absolutely not drool over Griffin if he showed up. And she would especially not make a fool of herself.

Too late, on both counts.

Again she attempted to get up, but Griffin put a big, tanned, work-roughened hand on her thigh, and she felt herself tingle.

Well, damn. Meg was right—too little sex fried the brain.

Clearly misunderstanding her body's response, Griffin squeezed gently as if trying to soothe, which of course had the opposite effect, making things worse. Embarrassed, she tried to pull free, but still effortlessly holding her, Griffin's steely gray eyes remained steady on hers.

"Take stock first," he said, voice low but commanding. "What hurts? Let me see."

Since the only thing that hurt besides her pride was a part of her anatomy that she considered No Man's Land, hell would freeze over before she'd "let him see." "I'm fine. Really," she added.

Griffin took her hand and easily hoisted her up, studying her in that assessing way of his. Then he started to turn her around, presumably to get a three-hundred-and-sixty degree view, but she stood firm. "Seriously," she said, backing away, "I'm good." And if she weren't, if she'd actually broken her butt, she'd die before admitting it, so it didn't matter. Bending to gather up her belongings, she carefully sucked in her grimace of pain.

"I've got it," Griffin said, and scooped up the duct tape and donuts. He looked like maybe he was going to say something about the donuts, but at the odd vibrating noise behind them, he turned. "Your phone's having a seizure," he said.

Panicked siblings, no doubt. After all, there was a camel to create out of thin air and a cheerleading top to locate, and God only knew what disaster her father was coming up with for breakfast.

Griffin offered the cell phone, and Kate stared down at it thinking how much easier her day would go if it had smashed to pieces when it hit the ground.

"Want me to step on it a few times?" he asked, sounding amused. "Kick it around?"

Startled that he'd read her so easily, she snatched the phone. When her fingers brushed his, an electric current sang up her arms and went straight to her happy spots without passing Go. Ignoring them, she turned to her fallen purse. Of course the contents had scattered. And of course the things that had fallen out were a tampon and condom.

It was how her day was going.

She began cramming things back into the purse, the phone, the donuts, the duct tape, the condom, and the tampon.

The condom fell back out.

"I've got it." Griffin's mouth twitched as he tossed it into her purse for her. "Duct tape and a Trojan," he said. "Big plans for the day?"

"The Trojans built protective walls around their city," she said. "Like condoms. That's where the name Trojan comes from."

His mouth twitched. "Gotta love those Trojans. Do you carry the condom around just to give people a history lesson?"

"No. I—" He was laughing at her. Why was she acting like such an idiot? She was a teacher, a good one, who bossed around seven- and eight-year-olds all day long. She was in charge, and she ran her entire world with happy confidence.

Except for this with Griffin. Except for anything with Griffin.

"Look at you," he said. "Little Katie Evans, all grown up and carrying condoms."

"One," she said. "Only one condom." It was her emergency, wishful-thinking condom. "And I go by Kate now."

He knew damn well she went by Kate and had ever since she'd hit her teens. He just enjoyed saying "Little Katie Evans" like it was all one word, as if she were still that silly girl who'd tattled on him for putting the frogs in the pond at one of his mom's elegant luncheons, getting him grounded for a month.

Or the girl who, along with his nosy sister, Holly, had found his porn stash under his bed at the ranch house and gotten him grounded for two months.

"Kate," he said as if testing it out on his tongue, and she had no business melting at his voice. None. Her only excuse was that she hadn't seen him much in the past few years. There'd been a few short visits, a little Facebook interaction, and the occasional Skype conversation if she happened to be with Holly when he called home. Those had always been with him in uniform on Holly's computer, looking big, bad, and distracted.

He wasn't in uniform now, but she could check off the big, bad, and distracted. The early gray dawn wasn't doing her any favors, but he could look good under any circumstances. Even with his baseball hat, she could see that his dark hair was growing out, emphasizing his stone eyes and hard jaw covered with a five-o'clock shadow. To say that he looked good was like saying the sun might be a tad bit warm on its surface. How she'd forgotten the physical impact he exuded in person was beyond her. He was solid, sexy male to the core.

His gaze took her in as well, her now windblown hair and mud-spattered leggings stuffed into snow boots—she wasn't exactly at her best this morning. When he stepped back to go, embarrassment squeezed deep in her gut. "Yeah," she said, gesturing over her shoulder in the vague direction of her car. "I've gotta go, too—"

But Grif wasn't leaving; he was bending over and picking up some change. "From your purse," he said, and dropped it into her hand.

She looked down at the two quarters and a dime, and

then into his face. She'd dreamed of that face. Fantasized about it. "There are two hundred ninety-three ways to make change for a dollar," she said before she could bite her tongue. Dammit. She collected bachelor of science degrees. She was smart. She was good at her job. She was happy.

And ridiculously male challenged . . .

Griffin gave a playful tug on an escaped strand of her hair. "You never disappoint," he said. "Good to see you again."

And then he was gone.

Chapter 2

Five minutes later Kate pulled up to her dad's place. One glance in the rearview mirror at her still flushed cheeks and bright eyes told her that she hadn't gotten over her tumble in the parking lot.

Or the run-in with Griffin.

"You're ridiculous," she told her reflection. "You are not still crushing on him."

But she so was.

With a sigh, she reached for the weekly stack of casserole dishes she'd made to get her family through the week without anyone having to actually be in charge. She got out of her car, leaving the keys in it for Ashley, who'd drive it to her private high school just outside of town.

Tommy stood in the doorway waiting. He wore a green hoodie and had a fake bow and arrow set slung over his chest and shoulder.

"Why are you all red in the face?" he asked. "Are you sick?"

She touched her still burning cheeks. The Griffin Reid Effect, she supposed. "It's cold out here this morning."

The seven-year-old accepted this without question. "Did you get the tape?"

"I did," she said. "Tommy—"

"I'm not Tommy. I'm the Green Arrow."

She nodded. "Green Arrow. Yes, I got the tape, Green Arrow."

"I still don't see how duct tape is going to help us make a camel," he said, trailing her into the mudroom.

She refrained from telling him the biggest aid in making a camel for the school play would've been to give her more warning than a panicked five a.m. phone call. Instead she set down the casserole dishes on the bench to shrug out of her sweater as she eyed him. She could tell he'd done as she'd asked and taken a shower, because his dark hair was wet and flattened to his head, emphasizing his huge brown eyes and pale face. "Did you use soap and shampoo?"

He grimaced and turned to presumably rectify the situation, dragging his feet like she'd sent him to the guillotine.

Kate caught him by the back of his sweatshirt. "Tonight'll do," she said, picking back up the casseroles and stepping into the living room.

Evidence of the second-grade boy and the high school–junior girl living here was all over the place. Abandoned shoes were scattered on the floor; sweatshirts and books and various sporting equipment lay on furniture.

Her dad was in the midst of the chaos, sitting on the couch squinting at his laptop. Eddie Evans was rumpled, his glasses perched on top of his head. His khakis were worn and frayed at the edges. His feet were bare. He looked like Harry Potter at age fifty. "Stock's down again," he said, and sighed.

Since he said the same thing every morning, Kate moved into the kitchen. No breakfast. She went straight to the coffeemaker and got that going. Ten minutes later her dad wandered in. "You hid them again," he said.

She handed him a cup of coffee and a plate of scrambled egg whites and wheat toast before going back to wielding the duct tape to create the damn camel. "You know what the doctor said. You can't have them."

His mouth tightened. "I need them."

"Dad, I know it's hard," she said softly, "but you've been so strong. And we need you around here for a long time to come yet."

He shoved his fingers through his hair, which only succeeded in making it stand up on end. "You've got that backward, don't you?"

"Aw. Now you're just kissing up." She hugged him. "You're doing great, you know. The doc said your cholesterol's coming down already, and you've only been off potato chips for a month."

He muttered something about where his cholesterol could shove it, but he sat down to eat his eggs. "What is that?" he asked, gesturing to the lump on the table in front of him.

"A camel." It had taken her two pillows, a brown faux pashmina and a couple of stuffed animals tied together with twine, but she actually had what she thought was a passable camel-shaped lump.

Ashley burst into the kitchen wearing a way-too-short skirt, a skimpy camisole top, and enough makeup to qualify for pole dancing. In direct opposition to this image, she was sweetly carrying Channing Tatum, the bedraggled black-and-white stray kitty she'd recently adopted from the animal center where she volunteered after school. Contradiction, meet thy queen.

Channing took one look at the "camel" and hissed.

"What the hell is that?" Ashley asked of the makeshift prop, looking horrified as she cuddled Channing.

"Don't swear," Kate said. "And it's a camel. And also, you're going out in that outfit over my dead body."

Ashley looked down at herself. "What's wrong with it?"

"First of all, you'll get hypothermia. And second of all, no way in hell."

Ashley narrowed her overdone eyes. "Why do you get to swear and I don't?"

"Because I earned the right with age and wisdom."

"You're twenty-eight," Ashley said, and shrugged. "Yeah, you're right. You're old. Did you find my cheer-leading top?"

Kate tossed it to her.

Ashley turned up her nose at the scrambled eggs, though she fed Channing a piece of turkey bacon before thrusting a piece of paper at Kate. "You can sign it or I can forge dad's signature."

"Hey," Eddie said from the table. He pushed his glasses farther up on his nose. "I'm right here."

Kate grabbed the paper from Ashley and skimmed it. Permission slip to . . . skip state testing. "No." Skipping testing was the last thing the too-smart, underachieving, overly dramatic teen needed to do.

"Dad," Ashley said, going for an appeal.

"Whatever Kate says," Eddie said.

"You can't skip testing," Kate said. "Consider it prac-tice for your SATs for college. You want to get the heck out of here and far away from all of us, right? This is step one."

Ashley rolled her eyes so hard that Kate was surprised they didn't roll right out of her head.

Tommy bounced into the room. He took one look at the camel and hugged it close. "It's perfect," he declared. Then he promptly inhaled up every crumb on his plate. He smiled at Kate as he pushed his little black-rimmed glasses far-ther up on his nose, looking so much like a younger, hap-pier version of their dad that it tightened her throat.

A car horn sounded from out front. Kate glanced at the clock and rushed Tommy and Ashley out the door. Ashley got into Kate's car and turned left, heading toward her high school. Tommy and Kate got into the waiting car, which turned right to head to the elementary school.

Their driver was Ryan Stafford, Kate's second-best friend and the principal of the elementary school.

And her ex.

He must have had a district meeting scheduled because he was in a suit today, complete with tie, which she knew he hated. With his dark blond hair, dark brown eyes, and lingering tan from his last fishing getaway, he looked like Barbie's Ken, the boardroom version. He watched as Kate got herself situated and handed him a to-go mug of coffee.

"What?" she said when he just continued to look at her.

"You know what." He gestured a chin toward the cup she'd handed him. "You're adding me to your little kingdom again."

"My kingdom? You wish. And the coffee's a 'thanks for the ride,' not an 'I don't think you can take care of yourself,'" she said.

Ryan glanced at Tommy in the rearview mirror. "Hey, Green Arrow. Seat belt on, right?"

"Right," Tommy said, and put on his headphones. He was listening to an Avenger's audiobook for what had to be the hundredth time, his lips moving along with the narrator.

Ryan looked at Kate. "Thought you were going to talk to him."

She and Ryan had once dated for four months, during which time they'd decided that if they didn't go back to being just friends, they'd have to kill each other. Since Kate was opposed to wearing an orange jumpsuit, this arrangement had suited her. "I did talk to him," she said. "I told him reading was a good thing."

"How about talking to himself and dressing like superheroes?"

Kate looked at Tommy. He was slouched in the seat, still

mouthing along to his book, paying them no mind whatsoever. "He's fine." She took back Ryan's coffee, unscrewed the top on the mug, blew away the escaping steam, and handed it back to him.

"You going to drink it for me, too?" he asked. He laughed. "Just admit it. You can't help yourself."

"Maybe I like taking care of all of you. You ever think of that?"

"Tell me this, then—when was the last time you did something for yourself, something entirely selfish?"